D1553586

REBEL WITHOUT A CLAUS

ABIGAIL DRAKE

Editor: Lara Parker

Proofreaders: Maria Thomas and Gwen Jones

Cover Art: Najla Qamber

To my oldest son, Timur, and his brand new wife, Kennedy.
Wishing you a lifetime of laughter, happiness, and love.

CHAPTER ONE

I hated reindeer.

Everyone assumed they were sweet, magical creatures, but most of them were total jerks. They sucked, and taking care of them sucked, too.

"Hey, Tinklebelle Holly. I've got a little itch. Can you scratch it for me?" asked Comet, lifting his leg to show me one of his giant...well, it sure wasn't a jingle bell.

They loved calling me by my full name, even though pretty much everyone who valued their life called me Tink —no relation to the fairy in *Peter Pan*. That Tink wasn't even a distant cousin, and she dealt with lost boys. I was up to my pointy ears in reindeer, creatures who took special joy in torturing me. They also got off on showing me their balls for some reason. It was like working in a high school locker room. It smelled like a locker room, too. The only thing missing was the scent of body spray and teenage hormones, but damp reindeer fur carried a uniquely horrible bouquet all its own. And they were always wet since it always snowed. Day in, day out, it never changed. Nothing but snow, cold, and smelly reindeer.

Being a RAT—a member of the Reindeer Assistance Team—was one of the worst jobs at the North Pole. I had to feed them, care for them, clean out their disgusting stalls, organize all their stupid games, and, most importantly, make sure their jingle bells sparkled in the moonlight.

Really? Who cared about shiny jingle bells?

Joy Berry, one of my favorite coworkers, wiped her hands on her neon green coveralls and gave me a wink. "Ignore them, Tink. They're not worth it. You don't want to get in trouble. Again."

She made a good point. My temper and lack of filter were what had gotten me assigned to this gig in the first place.

"You're right," I said. "But have I ever told you how much I hate reindeer?"

"Yes. Several times," she said with a laugh.

"And magical reindeer are the worst. The whole flying thing gives them delusions of grandeur, and the talking..." I shook my head in disgust. "What great mind thought talking reindeer would be a good idea? All they do is complain, joke about bodily functions, and make inappropriate comments. And I can't even file a harassment complaint against them because they're a protected species. Under our 'guardianship,' or whatever." I made air quotes with my fingers. "It's a crock of crap."

She put a hand on my arm. "You don't belong here, Tink. You're destined for greater things."

"Yeah, but unfortunately, I'm trapped. It's like being stuck in a never-ending nightmare."

"It's too early in the morning to be so cynical." Lifting one dark eyebrow, she studied me. "You forgot to eat breakfast again, didn't you? You know hunger makes you crabby, Tink. Here. Take this."

She handed me a brown paper bag. I opened it and inhaled the aroma of a homemade muffin, still warm from the oven.

"Is this chocolate?"

"*Double* chocolate. Your favorite."

"You are a lifesaver." My hands were clean, remarkably enough, so I pulled the muffin out of the bag and took a bite, moaning when the rich taste hit my tongue. "Oh, fleekity flock me. This is fantastic. You should be in the cookie department. Or even the Christmas cake department. You are wasting your talent, girlfriend. Why are you here?"

Her cheeks colored, and she turned away, tugging on one of her dreads. "Well, you know."

Sadly, I did know. Every elf assigned here had been in trouble of one kind or another. I didn't have to know specifics. I decided to change the subject.

"It's too bad you couldn't come out with us last night. It was fun. Well, except when Frank tried to proposition a cop. And when Puck got in a fight. But it was still a pretty good time."

"In other words, it was a typical Monday?" she asked with a smile. "I'll try to come next time. Promise."

I knew it wouldn't happen. Unlike the others in the reindeer division, Joy wasn't a partier. I'd never even seen her take a drink.

From across the paddock, Frankincense Yummy, aka Frank, winked at us, and I gave him the finger, but in a joking way. I'd known him since I was small and had hooked up with him once or twice, but it had never been anything serious. Frank would flirt with a rock.

"At least his name fits," I said under my breath. "He *is* yummy."

"Everything bad for you is yummy." Joy frowned. "Or is

3

everything yummy bad for you? Either way, Frank is trouble."

"I agree. But it doesn't stop me from admiring the view, though." We paused a moment, enjoying the sight of Frank leaning over, muscles bulging, as he picked up a bale of hay. "And he has a great—"

A voice boomed from behind me, startling me so badly I almost dropped my muffin. "Tink. I need to speak with you. Now."

Puck McHappy, the tattooed and burly manager of the reindeer division, indicated the door to his office with a filthy finger. He looked both irritated and hungover, his usual morning face. Having that face directed at me was never a good sign.

"I'd better go. See you later, Joy," I said.

"Not if I see you first." She winked at me, and I laughed.

Shoving the rest of the muffin into my mouth, I crumpled the bag and tossed it into the garbage. Wiping the crumbs off my face with the back of my hand, I gave a quick knock on Puck's office door.

"You wanted to see me?" I asked, poking my head inside. The clock on the wall above his head indicated both the time and the number of days until Christmas. We were a little over a month away, which meant it was crunch time.

"Yes. Dust off and come on in."

I patted my coveralls, causing a cloud of white dust to swirl around me. I went home covered in the stuff daily. Yet another perk to the reindeer gig—I smelled like poop and looked like a moldy, powdered sugar donut. But Puck looked even worse than I did in his green uniform, and, as usual, he was bleary-eyed, unshaven, and disheveled. Leaning back in his chair, he hefted his feet onto the desk. His boots, covered in reindeer poo, made me want to gag, but despite the gross factor, I liked Puck. As a boss, he managed to be both fair and direct. He was also great in a bar fight and usually good for a laugh, but he wasn't laughing now.

"This came from elven resources a few minutes ago." He tossed a paper at me over the desk. I caught it before it hit his dirty boots. "You've been reassigned. You have to report to company headquarters at ten."

"Wait, what? At ten? That's in an hour." I scanned the page, trying to figure out precisely what this meant. I put a hand over my mouth. "Holy snowballs. Is this about the job with the naughty list team?"

Last week, I'd applied for a managerial position overseeing the naughty list team, but it was a stretch. I never expected to hear back from them, but that didn't stop me from hoping.

Puck shrugged, the effect odd since he didn't have much of a neck. "I don't know, sweetheart. They don't tell me anything. But you'd be great at the naughty list job. Your skillset makes you uniquely qualified."

"My skill set?" I asked, confused.

"You're direct to a fault, Tink. It's your greatest asset but also your greatest liability. Mostly because you don't know when to quit. Or shut up."

"Well, we have something in common," I said wryly, and he chuckled because it was true. Puck was an intelligent guy, but he limited himself career-wise, mostly because he had problems respecting authority. He also seemed to enjoy working with the reindeer, unlike me. I guess it had something to do with the fact that as long as he did his job, no one bothered him.

I hated it here, and as I imagined moving to the naughty list team, hope blossomed in my chest. No more looking at

Comet's hairy testicles? No more smelling Donner's farts? No more inappropriate comments from Vixen? It was a dream come true.

Vixen was a pervert, by the way. I'd caught him playing reindeer games with Dancer's wife at the company Christmas party and wanted to pour bleach into my eyes. Once you see something like that, it can't be unseen. Trust me.

Puck twirled a pen between his fingers. Striped red and white, it looked like a grimy candy cane. "I knew you were too smart to last here. Too sparkly as well, even for a Christmas elf." He waved a general hand in my direction, and I tucked a lock of blonde hair behind my pointy ear self-consciously.

"Too sparkly?"

"Yes, well...oh, forget about it. I'm sorry I brought it up."

He sighed, scratching his big belly. Puck liked to scratch a lot. Maybe it was a guy thing because the male reindeer did it, too. The only one who didn't scratch, and wasn't a complete bully, was Rudolph. But Rudolph was...well, let me say, flying was the only thing he did straight.

Wink, wink.

"How old are you now, Tink?" he asked.

I frowned. "Twenty-seven," I said. "And a half...ish."

"You're still young. You still have a chance to change the trajectory of your life. Take my advice. Do it before you end up like me." He checked his watch. "You'd better scoot."

"Thanks, Puck," I said, jumping out of the chair to give him a spontaneous hug.

Puck hugged me back, his mud-brown eyes concerned, although I had no idea why. "Be careful out there, kiddo." I heard a catch in his voice. Puck McHappy was going to miss me, and I'd miss him, too—filthy fingers and all.

After whipping off my coveralls and tossing them into my locker, I grabbed my coat, punched out, and headed back to my apartment as fast as my feet would carry me. Shivering, I put up my hood. The biodome covering the entire metropolis of the North Pole kept things at a reasonably comfortable thirty-two degrees. Cold enough to snow but warmer than the surrounding area. A thousand years ago, our clever ancestors had tapped into an underground geothermal hot spring. They could have created a tropical paradise here, but no, they didn't. They were snow-a-holics, like all Christmas elves, and wanted to keep the whole ambiance going. Personally, I hated the ambiance. I'd leave here in a heartbeat if I could.

I sprinted up the steps to my apartment and flung open the door. My roommate, Noelle, sat on the couch eating cereal in her pajamas. A nurse at North Pole General, she worked nights.

"Uh-oh," she said, when I walked in, her spoon paused halfway to her mouth. "Did you get fired again?"

"No," I said, offended at the assumption. "Elven resources contacted Puck this morning. They're reassigning me."

"Good," she said, then considered it. "That is good, right? It's a promotion, not a demotion, isn't it?"

"Yes." I frowned. "Well, at least I think so. What could be lower than the reindeer division?"

Our eyes met, and I cringed. There *was* something lower than the reindeer division, but I didn't even want to go there, and obviously, neither did Noelle.

"I'm sure it's a promotion," she said, tugging on her long, brown ponytail. She only tugged it when she was nervous, and the gesture made me nervous as well.

"I have to get ready," I said. "I smell like reindeer dung."

7

She yawned. "I'll be going to bed soon. If I don't see you, good luck."

"Thanks," I said, heading toward the bathroom, but Noelle stopped me.

"And Tink, try to be...normal, okay?

I narrowed my eyes. "What do you mean?"

She waved her spoon at me. "Happy thoughts. Christmas joy. You need to amp up your spirit quotient. They love cheerful elves at company headquarters. Keep smiling, and keep your mouth shut."

I gave her a thumbs up. I'd known Noelle since kindergarten. She'd earned the right to say those things, and she happened to be correct. I did need to amp up my spirit quotient.

After taking a quick shower, I bypassed my usual jeans and T-shirt combo and put on my favorite red skirt. On the North Pole, most of our clothing was red, green, or covered in bling. Like housewives in New Jersey, Christmas elves were all about the bling. But today, I went for something more professional.

"Look the part until you get the part," I said to my reflection in the bathroom mirror. As Noelle had suggested, I tried practicing a smile, but it came out more like a grimace. Maybe I'd keep my mouth shut and forget about the smiling part. It made me look creepy.

I glanced at my watch. It was already 9:30. "Oh, figgy pudding," I said, slipping into a pair of heels and tossing my coat over my shoulders. I grabbed a copy of my resume from the printer and shoved it into my briefcase. My grandmother, Gingersnap Holly, had given the briefcase to me when I graduated from college. I'd been first in my class, and she'd assumed I'd end up with a high-powered job.

That didn't happen, but maybe my luck was about to change.

North Pole company headquarters was only two subway stops away from my apartment. As I rode in the car, hanging onto one of the overhead straps, Christmas music blared over the loudspeaker, and advertisements for candy canes, sledding lessons, and tropical travel destinations decorated the interior. Unlike the South Pole, which sits on top of the continent of Antarctica, humans saw the North Pole as a floating sheet of ice. They were wrong. The same elves who figured out how to build a biodome and use geothermal energy to heat our city also figured out they could use the North Pole's magnetic properties to disguise it from prying human eyes. And other than once or twice when a whaling ship bumped into us by accident, it had worked.

Hooray for our forward-thinking and technically superior ancestors. They were much more intelligent than the average elf today, but I wished they'd made the temperature about forty degrees warmer. If they had, it would have been perfect. But who knows? Maybe with global warming being what it was (thank you, humans), I might someday get my wish.

I sighed as I looked at a poster of a palm tree and a white sand beach next to the window of the subway car. I needed a vacation. The last time I'd been anywhere was spring break over five years ago, and I'd been too drunk to remember most of it. But first I needed a new job.

I hopped out of the subway car and ran up the steps. A large clock on the wall indicated I had ten minutes left. Like every clock in the North Pole, it also showed the countdown to the big day. It was closing in fast, and right now, we all felt the pressure.

"Tink?"

The familiar voice made me stumble. I turned, plastering a big, fake smile on my face as I greeted Winter Snow III. My fabulous ex-boyfriend.

"Hey, Win. How are you?"

He grinned, all white teeth and blond hunky handsomeness. "I'm great. How are you? You look amazing." We'd broken up a few years ago, but when his eyes scanned my body, I experienced a familiar flutter in my chest. Old habits die hard, and Win was a hard habit to break.

"Thanks, Win. I'm fine."

Win was perfect—perfect face, perfect hair, perfect body, and a perfect smile. He was kind, too. And super smart. All in all, the man had no flaws, which was incredibly annoying, and he was successful as well. He had a high-level position in supply chain management, and some, including Win himself, thought he might be in line for the big job when the current Santa retired.

I frowned. Having seen Win naked, I had trouble imagining him as the next Santa, but it seemed likely he'd end up with the job. And that was one of the reasons I'd broken up with him. Frankly speaking, I could never picture myself as a future Mrs. Claus.

I would be the *worst* Mrs. Claus.

"Do you want to grab a coffee or something?" he asked, his blue-eyed gaze scanning my face like a caress. Even after all this time, he still acted as if he missed me. The man had issues.

"Sorry. Not today. I've got to run. I have a meeting." I pointed at the giant clock. "And I don't want to be late."

He leaned close and brushed my lips briefly with his before stepping away. "Call me sometime, okay? I miss you."

"Sure," I said, knowing I'd never do any such thing. Our

relationship had ended when I caught him kissing an elf named Candy Holiday under the mistletoe. I'd accused him of stuffing Candy's stocking. He denied ever doing any such thing, and it turned out he was telling the truth, but I keyed his shiny new red sleigh anyway. He called me a jealous, spiteful bitch, and the rest was history.

Basically, it was a typical breakup in the world of Tink Holly.

Truth be told, I'd been looking for a reason to end things. Candy Holiday provided me with the perfect opportunity. I was at a terrible point in my life. It happened not long after I'd been assigned to my current position on the Reindeer Assistance Team, a massive blow to my ego. Win's star had gone up as mine had crashed in a pile of soot and reindeer poo. None of it was Win's fault, but his success was a constant reminder of my failures. And, to make matters worse, the jerk got better looking every single day. Even now, two full years after our breakup, he could still make me all hot and bothered with a single look, and I suspected he knew it.

He grinned again, flashing his megawatt smile. "See you later, Tink. Good luck with your meeting."

With a wave, he marched down the steps. Several female heads turned to look in his direction, a common occurrence. Win Snow was elf bait, plain and simple. But I had other things to focus on right now.

Walking into the suite on the fourth floor without a minute to spare, I took a deep breath and tried to control my racing heart. Nerves, plus the chocolate from Joy's muffin, plus seeing Win, had gotten me wound up. I needed to calm myself. Pronto.

"Ms. Holly?" The receptionist's eyes narrowed disapprovingly at the length of my skirt. I attempted to adjust it discreetly. A small black sign with gold lettering on her desk read, *Mince Mingle*. I shot her a pained smile.

"Yes, I'm Tink Holly."

"We've been expecting you," she said, pursing her lips like she'd sucked on one too many sour lemon drops. "Follow me."

She ushered me into a large office and closed the door softly behind me. The room was dark, illuminated only by a small lamp in the corner. It took a second for my eyes to adjust, and when I saw the man sitting behind the big, shiny desk, my heart sank.

"Cookie Wassail," I said, my voice barely a whisper.

Cookie and I went way back. He was the same elf who'd fired me from my job in the letter-writing department. And the packaging team. And the distribution center. And (colossal shock) the elven resources department. This was bad. Like, really bad.

Amp up the spirit quotient. Amp up the spirit quotient.

I shook his hand, hoping my palms weren't sweaty and forced a non-creepy smile onto my face. At least, I thought it was non-creepy. I didn't have a mirror handy to check.

"Mr. Wassail. Nice to see you again."

He sank back into his chair, his bald head shining in the dim light and his expression grim, and indicated I should sit, too. "I wish I could say the same, Tinklebelle."

I swallowed hard, my spirit quotient going down faster than a sled greased with pig fat. "Am I in trouble, sir?"

"No, not this time. But is there something wrong with your face?"

"What do you mean?" I asked, smiling so hard I could barely move my lips.

"You're grimacing."

"I'm not grimacing. I'm smiling," I said, sending him a dirty look. An elf could only fake happiness for so long.

Cookie let out a long sigh. "Fine. Be that as it may, I called you here to give you an opportunity."

"What kind of opportunity?" I asked, getting suspicious. If Cookie Wassail suggested having a merry little fun time while naked in his office, I was going to kick him right in the icicles.

He shuffled through the papers on his desk until he found what he wanted. "You recently applied for a job with the naughty list team, correct?"

I nodded, almost afraid to speak, but I managed to produce a few words. "Yes, I did," I said, swallowing hard. "Sir."

Was I getting fired or hired? I had no idea, but the "sir" at the end was a nice touch.

Cookie studied my face. "I want to give you a chance, but you're going to have to prove yourself."

"How?" I wondered again if this did, indeed, involve getting naked, but Cookie's answer caught me off guard.

"This morning, someone showed up from Elven High Council to conduct a surprise audit. We don't like surprises." He adjusted his glasses. "He needs a tour guide. Since you've worked in nearly all the departments on the North Pole, who could be better? Also, you're smart enough to show him only what we want him to see, if you know what I mean."

"I do," I said, even though I really didn't.

The Elven High Council, our governing body, was made up of the best and brightest the elven world had to offer. They met in Elf Central, the capitol, which located in a veiled dimension overlapping the human city of Las Vegas.

A few decades ago, some wise elf had figured out Vegas would be one of the only places where a random elf would likely go unnoticed if spotted by accident, and she'd been right. Elf Central was a bustling metropolis but hidden from human eyes. The council building was close to many other governmental agencies, like the Elven Bureau of Investigation and the Toymakers Union. Thanks to strict rules, we'd existed there, side by side with humans, for years without a major incident. The Elven High Council made those rules, as well as all our other laws. What the heck would Cookie have to hide from them?

Cookie continued. "It's only for a week—two at the max. If you can manage not to mess this up, the position you applied for is yours. Am I clear?"

"Crystal. Do what you say, and I get the job."

"Exactly," he said, as a knock came at the door. "Ah. Here he is now."

I turned around to see who I'd have to play nice with for the next few days, expecting a balding bureaucrat. Instead, a tall figure with broad shoulders, silky black hair, and pale skin entered the room.

Not at all what I anticipated. This guy was a dark elf. *Holy roasted chestnuts.*

CHAPTER TWO

I'd never seen a dark elf in person before and didn't expect to meet one in Cookie's office, but I did my best to keep my expression neutral. The last thing I wanted to do was insult anyone, especially the person who now held my future in his big, pale hands, so I took a calming breath. I needed to implement some elf-control, or things could go South Pole quickly.

I racked my brain, trying to remember what I knew about dark elves from the Elven World Cultures class I took freshman year of college. It was, unfortunately, an early morning class, so I often slept through most of it, but I recalled bits and pieces.

Although we were all members of the same ancient, magical species, the elven tribes had several essential differences. Some of those differences were physical, and others had more to do with the chosen professions of each tribe.

Unlike how humans depicted us in their folklore, we weren't tiny. We were the same size as humans, and Christmas elves like me were, in general, happy, sparkling, toy-making robots.

Nature elves lived in forests, parks, and jungles. They were the most environmentally conscious tribe, a bunch of hippie tree-huggers who preferred to be naked most of the time. Their "villages" were glorified nudist colonies, and they smoked a lot of weed. I mean, a lot.

Water elves had gills and lived anywhere there was water—rivers, lakes, oceans, and sometimes bathtubs. Even though they were perfectly capable of breathing air, they built their homes in vast underwater cities. Their primary industry was tourism, and since they usually inhabited areas that were warm, tropical, and pricey, they made a lot of money. Well, except for the bathtub-dwelling water elves. Who'd want to visit a bathtub?

Air elves were useless, the penguins of the elven world. They had wings, but they couldn't fly—they sort of hovered. It was pretty pathetic. They were the smallest of all the elven species, lived in gardens, and interacted with humans far more than they should. Thanks to the veil between the human world and the elven world, we could see humans, but they couldn't see us unless we allowed it. And although air elves weren't nudists like nature elves, they were exhibition-ists. They loved being seen. Also, they were biters. Puck got in a fight with one once and nearly lost a finger. It was ugly.

Snow elves lived on the South Pole. You'd think North Pole elves would be snow elves, too, but we weren't. We lived in a snowy climate, but we didn't get off on snow like our brothers in the south. And by that, I mean they literally got off on it, but I'll spare the details. South Polers were rude, unfriendly, and drank a lot. They lived in cities made of ice, and they were polar opposites (get it?) from Christmas elves. They did sparkle, though, because they were partially frozen most of the time. Oh, and they ate baby seals. Gross.

Last, but not least, were the dark elves. No one knew what the dark elves did because no one interacted with them. Mysterious and strange, they lived in a vast network of underground caves and weren't the kind of folk you invited to cocktail parties. Or any parties. They were just plain scary. And possibly psychic. And I stood next to one right now. Was he reading my mind? Crap.

Cookie spoke, snapping me out of my thoughts. "Tinkle-belle Holly, this is Jax Grayson."

Jax Grayson's eyes met mine, and I had to force myself again not to stare. A dark elf working for the high council? Unusual, but everything about this guy was unusual. And intriguing. And, well, sexy. Okay, fine, I'll admit it, the guy was one hot elf. But he didn't seem happy to see me. He looked disturbed.

"Nice to meet you, Mr. Grayson." Remembering dark elves preferred not to be touched by strangers, I didn't extend a hand to him. Instead, I stood there, awkwardly, and, unable to come up with a better idea, I curtsied. Like I was meeting the queen. I was officially an idiot.

He didn't acknowledge my curtsy. He didn't acknowledge me at all. Instead, he spoke directly to Cookie. "You're kidding, right?"

Cookie raised an eyebrow. "Whatever do you mean?"

The dark elf's eyes narrowed. "You can't expect me to work with this." He still wouldn't look at me, but he lifted a hand to indicate my body from head to toe. "I need a serious guide, not a cruise director."

He thought I looked like a cruise director? Not what I'd been going for at all. "Wait a second, buddy—"

Cookie stopped me in mid-sentence. "You will find Ms.

Holly quite capable. You can accept her assistance, or you can reschedule the audit. Your choice."

With a growl, Jax slammed a fist on Cookie's desk, making both of us jump. "Fine, but your superiors will hear about this, Mr. Wassail."

"My superiors are the ones who chose Ms. Holly for this... honor." Cookie handed me a thin, red folder, and I accepted it, controlling my trembling hands by sheer force of will.

"Thank you, Mr. Wassail," I said. "I'll do my best."

"I know you will." He gave me a smarmy smile. "I've prepared a detailed itinerary for you. Please follow it exactly. No deviations. We wouldn't want Mr. Grayson to, uh, miss out on anything."

I opened the folder, my eyes scanning the pages. If I had to show a rude and yet extremely good-looking elf around for a few days to get away from the reindeer department and onto the naughty list team, I'd take it.

Coming up with the biggest smile I could muster without looking insane, I turned to him. "Well, Mr. Jaxon. I mean, Mr. Grayjax. I mean Mr. Grayson." *Fudgity fudge cake.* "It's a long list, and we don't have a lot of time. Shall we?"

He nodded. "I suppose we have no other option, Ms. Tinklewinkie."

Was that a joke or an insult? I had a feeling it was the latter. Despite my obvious charms, or at least those accented by my short skirt and tight top, Jax didn't like me. Maybe he hated Christmas elves in general. Either way, it didn't matter. I had a job to do, and I would do it to the best of my abilities. I was getting that spot on the naughty list team. Mr. Crabbypants would have to deal with it.

We left Cookie's office and walked down the hall in

silence. Like all the North Pole buildings, our company headquarters kept with the theme, meaning it looked like a giant Bavarian chalet. Five stories tall, it was all gingerbread house on the outside, and plain, boring, offices and cubicles on the inside.

"And here we are—the first stop on Mr. Wassail's itinerary. The accounting department," I said when we reached our destination.

"How thrilling." Jax had a deep, whisky-rough voice. It sort of rumbled when he talked and held more than a hint of annoyance, but I kept my neutral expression in place.

"It's on the same floor as his office, which is, I imagine, why he listed it first. We'll hit a few of the departments in this building today and tackle the bulk of the schedule tomorrow. Does that work for you?"

"Do I have a choice?"

"Not really." My eye started to twitch.

He muttered something under his breath, which I suspected was not Merry Christmas, but continued to follow me. "May I ask, Ms. Holly, why are you the one giving me the tour?"

I frowned, not liking his tone. "Well, Mr. Grayson, I've worked in every office you're going to see, and perhaps Mr. Wassail thought my insight would be valuable."

"Your insight, huh?"

People, especially males, looked at me and saw someone fluffy, blonde, and pretty. They never expected me to have a brain, and it ticked them off when they found out I did. I'd been fighting this attitude my whole career. Jax was exactly like all the others I'd had to deal with, and I could handle him. I could handle anyone. Even if I did want to smack him upside the head, I did not indicate my feelings in my response. I even managed a smile.

"I'm doing my job, Mr. Grayson. If you have an issue with Mr. Wassail's itinerary or anything else to do with your tour, I encourage you to take it up with him. If you have an issue with me, that's a different story. Now, are we going into the accounting department or not?"

"Call me Jax," he said. "It's simpler. And lead the way, oh, insightful one."

I couldn't tell if he was teasing me or not, but it didn't matter. Jax Grayson was officially on my naughty list, and not in a good way.

Be nice, be nice.

Resisting the urge to step on his foot with the heel of my bright red pump, I ushered him into the accounting department, a giant room full of elves tapping away on their computers. Jax studied them, hands clasped behind his back. The elf closest to us, a heavy-set, middle-aged woman named Pepper Minstix, glanced up at us and gasped. At first, I thought her reaction came from shock at seeing Jax. But when she grabbed her blinking miniature Christmas tree off her desk and shoved it onto the floor next to her chair, I realized her behavior had nothing at all to do with seeing a dark elf in her office.

"Tinklebelle Holly. What are you doing here?" she asked, spitting out the words. She had on a purple dress covered in snowflakes, purple eyeglasses, and purple earrings dangling from her pointy ears. Even her curly hair had a faintly purple tinge. It was her signature color.

"Hi, Pepper. It's been a long time."

"Not long enough."

A few of the other elves noticed me standing there and reacted in the same way Pepper had—by hiding their Christmas decorations under their desks. This was so embarrassing.

"Ha. Funny. Sorry to bother you all. Pretend we aren't here. I'm giving Mr. Grayson from Elven High Council a tour. Official business. You get it. Carry on."

It was like they all noticed Jax at once. Twenty sets of elven eyes locked on him. Pepper got the hiccups, a nervous tick. "Official..." (hiccup) "Business?"

"Yes. Mr. Grayson is conducting an audit."

If you want to freak out accountants of any species, all you have to do is mention the word "audit." They immediately ducked their heads and went back to work. I noticed several of them switched their screens from solitaire games back to accounting spreadsheets, and they all pretended to be incredibly busy.

When I noticed Jax studying them, a perplexed wrinkle on his brow, I asked, "What is it? You look confused."

"I am," he said. "Could you give me a run-down of how this department works and how it interacts with the other divisions here?"

"Uh, sure." I double-checked Cookie's secret notes to see how much I could tell him about the accounting department, but Cookie had written nothing except "Keep all numbers confidential." Easy, since I didn't know any numbers.

"Tell me, Mr. Grayson, how much do you know about the banking and financial systems of the North Pole?"

"I asked you to call me Jax," he said, his voice monotone. "And assume I know nothing."

I doubted that was the case, but I told him what I knew, paying attention to the talking points Cookie highlighted on the agenda. "Okay, *Jax*. The North Pole is a financially self-sustaining entity. We don't get paid for the toys we distribute to children, but centuries of smart investing, branding, and the purchase of several large manufacturers in the human world are what keeps us in business. We also patent all the toys we perfect in research and development, which adds to our income. That money covers the materials needed to create our toys, as well as our salaries and other benefits."

"What sort of benefits?"

"Health care, for example. Every elf is covered. And education. All Christmas elves attend college free of charge."

"A nice perk," he said.

"It is. As long as you work hard, you will be rewarded." *Usually.* "And we are all required to work at our assigned positions until we turn fifty or die. Kind of like indentured servitude." He blinked in confusion. I continued speaking, trying to cover up what I'd said. "The, uh, money is also used for housing and food subsidies, infrastructure, libraries, etc."

"And the funds are limitless? That's how the elves see it in other tribes."

I smiled graciously, telling him what everyone already knew. "Nothing is limitless, but do we have enough money? Yes. Are we greedy about it? No. Despite what we do here, Christmas elves are not materialistic in general."

"Despite what you do here?"

I indicated the positive Christmas messages displayed on posters all over the walls. "We create the magic of Christmas through the production and distribution of material goods. Our customer base is materialistic. Our employees are not."

He seemed confused by my words. I needed to stop the unfiltered commentary, or I risked serious trouble.

"Next question," he said as we left the accounting department and rounded the corner to head to the elevator.

"Why did they hide their Christmas decorations when we came in? Did they think I'd be offended?"

I waved my hand at his question. "Oh, no. They hid them because of me."

"Excuse me?"

I sighed. Better to be honest. "I used to work in the accounting department. It was a long time ago. I had an itty-bitty problem with a coworker, Tinsel McFly. He grabbed my..." I cleared my throat. "Well, he touched something he shouldn't have, and I responded by beating him over the head with the Christmas tree on his desk."

"Sounds reasonable."

"Doesn't it?" I shook my head at the memory. "Unfortunately, I hit him a lot harder than I intended. He required medical attention. The tree was covered in glitter, so it was like a Christmas bomb exploded in the middle of the office. All the desks were covered with it. People sparkled for months." I lowered my voice. "Glitter is like herpes. Once it's on you, it's almost impossible to get rid of it."

He made a slight choking sound, and for a moment, I thought he might laugh. He recovered, however, and managed to look sullen once again. "*You're* the reason they all look so nervous?"

"Yes, I believe so."

Tinsel came out of the breakroom, and when he saw me standing there, he froze. He was still wearing an eyepatch. Could something as minor as a scratched cornea seriously take so long to heal?

"You can't be here," he said, backing away. "The restraining order is still in effect."

I rolled my eyes. "Come on, Tinsel. Get over it. It was three years ago."

"Get over it?" He lifted his eyepatch to show us his red, swollen eye.

I flinched involuntarily. "Yikes."

"Yikes? I have glitter embedded in my eyeball, thanks to you. It scratches me all the time."

I winced. "Which sounds horrible, but how is it my fault? You grabbed my—"

"Don't say it," said Tinsel, raising one finger. "You are a menace, Tink Holly, and we all know it. You're lucky I didn't press charges. You'd be in jail right now."

I wanted to say Tinsel could be in jail, too, but I kept my mouth shut. I nearly broke my jaw from clenching it, but at least I didn't say anything that might embarrass me further.

"We should move on." Jax's voice cut into my thoughts. "We're going to be late."

Jax stood between me and the job on the naughty list team. I had to focus on this audit instead of on Tinsel or any of my other past mistakes.

"Yes," I said, putting a tight smile on my face. "We need to go to the collections department, which is always a delight. Bye, Tinsel. It was a real pleasure."

As we walked out of the elevator and headed to collections on the first floor, I was still fuming. When Jax spoke, his words nearly floored me.

"Although it doesn't matter much, in my opinion, Tinsel deserved what he got."

"What did you say?"

He ducked his head, almost like he regretted his comment, but he continued anyway. "His behavior was unacceptable. You were right to fight back."

I gave him a grateful nod. "And yet I'm the one who got fired over it."

"Why?" he asked, tilting his dark head to one side.

24

I hugged the red folder from Cookie to my chest. "The head of the department is his cousin, Wally Slumpkin. Pepper, the receptionist, is his sister-in-law. It's a family business."

"Ah," he said. "Good old nepotism."

"It's not unusual here on the North Pole. Many of us are related in one way or another. We're a close-knit community. The gene pool is shallow here if you know what I mean." I gave him an overly dramatic wink.

His eyebrows nearly went up to his hairline. "Are you suggesting Christmas elves are inbred?"

I winced, desperately trying to think of something else to say. "No. Definitely not. But it's a good thing they hid their decorations. I was tempted to whack Tinsel again. Ha, ha." My laughter sounded so forced it embarrassed me. "Not seriously. I'm teasing. I'm usually not a violent person."

I needed to shut up. Now. But I couldn't seem to do it. I pressed my lips together so hard they may have turned white.

Jax watched, his eyes crinkling with what looked a lot like amusement. "Which is exactly what a violent person would say, Ms. Holly. Can we continue with the tour now, or will we have to deal with any of your other former victims first?"

"I don't have other former—"

"Oh, hello, there. Twice in one day. It's a Christmas miracle."

Crap on a cookie. I turned to see Win approaching us with a welcoming smile.

"Hello, Win."

"Who's your friend?" Win asked, extending his hand. Jax stared at it a long moment before accepting it and

25

shaking it. Win obviously didn't know about the whole dark-elves-don't-like-to-be-touched thing.

"You must be our visitor from Elven High Council. Nice to meet you. I'm Winter Snow III. Call me Win."

"I'm Jax Grayson," he said, wiping his hand on his jacket in a move so subtle I doubted Win noticed. "Call me Jax Grayson."

Win laughed, but I saw a flicker of irritation in his bright blue eyes, which was odd. Win never got irritated. "Funny guy."

"Yes, I'm hilarious," Jax deadpanned.

Jax was taller, broader, and a lot darker in the aura department than Win. In fact, he looked like his face might crack in half if he grinned. He and Win could not have been any more different, in looks or personality. The only thing they had in common was their mutual gorgeousness.

There was an awkward silence, which I filled, because that's what I do. I talk, and I keep talking. It was like a nervous tic.

"Win works in supply chain management," I said brightly.

"I'm the Vice President of Logistics," he said, puffing out his chest. "Overseeing everything coming in and out of the North Pole."

"Sounds like a big job," said Jax.

"Oh, it is."

They had what looked like a stare down. Unsure what to do, I tried smiling again. Win shot me a confused frown.

"Is there something wrong with your face? You look weird."

I stopped smiling. "I'm fine. We'd better go. Bye, Win."

As soon as we were out of Win's earshot, Jax spoke. "Another former victim?"

"Another former something." I narrowed my eyes at him. "Wait, how did you know? Was it because of your...you know?" He seemed confused, so I spoke softly in case anyone was listening. "Is it true what they say?" I tapped a finger on my temple several times.

He lifted an eyebrow. "About dark elves having psychic powers?"

"Yes." If it were true, Jax might know a great deal about me by now. And if he read Win's mind, most of his information would be X-rated.

Jax leaned closer, so close I felt the warmth of his breath as he whispered in my ear. "It's not true, but don't tell anyone. I prefer to keep them guessing."

I eyed him suspiciously. "How did you know about Win being my ex?"

"It was obvious, both by how he behaved and how you treated him. I'm not a mind reader. I am, however, observant. And a great judge of character."

"Oh, yeah? So what did you think of Winter Snow III?"

"He's a pretentious wanker."

I let out a bark of laughter. His words were harsh, but there was some truth to the pretentious part. "And what do you think of me?"

"You are not a wanker, and you're definitely not pretentious, but the jury is still out."

I grinned and nudged him hard with my elbow. "Well, aren't you the smooth-talking dark elf?"

He seemed thrown off by my words, or maybe by the nudging. I couldn't tell which. "Excuse me?"

"You aren't as crabby as you seem, but I don't want to embarrass you with any more flattery. I might make you blush."

"Dark elves don't blush," he said, his expression serious. "Ever."

"Do dark elves eat?" I glanced at my watch. "Because it's almost lunchtime."

"We do eat," he said. "But only babies and virgins. And we like to drink the blood of our enemies."

He was joking. Or at least I hoped he was joking.

"No babies for lunch, and not a virgin in sight," I said. "Sorry to disappoint you. How about a burger instead?"

CHAPTER THREE

Even though it wasn't on the official itinerary, we went to my friend Sugarplum Happypie's place for lunch. She called it, accurately enough, Happypie's Hamburgers, and Sugarplum made the best burgers and fries on the North Pole.

"Happypie's?" asked Jax, tilting his head to study the sign.

"The owner's last name."

"But they don't serve actual pie?"

"Nope." I'd never thought about it, but they didn't. "But pie would be so good right now, served warm, with ice cream. Maybe I'll recommend it."

"I'm still trying to wrap my head around the idea of someone with the surname of Happypie."

"Do you know about the names here?" When Jax shook his head, I continued. "There were originally five families of Christmas elves. They're known—creatively—as the first five, and their last names are traditional. Like Kringle, and Snow."

"As in Winter Snow III?" The way he said Win's name made it sound like an insult.

"Yes."

"What were the others?"

"Ivy, Tannenbaum, and, uh, Holly."

His jaw dropped as my words sank in. "Wait a second. You're descended from one of the first five?"

"Yes." I hated talking about it, but Jax seemed curious. "Other families can choose their own names, and they can select anything except the names belonging to the first five. That is strictly forbidden. Ridiculous, but true. The only requirement in picking a name, first or last, is for them to be 'joyful' and 'Christmas-themed.' Happypie is an example."

"We're taught the North Pole is a meritocracy, but it sounds like your Christmas elf society is an aristocracy."

"Oh, it is a meritocracy—mostly. Santa is elected, kind of like the pope. But members of the first five are always part of the governing body selecting him. Not me, of course. Others." I bit my lip, not sure I wanted to say any more. "But what about dark elves? Don't you have a king and a royal family and stuff?"

"We do. As do all the other elven tribes," he said, his mouth set in a tight line. "Only Christmas elves are different."

I couldn't help myself; I snorted. "A good word for it."

As we waited to be seated, Jax's phone buzzed with a text. He looked at it and frowned. "Apologies, but I must meet with someone after lunch. May we tour the collections department tomorrow instead?"

I considered his question. "I guess. Cookie was pretty adamant about sticking to his schedule."

"If he has an issue with it, I'll take the blame."

I tried to imagine Cookie's reaction and knew I'd be

blamed no matter what, but I didn't see any other options. Jax was the VIP here.

"At least let me take you where you need to go."

"They'll meet me here," he said. "So I guess you now have the afternoon off."

"Lucky me."

Christmas music played as we slid into a booth with red leather seats and gazed at our menus. I pondered whether I should contact Cookie and tell him about the change in plans but decided it could wait. I was starving. I felt like I'd eaten the chocolate muffin from Joy a year ago instead of this morning. A lot had happened in a short period, and stress always made me hungry.

"What do you recommend?" asked Jax.

"Everything. Seriously. I've tried every item on the menu, and it's all good. I recommend all of it."

Sugar came up to the table, smacking her gum and twirling a pen between her fingers. She'd been close friends with my late mother, and she'd adopted me a long time ago as one of her own. We went way back.

"Hey, kiddo. What are you doing here? I haven't seen you in ages." She kissed my forehead and pulled out a notepad to take our order. When she turned to direct her attention to Jax, she dropped the notepad.

"Sugar, this is Jax. He's a visitor from the Elven High Council, and I'm showing him around."

She seemed momentarily stunned. "Showing him around?"

"For work." I gave her a meaningful look, trying to psychically convey "showing him around" was not a euphemism for boinking him. She seemed to get it.

"Oh. Well, cover me in chocolate and call me a sundae. This is exciting. I've never met a..." Her voice trailed off, but she recovered quickly. "A person from Elven High Council before. Nice to meet you, Jax."

Good save. I loved Sugar. She had flaming red hair, a quick wit, and a skirt so short she nearly flashed us when she bent over to pick up her notebook. Jax averted his eyes, which was wise. He avoided seeing Sugar's red ruffled panties.

"Nice to meet you, too, Ms. Happypie."

His words made both of us giggle. "Everyone calls me Sugar, sugar." She gave him a saucy wink. Her lashes were fake, blue, and sparkly, but still looked great on her. In another life, Sugar may have been a stripper. "What can I get for you two?"

"I'll have the bacon double cheeseburger, the mega fries, and a chocolate milkshake." I frowned. "No, I had chocolate for breakfast. Make it strawberry. That's healthier."

"It is a fruit," said Sugar diplomatically, scribbling on her notebook before moving on to Jax. "And what about you?"

"The, uh, same. I guess. But maybe skip the milkshake."

Sugar and I both shook our heads. "No, baby," she said. "You don't want to skip the milkshake. Trust me. They are addictive."

I agreed. "Milkshakes are my drug of choice. What about Jax, Sugar? What flavor would suit him best?"

"Well, we need to start with the basics. You look like a strictly vanilla kind of guy."

We giggled again, but Jax didn't seem to find any of it amusing. "It's okay," I said. "Vanilla is yummy, too."

Sugar jotted down our order, a smile playing on her ruby red lips. "Speaking of yummy, how's my sweet nephew Frankie doing?"

"He seems good. I saw him a few hours ago." When Jax

looked confused, I explained. "Her nephew's last name is Yummy."

"And it suits him," said Sugar. "He may be lazy and a little promiscuous, and he makes the worst possible decisions, but he's a nice-looking kid. I'll give him credit where credit is due."

On paper, Frank and I sounded a lot alike. In truth, I was more unmotivated than lazy and more flirty than promiscuous. Or at least I hoped so. But the part about making bad decisions? We shared that trait for sure.

Sugar shot us one last grin before grabbing our menus and leaving to place our order. Jax gave me an odd look.

"His name is Frank *Yummy*?"

"Yep. Frank is short for Frankincense. His middle name is Figgypudding."

"Are you serious?" he said with a puzzled frown. "Excuse me for saying this, but the first names are also bizarre here."

"What do you mean?" I pretended not to understand, and his jaw dropped, abashed.

"I'm sorry, I—"

I laughed at him. "I'm kidding, dude. Relax. They're goofy AF. But some are a lot worse than others."

"Such as?"

"Oh, let me think." I tapped a finger to my chin. "I went to high school with a guy named Gingernuts Jollyfun."

"You're kidding, right?" He grinned, and once again, the effect was astounding. It brightened his entire face and made him look much better than when he was all broody and crabby. I wanted to keep him smiling, so I kept talking.

"It gets worse. I once worked with a gal named Bushy Evergreen."

"No."

"Yes. And how about Nippy Nibblewrap? How'd you like to have that one for your whole life?"

He laughed so hard his shoulders shook. "Why would someone do such a thing to their own child?"

I shrugged. "You get bored with hearing the same old names over and over again. And Christmas elves aren't great with original thought."

He gave me a curious look. "But you make toys, which is all about creativity."

"We put together toys. It's a different skillset. We like sticking to a formula. There are a few geniuses in research and development, but most of their work involves taking an idea from the human world and expanding on it. We spy on human children constantly. The whole 'He sees you when you're sleeping' thing is no exaggeration. They are under constant surveillance, and not only for behavioral issues. We observe them and calculate trends. We process information to see what might interest them in the future and spend countless dollars on advertising to make sure a toy we patented is the hot gift item each year."

He frowned. "But doesn't Santa bring the toys?"

"He does, but only the more traditional and less expensive items. The high-ticket ones? Those are all on the parents to purchase. We bring the kid a teddy bear worth about five bucks, and the parents pay hundreds for a gaming system we developed. The toy we provide is almost like a gift with purchase."

His frown deepened. "And the naughty list?"

"Oh, it still applies. Naughty kids never get gifts from Santa, but we make sure the parents feel compelled to buy them the most expensive item possible using marketing and manipulation." I shook my head in disgust. "It's all about the elf bucks. Nothing else matters."

He studied me, his expression unreadable. "Do other Christmas elves think like you?"

I snorted. "Nope. Most are normal, happy, sparkly, and oblivious. Because ignorance is bliss, right?"

"I suppose."

We were quiet a moment, and I noticed the other elves in the restaurant staring at Jax. One elf a few tables away whispered something about "cave dwellers" and "slug eaters" and my face got hot. Jax didn't say anything, but I could tell he'd heard them by the way his body stiffened. I didn't necessarily like Jax Grayson, but the rudeness of my fellow Christmas elves made me angry. And I'd never been one to hold back my feelings, so I looked directly at the elf who'd commented, a chubby guy wearing a dark green production line uniform and gave him the stink eye.

"Shut it," I said. "Or else."

"Or else what, sweetheart?" he asked with a sneer. The entire restaurant had grown quiet, and the other patrons now stared at us, but I didn't care. I hated bullies, and this guy was a bully and a racist.

"Or else I'm reporting you directly to Santa. I mean it. But that isn't all I'll do."

He laughed, but the guy sitting next to him, a skinny elf with dark hair and a name tag reading Skittle Pinklepot, nudged him. "Don't mess with her, Fizzy. Don't you know who she is?" When Fizzy looked at his friend in confusion, Skittle continued. "That's Tinklebelle Holly."

Fizzy paled. "You're kidding, right?" Skittle shook his head. "The same Tinklebelle Holly who..."

He whispered the rest of his words in Skittle's ear, but I could imagine he was talking about the incident with Tinsel and the tree. Or the time I kicked my manager in the letter-writing department so hard, I may have loosened one of his jingle bells. Or the time... well, there were a lot of possibilities. Sure, I usually acted first and considered the consequences later, but the fact of the matter was, most of the times when I lost it on people, they deserved it. No one ever mentioned that part, however.

Fizzy looked at me, and for a second, I thought he might cry. "Apologies, Ms. Holly. It won't happen again. Please don't mention this to you-know-who."

"Elf off," I said, not impressed.

He and Skittle took me seriously. They got up quickly, threw some money on the table to pay for their meal, and took off, bowing to us before they left. The other customers in the restaurant watched them go, and when the conversations resumed, they weren't talking about Jax anymore. They were talking about me, but it didn't matter. I was used to it.

"I'm sorry," I said as Sugar brought out our burgers. She glanced at the empty table Fizzy and Skittle had just vacated.

"Everything okay here?" she asked. I nodded, ducking my head sheepishly. Sugar put a hand on her hip. "Tink. Are you scaring away my customers again?"

"No." I shook my head vehemently. "They were rude to Jax. I told them to stop it."

"Oh." Sugar gave Jax an apologetic look. "Sorry, sweetness. You shouldn't have to deal with that sort of thing on your first day in the North Pole. Your meal is on me."

She pinched his cheek, and he eyed her curiously as she walked away. "How did she know it was my first day here?"

"Maybe because you have 'newbie' written all over you?" I laughed at the expression on his face. "I'm kidding. Sugar knows all. Accept it and move on. And she must like you because she never gives anyone a free lunch. Speaking of which, please eat. There is nothing sadder than cold French fries, you know."

We ate, and the food was fantastic as always, but I still burned with embarrassment over how those elves had treated Jax. He seemed to be thinking along the same lines.

"You didn't have to stand up for me. I can handle things on my own."

"But you shouldn't have to." I tried to explain. "It's no excuse, but they've probably never seen a dark elf in person before."

"And you have?"

"Well, no," I admitted.

"So don't make excuses for them," he said. "I suppose I do stand out here. It's normal for some elves to be uncomfortable around me. I expected it."

Members of the various elven tribes had notably different physical attributes. Christmas elves, who represented all the human races, were cute and sparkly. Nature elves never cut their hair or shaved, and since they hated both clothing and societal rules, they tended to be free spirits (and even more promiscuous than Frank Yummy). Water elves had gills, flowing hair in shades of blue and green, and a bluish tinge to their skin. Air elves were small, with tiny, useless wings, and they always seemed to be compensating. As the old elven saying went "Small wing-a-lings equals small ding-a-lings." I had no idea if it was true or not but never cared to test the theory.

Snow elves had no ding-a-ling issues, but they were hairy, so hairy they seemed to be covered in fur. They reminded me vaguely of wooly mammoths. Or maybe long-haired guinea pigs.

Dark elves weren't funny or furry, and they didn't have wings or gills. They had pale skin, dark hair, dark eyes, and a dark aura. And they mostly kept to themselves, which only added to the mystery and misconceptions surrounding them.

Jax had the dark elf coloring and the aura of darkness, but he was not a typical High Council elf. They were usually pretty full of themselves, but Jax exuded confidence, not arrogance. And despite my first impression of him, he wasn't a prick.

"Do you like the burger?" I asked as he took a bite. He responded with a groan. Sugar knew what she was doing. "I'll take that as a 'yes.' And I'm sure it's much tastier than babies or virgins."

He shrugged. "Debatable," he said.

"Aha, dark humor."

This time he laughed out loud. "I guess it goes with the territory, but I'm curious. Were you serious when you said you'd never met a dark elf before, Tinklebelle?" he asked, studying me as I tried to suck up some of my milkshake. Sugar was known all over the North Pole for her delicious milkshakes. Mine was so thick, in fact, I couldn't get any through the straw, and it felt vaguely like I was attempting to give the straw a blow job. I took the lid off my cup and used my spoon instead. Jax followed my lead. I had to guess he didn't want to look like he was giving a straw a blow job either.

"Nope. You're my first. And please call me Tink. I hate being called Tinklebelle. It makes me sound so fluffy and vapid and Christmas-y."

"You don't want to be Christmas-y?"

"No, I'm not a fan," I said, feeling the old familiar pang in my heart. "As you may have guessed."

"A Christmas elf who isn't into Christmas?" He studied my face with a hint of amusement in his eyes. "And who barely blinked when she met her first dark elf? You're unusual, Tink, and not only because you didn't scream and run away when you saw me."

"Don't flatter yourself," I said, unable to resist. "I've seen far scarier things than you, buddy—"

My words were cut off by a series of screams coming from outside. Jax and I stood up in time to see a woman convulsing on the ground, blood trickling out of her nose, mouth, and her pretty, pointed ears.

Pretty, pointed, *familiar* ears.

"Oh, no." The elf on the sidewalk was Joy Berry. My sweet, muffin-making coworker.

I grabbed napkins from our table and ran outside. Christmas elves were not good in emergencies. We tended to run around and scream a lot, which was what most of the other elves were doing right now. I'd never been one to panic, but as I knelt next to Joy and grabbed her clammy hand, I started to freak out. She was so pale she looked ash gray, but her fingers were an odd shade of purple. The remains of a shake from Happypie's lay on the ground next to her, but I didn't know if it was Joy's or if a bystander had dropped it. The cold liquid from the melting shake mixed with Joy's blood on the sidewalk. I had to fight the urge not to run around and scream, too. Instead, I tried to focus on her.

"Hey, Joy. It's me, Tink. I'm here, honey. Don't worry. You're going to be okay."

It was a lie. Poor Joy. She did not look okay. Not by a long shot.

I tried to use the napkins to wipe off her face, but soon they were saturated. The blood kept pouring out. Her eyes met mine for a brief second, and she opened her mouth as if to speak but only a strange, gurgling sound came out.

I gripped her hand even harder. "Hang on. Please."

Her body spasmed once more before stiffening and going still. Her eyes remained open, but they were lifeless. A hush filled the crowd surrounding us as Jax placed his fingers on her neck to check her pulse.

"Please help," I begged him. "I...I don't know what to do."

He gave me a steadying look, and oddly enough, it helped. "She needs medical assistance. Call for an ambulance."

I pulled out my cell phone as Jax performed CPR. It took only seconds for the operator to answer, but it felt like hours.

"Ho, ho, hello. What is your emergency?"

Even the freaking emergency dispatchers were cheerful. "We need an ambulance. A woman is unconscious on the sidewalk in front of Happypie's Hamburgers. Her name is Joy Berry."

Jax gave me a sharp look, but I had to focus on what the dispatcher was asking me. And Jax had to focus on the chest compressions.

"Age?"

I rubbed my head. "I don't know. Twenty-four...?"

"Is she breathing?"

Jax's eyes met mine, and he gave a slight shake of his head, his expression grim. "No," I said, blinking away tears. "Someone is administering CPR."

"Good. How long has she been unconscious?"

"Minutes. Look, she's in bad shape. Will you please stop asking me stupid questions and get her some help? Jiminy Christmas."

The people around us gasped. The operator seemed shocked as well, although he must have heard worse in his line of work. "There is no need for profanity, miss. I've already dispatched the ambulance. I'm asking you questions because they're important. I want to be sure I'm sending the right sort of help for your friend. Do you understand?"

"Yes," I said, trying to calm myself. "I'm sorry."

"It's all right. Is the person still performing CPR?"

"He is," I said.

"The ambulance is on its way. I'll stay on the phone with you until they get there."

"Thank you."

Jax continued doing chest compressions, counting softly with each push on Joy's sternum. He seemed so determined as he fought to keep her heart beating, but it looked bleak.

The whine of an ambulance siren signaled the arrival of the elf medical team, but I knew it was already too late. The EMTs tried to revive her, but there was nothing anyone could do. They called the time of death at 12:46 pm, and Jax turned to me, his dark eyes full of sympathy.

"I'm so sorry. I tried—"

Even though I knew I wasn't supposed to touch him, I squeezed his hand. It was much warmer than I expected.

"I know you did. Thank you."

"You're welcome," said Jax, his voice hollow and sad. "You knew her?"

"Yes," I said as they carried her off on a gurney, a white sheet covering her face. "She worked with me."

"At the reindeer department?" When I nodded, he continued. "When did you last see her?"

"A few hours ago," I said, confused by his questions. "Right before I got called to Cookie's office and assigned as your tour guide."

"Did anything unusual happen? Did she seem all right?"

41

I lifted my hands, staring at my bloody palms. "She was fine. Normal. It was a typical Monday."

"Can you tell me step by step what happened?"

"I saw her as soon as I got to work. She gave me a chocolate muffin."

"And that was typical?"

"Yes. Joy always brought an extra one because she knew I never woke up in time for breakfast. She said I got crabby if someone didn't feed me at regular intervals." I looked up and saw Sugar standing a few feet away, dabbing her eyes with a tissue. She sent me a sad smile, and I sniffed, wiping away the tears on my cheeks with the back of my hand. "I don't see how a perfectly healthy young elf could be baking muffins one minute and dead the next. It doesn't make any sense. What happened to her?"

My voice increased in volume. Jax put a hand on my shoulder as he glanced at the crowd of elves surrounding us. "I may be able to answer your question, but can we discuss it somewhere more private?"

"Why can't we discuss it right here?"

He leaned closer, so close his lips brushed against my ear as he spoke. "Because Joy Berry is the person I was supposed to meet today after lunch. And I don't think her death was an accident."

CHAPTER FOUR

I took Jax to my favorite bar, Nick's, only a few blocks away from Happypie's. I needed a drink. Or maybe multiple drinks. And Jax looked like he could use one, too.

"Hey, Tink," said Nick as we walked through the door. An older elf with dark hair and a bulbous nose, he'd been serving me drinks since before I was even legal. Nick and I went way back.

"How's it hanging?" I asked.

"By the chimney with care," he answered, as he always did, pointing to a fake cardboard fireplace in one corner of his bar. On it were stockings with the names of his favorite customers on them. Mine was front and center.

"Good man. I'm still up there."

"I'd never take your stocking down, sweetie. Who's Mr. Tall, Dark, and Gloomy?" he asked, tilting his chin to indicate Jax.

"This is my friend Jax. Can we have the table in the corner?"

"Sure." He glanced at my hands. "Is that blood?"

"Yep."

"Is it *your* blood?"

"Nope."

"Okay. What do you want to drink? The usual?"

"Of course."

"And what about you, Mr. Jumping Jax?"

Jax seemed confused, but Nick gave all his patrons a nickname. It was his signature thing. And Nick's nickname was Nick, but that was a long story.

"I'll have a whiskey, please. On the rocks."

I pointed Jax to the men's room and went to the ladies' to wash up. It was a ridiculously small and awkwardly appointed facility but a place full of memories. I'd shared confidences with friends here, comforted crying drunk girls I didn't even know, and argued with others I'd just met. I'd thrown up here once or twice, too, but most of the memories it held were good ones. Happy ones.

Glancing to the right of the sink, I saw the words *T loves W* carved into the wood paneling. Tink loves Win. It was still there, even after all these years. So much had changed, but that remained. Weird.

After scrubbing my hands until they were nearly raw, I joined Jax at the table in the corner. When our drinks arrived, he studied my bright green concoction with a raised eyebrow. "What are you drinking?

"The Grinch," I said, taking a long sip. "It may look disgusting, but I like it. I think of the Grinch as my spirit animal."

His lips curved into a smile, which he quickly hid behind his drink. "You really do hate Christmas stuff, don't you?"

"I really do."

"To the Grinch." He raised his glass, and we both drank deeply.

"I needed this. Thanks."

"It's been a rough day."

I took a long sip. "Tell me what's going on, Jax Grayson. If that's honestly your name."

He bit his lip, looking both super-sexy and mischievous at the same time. "That is, indeed, my name, but let's talk about Joy first. How well did you know her?"

"Hmmm. Well, I knew she was a great baker, with a dry sense of humor and a kind heart. Her mom's name was Holly, like my last name, and her father's name was Jolly. It's hard to forget a couple named Holly and Jolly Berry." I steadied myself. "Joy still lived with them on the West Side."

"The West Side?"

"Yes, it's kind of a blue-collar area—filled with middle-class families and factory workers. But it's nice and convenient, especially for people working in the reindeer department."

I'd grown up on the East Side, the bougee part of the Pole. I didn't live there now, however—I couldn't afford it. Noelle and I lived on the South Side, which was shabby but safe, and a popular place for students and young people. Most of the best bars were on the South Side, too. Nick's was one of the few I liked here in Central City.

"Joy talked about getting her own place, but..." My voice trailed off. Joy would never have a chance to do any of the things she'd planned. I cleared my throat. "Anyway, we'd only worked together a few months, but I liked her. She was a nice kid."

"Did she ever talk to you about problems with her job?"

I shook my head. "No, but there has to be a reason you're asking."

"There is."

"And do you plan to share it with me?" He hesitated. Only for a second, but I caught it and jumped in before he could respond with something vague again and annoy me. "What's going on, Jax? Please tell me the truth."

He let out a sigh. "I don't even know where to start."

"Maybe with the obvious?" I leaned closer and narrowed my eyes at him. "Jax Grayson...what's a nice boy like you doing in a place like this?"

He gave me a crooked smile. "A place like this?" he asked as he glanced around the bar decorated with twinkle lights and fir branches. Mistletoe hung from the ceiling, convenient for drunken make-out sessions, and instead of stirrers in our glasses, we had candy canes. Even Nick, the owner of this fine establishment, took the holiday theme to the next level, but Jax didn't seem to mind. It was almost like he enjoyed it. But we weren't here to discuss décor. We had something else to talk about entirely.

"I'm not here to do an audit, Tink."

"I figured as much."

"I'm here to investigate something, and I'm pretty sure Joy's death is connected."

"What do you mean?" He pulled his wallet out of his pocket and flashed something at me—a badge. I looked up at him in shock. "Elf Enforcement?"

"Yes, the narcotics division."

I nearly knocked over my Grinch. "Oooh. You're a dark narc?"

He let out a laugh. "Yes," he said, glancing around as if to make sure no one was listening. "I am."

I frowned, confused. "What does this have to do with Joy's death?"

"It's connected. Did you notice her fingers?"

"I did. They were purple."

"That's a sign of something very particular. I know because I've seen it before—many times."

"What are you talking about?"

He lowered his voice. "Joy Berry died of an overdose."

"An overdose?" I stared at him in disbelief. Other than the muffins, Joy was super health conscious. She ate organic food and ran five miles a day. She got high on endorphins, nothing else. "No way. Joy didn't do drugs. I'm sure of it."

"I don't think she took the drugs on purpose, Tink. Someone gave them to her without her knowledge. Someone killed her."

I choked on my Grinch. "Joy was murdered?" I asked, still gasping. I took another sip of Grinch to recover, which may have seemed counterintuitive, but it worked.

"Are you alright?" he asked. When I reassured him with a wave of my hand, he continued. "Back to Joy, she contacted me with information about a possible drug ring on the North Pole. She died moments before she could share it."

"What kind of drugs are you talking about?" I asked.

"Candicocane." This time when he spoke, his voice was so soft I thought perhaps I'd misheard him.

I leaned closer. "You're kidding, right?"

"I am not." He looked at me, his dark eyes steady in his pale face. "I wish I were."

I'd heard about the candicocane problem on the news, but I never knew of a Christmas elf using it. We didn't do the hard stuff. Our idea of a fun time was drinking hot cocoa spiked with too much peppermint schnapps. Yes, it made you puke, but it didn't make you die.

And Joy wasn't even the type for the peppermint schnapps. "This doesn't make sense. First of all, Joy is the last person I'd expect to be involved in drugs. But, for the sake of argument, let's say all of this is true, and someone killed her by giving her a fatal dose of candicocane. Why was there so much blood?"

"Someone is lacing candicocane with telazol. It's a cheaper high, but it can easily turn deadly. As you witnessed today."

"Telazol?" I frowned. "Reindeer tranquilizer?"

"Yes," he said. "I take it you're familiar with it?"

"I am."

I stayed so calm I impressed myself. With the wave of a hand, I ordered another Grinch, and focused all my slightly inebriated attention on the elf in front of me.

"Doping up deer is one of my many RAT duties." I took a long sip of my Grinch. "Or, I should say it *was* one of my duties until this morning when you showed up. What an odd coincidence."

The last word came out slurred. It sounded more like *co-in-she-dance*. I tried to say it again, but it came out the same. He interrupted me before I could try it a third time.

"You may have had one Grinch too many."

"Or maybe one Grinch too few," I said, lifting a finger.

The door to the bar opened, and in came a bunch of my friends from the Reindeer Division, led by the one and only Puck McHappy. When he spotted me, he made a beeline for my table.

"Are you okay, kid?" he asked, his brown eyes sad. "I heard the news. I gave the guys a few hours off so we could have a drink. What a shock."

"It was." I sniffed but managed not to cry. "But I'm fine."

"She was so young. Such a waste."

I glanced over at the bar, where several of my former coworkers were ordering drinks. Even the ordinarily cheerful Frank Yummy seemed oddly quiet. His handsome face was drawn and pale, and his shoulders slumped with grief. When he caught me studying him, he lifted his beer to me.

It was Mug-a-Lug Monday, which meant a mug of beer was half price. The last time Frank and I had both been here on a Monday, we'd ended up making out next to the antique jukebox by the wall.

He was a naughty elf, and we both knew it, but he was a good guy at heart. And Joy's death had upset us all, including our manager, who currently looked like he might burst into tears or hit someone. Or maybe both. I reached out to pat his arm, and Puck sighed.

"I need a beer, and I suppose I should say a few words."

"That would be nice."

He nodded before bellowing over his shoulder in the general direction of the bar. "Get me two mugs, Nick. I need one for each hand."

Nick responded without missing a beat. "If I give you one for each hand, do you promise you won't punch anyone today?"

Puck shrugged. "I don't make promises I can't keep, Nick-Knack."

With a laugh, Nick brought Puck his drinks. Puck lifted one beer and chugged nearly half of it before speaking.

"Hey, you dirty RATs." The bar went silent. "It's true what they say. Only the good die young, and Joy was better than us all." He cleared his throat, struggling to contain the

49

emotion before lifting his glass. "A sunbeam to warm you. A moonbeam to charm you. And a sheltering angel so nothing can harm you. To Joy."

The rest of us spoke in unison, raising our glasses as well. "To Joy."

I took a long swig of my Grinch, my mind on my friend. "How did you hear about what happened?" I asked Puck.

"Frank told us. He heard the news from his Aunt Sugarplum. She said you were there when it happened."

"We were."

"Do you know how Joy died?" he asked softly. "I heard it may have been a brain aneurysm or something."

I opened my mouth to answer, but Jax stepped in. "I imagine it's too soon to tell, but it was a terrible thing to witness."

Puck eyed Jax. "You're the guy from Elven High Council, right? Sugarplum said you tried to help poor Joy today. Thank you."

"You're welcome," said Jax. "I wish I could have done more."

Puck's eyes grew misty with tears. I patted the seat next to me. "Would you like to join us?"

"Sure," he said. "For a minute." He plopped into the chair, his hands wrapped around one of his beers. The other was already empty. "It's a sad day. One minute you're here, and the next you're gone. And it happens in the blink of an eye."

"Jax thinks—" I got a sharp kick under the table from Jax. "Ow." I shot him a look. I'd wanted to mention his theory, but something in Jax's expression told me not to say any more. I scowled at him, both for the kick and because I had no idea why I couldn't tell Puck.

"Jax thinks what?" asked Puck with a frown.

"It's a tragedy," Jax said.

"A tragedy. I agree." Puck drained his beer and let out a loud belch. "I have to go back to the paddock and tell the reindeer about Joy. They aren't going to like it. They're already pissed off because you left, Tink, and they hate the new girl. Her name is Fiddlesticks. They already made her cry. Twice."

"Oh, fiddlesticks," I deadpanned, and Puck laughed, but I felt kind of bad for the girl. "Was it Comet? He's usually the instigator."

"Oh, yes. The biggest, baddest, meanest reindeer of them all. But there always has to be an alpha, right? That's nature for you. Alphas and betas. Predators and prey. And even though reindeer are supposedly cognizant, domesticated beings, there is still a bit of wildness in them. I guess there is wildness in all of us." He gave a sad shake of his head. Puck always got philosophical after the second beer. It wasn't until the fifth or sixth that we saw the wildness in him.

"What are the other reindeer like?" asked Jax.

"Well, Prancer and Vixen are friends with Comet, and they're both evil." Puck took a sip of his beer. "The rest are okay. Dasher and Dancer are brothers. They're solid. Cupid is a bit of a flake. Donner has anxiety issues. Blitzen drinks too much. Like me," he said with a laugh.

"Which is your favorite?"

Puck and I answered together. "Rudolph."

"Really?"

"Yep. He's the most famous reindeer of all. For good reason." One of the other RATs called Puck over to the bar. "I'd better go. Good to meet you, Jax."

He went back to have another drink and carouse with his friends. Normally, I would have been drinking and carousing with them. I grabbed my Grinch and sucked more down. It went straight to my head.

Even after all these years, I still had no idea what was in my favorite drink, and Nick wouldn't tell. Once, I found a cherry in my glass, and I was so excited because I love maraschino cherries. Sadly, it ended up being a plastic fake berry from one of the decorations on the bar, and I nearly choked on it. Not a pleasant experience, but did it stop me from ordering a Grinch when I came to Nick's? Heck no. I, for one, valued the importance of tradition. I also valued the importance of cheap drinks that got me intoxicated as quickly as possible.

The guys from the Reindeer Team went back to work, waving goodbye as they left. I waved back, calling out to each of them by name. Frank blew me a kiss.

Good old Frank. Yes, he was shallow and possibly a sex addict, but he'd gotten me through some rough patches. Well, Frank and Win together. We'd been close friends once upon a time but had drifted apart when Win and I went to college and Frank set out to become a professional skier. After a knee injury, he'd had to give it up, and when he returned to the North Pole, things were different. We didn't connect anymore.

Well, other than the occasional hookup. We definitely connected in that way.

It never led to anything, though, other than some furious make-out sessions and a few hickies. Frank and I hadn't discussed it, but the whole thing seemed wrong. Even though my hookups with Frank happened long after Win and I broke up, they brought on a surprising surge of guilt, and I had a feeling Frank experienced the same thing.

Win and I had broken up more than two years ago, and I hadn't been in a serious relationship since. I wondered if

I'd ever be in a real relationship again. Wow. How depressing.

When I turned back to Jax, he was deep in thought, and it gave me a chance to study him. In appearance, he differed significantly from a Christmas elf. We tended to have softer features and brightness filled us, like we carried eternal sunshine around with us wherever we went, but Jax wasn't filled with the same light. Not that he didn't glow in his own way. It was simply different—more luminous, like the radiance of a full moon on a cloudless night.

I sighed, realizing I'd nailed it. Jax Grayson was moonlight. He looked up at me questioningly, probably due to all the sighing, and I shook my head to indicate it was nothing. He'd almost busted me, but I couldn't help being interested. I'd never met anyone like him before.

He wore his long hair tied in a neat ponytail. Simple and severe. Christmas elves favored ribbons and curls and fancier styles, even the guys, but not Jax. His clothing was simple. No sparkles. No appliqué. No plaid. Definitely no sequins. He wore only plain black, from his elegantly cut suit to his leather shoes. Even his shirt and tie were black, which seemed excessive, but he wore it well. Everything about him was both attractive and dangerous, but I couldn't tell if he was dangerous because he was attractive or attractive because he was dangerous. It was a conundrum. And I was wasted.

Jax rubbed his chin with one hand, an unreadable expression in his dark eyes. "I hate to ask, but I must." He leaned closer and took a glance around the bar as if to make sure no one was listening. It was quiet now, since the RAT guys were gone. A drunk old elf was nursing a beer at a table by himself, and two were at the bar chatting with Nick, but that was it. There was no need to worry about being overheard. Even so, when Jax spoke, he kept his voice soft.

"I need your assistance, Tink. Cookie has effectively tied my hands by making you my guide, which is what happens whenever a dark elf visits the North Pole, but perhaps this is a twist of fate which could work in my favor."

"What do you mean?"

His intense gaze locked on mine. "Help me figure out what's going on here."

I attempted to gaze back at him just as intensely, but since there were currently two Jax Graysons in front of me, it was challenging to do. I squinted, trying to focus.

He must have understood my predicament because he ordered coffee and gently pushed my second Grinch to the side. I didn't protest. I was nearly done with it anyway, and the bottom part was always questionable. Whatever made it tasty on the top also made it sickly sweet and sludgy toward the end.

Nick brought our coffee in chipped white mugs. Despite adding two creams and four sugars, the coffee was still dark and tasted like tar. It had probably been sitting on the burner since last night. I drank it anyway. I needed to sober up, and I needed to do it quickly.

"You seriously want me to help you?" I asked.

"I do. What happened to Joy is only going to happen again. We need to put an end to the situation before it gets worse."

I weighed my options. I recognized trouble when I saw it, and Jax Grayson was trouble. It was the last thing I needed right now. If I screwed up, I'd lose the job on the naughty list faster than I could say "Ho, ho, ho," and end up right back with the reindeer.

But this wasn't about me. It was about all of us. And it was important.

I pictured Joy's lifeless face and the blood trickling from her ears. If I could help bring whoever had done this to justice, I owed it to her to do it. I was not the queen of making good decisions, but this time, I didn't care if the decision was good or bad. I had to do it. I had no choice.

I gazed up at Jax, decision made. "How can I help?"

CHAPTER FIVE

A fter deciding our best option was to stick to Cookie's schedule as much as possible, we headed to the collections department. I was still shaky after what had happened to Joy, but the coffee sobered me up nicely, and I now had some questions for Jax. Important questions. Questions I should have asked him before, but I managed to get some of them in as we made our way back to company headquarters.

"As much as I'm flattered by your request, Mr. Mysterious, what can I do to help you? I don't have a high-ranking job, nor am I privy to any top-secret information."

He snorted at my newest nickname for him but answered my question. "Showing me around and giving me your honest opinion would be useful. No one else seems inclined to do it."

"Well, I'm always a little too honest, so I don't foresee a problem," I said with a wry smile.

"Good." He shot me a sidelong glance. "Tell me about the next stop on our itinerary. The collections department."

"Fine, but I doubt the collections department has anything to do with drugs or candicocane."

"What do they deal with?" asked Jax.

"Billing and accounts receivable," I said. "It's complicated because we deal in different currencies, distribute to different tribes, and collect from different worlds. But it's all about the toys."

"In what way?"

"As a side hustle, we sell genuine North Pole toys to shops and distributors in the human world, as well as to the other elven tribes. It's a lot to keep track of, and the collections department is under the umbrella of accounting."

Collections was also one of the most depressing, colorless offices in the North Pole. Jax caught the vibe as soon as we stepped through the door. "Such a cheery place," he said, taking in the drab walls and the equally drab employees.

"Collections is not a party," I said quietly. "It's more like a wake."

"Tink." The voice came from directly behind me. I turned around with a smile.

"Nippy?" I said. "Wow. How strange. We were just talking about you over lunch. Jax, this is Nippy Nibblewrap. What a coincidence, huh?"

Jax seemed momentarily stunned. Maybe he thought I'd made up the name. I nudged him. Hard.

"Hello," he said, as he came out of his stupor. "Nice to meet you."

"You, too," said Nippy. "And it's good to see you as well, Tink."

"Yes, it's been too long."

Nippy adjusted his glasses. "Eighteen months and two days, to be exact."

Nippy was tall, thin, and kind, having somehow managed to maintain his soul, even after working in collections for over a decade. He didn't seem to notice Jax's awkward pause at his name, but he wasn't the kind of person who noticed awkward pauses. Or awkward people. Or awkward anything.

He turned back to Jax. "Are you here on vacation?" He glanced around. "Not here in the collections department obviously," he said with a snort. "That would be the worst vacation ever."

"True," I said with a laugh. "Jax is here for work. He's from the Elven High Council."

Nippy smiled. "Well, we're happy to have you here, Jax."

"Thank you." Jax studied him as if looking for some hint of sarcasm in Nippy's words, but he wouldn't find it. Nippy didn't have a mean bone in his body.

I gave Nippy a playful poke in the arm. "What have you been up to? Staying out of trouble?"

Nippy laughed, a sound reminiscent of a donkey braying. "You're such a card, Tink. I work in the shipping department now. I'm here to check on a few discrepancies I found in some billing documents. I handle international bills of lading now, which is a hoot."

Only Nippy would think paperwork was fun. "Good for you." I turned to Jax. "But, if you have any questions about collections, Nippy is the man to ask. He worked in this department longer than anyone else I know."

"Tink's right. It might have been a record. But you also set a record, didn't you Tink?"

"A record?" asked Jax, shooting me an amused glance. "What for?"

Nippy pointed a finger at me almost proudly. "Shortest time ever working in collections. How long did you last?"

"Twenty-seven minutes," I said. "Well, thirty if you count how long it took me to get my coffee and sit at my desk."

Jax's lips twitched. "Dare I ask what happened?"

"I was just unlucky. The first person I had to call was an old lady. She was a nature elf and so sweet and mellow."

"They're always mellow," Jax deadpanned. "Because they are always high. Please continue."

"Well, she was nice and old and didn't have much money. She bought a toy for her grandson and couldn't pay for it. She told me he had learning issues. And she was a widow. And her dog ran away. And she was on the verge of losing her house."

Jax had a twinkle in his eyes. "In other words, she scammed you."

"Yep," said Nippy with a grin. "Total scammer."

"What did you do?" asked Jax. "Write off her debt or something?"

"No," I said, covering my face with my hands. "I paid it myself—using my own personal credit card. And they fired me."

"But it doesn't stop there," said Nippy with another snort.

I sighed. "He's right. The old forest bitch got my credit card info and used it to buy a freaking hot tub. It took months to get it sorted out, and my credit score ended up being naughty list material because of it. I can't believe I was so stupid."

"You were compassionate," said Nippy. "Not stupid."

"Really?" I asked, narrowing my eyes at him.

He laughed. "Okay. You were kind of stupid, but mostly

you were young and inexperienced. And you learned from it, right?"

"I learned I hated collections," I said. "And I also learned never to trust a person whose life sounds like a bad country music song."

"Oh, something like, 'I lost my job after twenty-seven minutes, and they stole my credit card,'" sang Nippy in a fairly decent imitation of a country music star.

I punched him lightly on the arm. "Shut it. But you're right. I concede your point. Nice voice, by the way." I turned back to Jax. "Do you have any questions for Nippy?"

He shook his head. "I don't think so."

"Jax is doing an audit," I explained.

Nippy's face turned even paler than usual. "An audit? Are we in trouble?"

"No," I said. "It's procedural stuff. Right, Jax?"

"Right," he said, glancing around the room at the people working in their cubicles. "We have all the information we need for now. Thank you for your time, Mr. Nibblewrap."

"You're welcome. And please call me Nippy. All my friends do."

When we stepped outside, Jax glanced down at me, perplexed. "Your friend is a sincerely nice person."

"He is," I said. "Does it surprise you?"

"No," he said. "But most of the Christmas Elves I meet at Elf Central aren't the same. They're pompous and arrogant, if you want to know the truth."

"They're politicians. I guess it goes with the territory." I glanced up at the darkening sky. The dome covering the entire city kept the temperature livable. It also provided fake daylight to make sure our circadian rhythms stayed in check, but there was no sunset. Just a gradual fading of light, indicating it was around five o'clock.

"Did you have anything else you wanted to ask?"

"Not at the moment." Jax glanced at his watch. "But it's getting late. We should wrap it up for the day."

"Sounds good. Let's meet first thing in the morning in front of Cookie's office. Does nine work for you?"

"It does."

"Okay. Bye, Jax."

I turned to leave, but he stopped me. "You were brave today, Tink, and I found your candidness refreshing. Thank you for your work and for agreeing to help me. Not every Christmas Elf would do so."

With a bow, he turned and left, the wind ruffling his dark hair, and his stride determined.

Determined.

If Nippy was sincere, and I was candid (an excellent way to say I couldn't keep my mouth shut), the best way to describe Jax was determined. If something was going on here, be it candicocane or not, he would figure it out.

When I got home, all the stress and pressure of the day hit me at once. I dropped my briefcase and slipped out of my shoes before heading down the hall to seek out my roommate. Noelle stood in front of the bathroom mirror, wrapped in a towel, and applying mascara as she got ready for work.

"How did it go?" she asked, pumping the brush into the mascara tube. "Did you get a new job?"

"Not sure yet," I said.

She frowned, her gray eyes worried, as she studied my face. "What happened? You look upset."

"I am." As I let what had happened sink in, my chin wobbled. "Joy Berry died today."

She gaped at me. "Your friend from work?"

"Yes." I told her the whole story, from being assigned to

Jax to watching Joy die in front of Happypie's. I faltered slightly on the last part.

She gave my arm a gentle squeeze, her eyes kind. "Oh, Tink. I'm so sorry,"

"Thanks," I said, my voice thick with emotion.

Noelle glanced at her watch. "I wish I could call off work, but we've been so short-staffed lately. Will you be okay?"

"Of course." I followed her from the bathroom to her bedroom and leaned against the doorjamb as she dressed in pink scrubs and pulled her dark hair into a neat bun.

"Did the EMTs tell you what happened?" she asked.

I shook my head. "No but Jax says it looked like a candicocane overdose."

She paused in pinning up her hair to give me a shocked look. "Joy didn't seem like the type. At all."

"That's what bothers me. Well, in addition to watching her die on the sidewalk." I shuddered at the memory. "Have you ever seen a candicocane overdose in the ER?"

She hesitated, but only for a moment. "I have. It's been like an epidemic lately. The numbers are going up week to week. They're trying to keep it hush-hush, from what I can tell, but three people died from it last night."

I sank onto the corner of her bed. Her room was always so neat and tidy. Mine looked like the aftereffects of a pipe bomb explosion.

"Why would anyone want to hide it? Doesn't that seem weird?"

"This close to Christmas?" she asked with a snort. "Not weird at all." She paused while slipping into her nursing clogs. They were also pink and matched her scrubs. "But do you know what's troubling me about the whole thing? We've always had drug issues on the North

Pole. It's not a big secret. But usually, the people who over-dosed were junkies and sex workers. Right now, however, it's a free-for-all. The patients I've seen are a mix—executives and homemakers and people like your friend Joy. She doesn't fit the stereotype at all. There is something strange going on."

"Jax said the same thing. He asked me to help him figure it out."

"He did?" Noelle gave me a funny look. "Why?"

I frowned, not liking her tone. "Because he needs help, I guess, and because I'm familiar with how things work here. And we bonded when Joy died."

"But you met him this morning?"

"Yes. Why are you looking at me like that?" A thought occurred to me. "Wait. Is this because he's a dark elf? I cannot believe you'd judge someone by their tribe, Noelle."

"No," she said, sounding exasperated. "It's not because of his tribe. It's because he's from Elf Central, and you don't know him or his agenda. You're in line for a job you want and pissing off Cookie Wassail is not the way to get it."

She had a point. Actually, she had several points. "What do you suggest I do?"

Noelle put her hands on my upper arms and stared straight into my eyes. We were the same height, so it was easy to do. "Tell Cookie what happened. All of it. And let him know Jax asked for your help."

"That feels like betrayal."

She let go of my arms and grabbed her purse and ID. "It's not betrayal. It's elf-preservation, kiddo."

"Ugh. You're right. I know you're right, but I'm exhausted. I want to curl up in a ball and sleep for the next two hundred years."

"That'll have to wait," said Noelle, as she put on her

coat. "It's Monday. Don't you have to go to Grandma Gingersnap's for dinner?"

"Oh, no. I forgot." I winced. "Do you think she'll let me get out of it this one time?"

Noelle laughed, but we both knew the answer. I had to go to my grandmother's for dinner at least once a week. If I couldn't make it on Sunday with the whole family (which I tried to avoid whenever possible), I had to be there on Monday at precisely 6 pm, no exceptions, and it was already 5:30.

"Jiminy Christmas," I said, slipping back into my heels.

"Watch your language," said Noelle giving me a peck on the cheek. "And if I don't see you tomorrow morning, remember what I said. Be careful, Tink. You're running out of options. This might be your last chance, so don't screw it up."

Don't screw it up. Great advice. If only I could learn to follow it.

Twenty-eight minutes later, I was at Grandma Gingersnap's front door. She opened it before I even knocked. "You're late."

"No, I'm not. I'm two minutes early," I said, bypassing a row of suitcases to follow her into the kitchen. The smell of roast beef and potatoes wafted through the air. I was starving. I'd had a big lunch, but stressful events always made me ravenous. "Going somewhere?" I asked, tilting my head to indicate the suitcases.

She let out a huff. "Tinklebelle Holly. How many times do I have to tell you? I'm going on my annual pre-Christmas cruise with my lady friends. I leave tomorrow morning, and I'll be gone two weeks."

"So I don't have to come to dinner next week?"

"Is it such a chore?" she asked, a catch in her voice. I immediately experienced a stab of guilt.

"I was kidding. Can I do anything for you while you're gone?"

"Well, you could pick up my mail every couple of days, if you don't mind. Put it on the table by the front door. And if I get any packages, put those on the bench in the mud room. The Snows promised to keep an eye on the place, but I'll let them know you'll be stopping by, too."

"Sounds good." I tried to grab a cherry tomato out of the salad, and she swatted my hand.

"What are you doing? Were you raised by wolves?"

"Close enough," I said, popping the tomato into my mouth when she wasn't looking. "I was raised by you."

She sent me a sharp look. I tried hard to make it seem like I didn't have a cherry tomato in my mouth, but Grandma Gingersnap somehow knew. She shook her head and let out a huff before turning to take the roast out of the oven. I rolled my eyes in annoyance. She somehow knew about that, too.

"Stop rolling your eyes at me, young lady."

I nearly choked on the tomato. "You weren't even looking at me. How could you possibly see what I was doing?"

"When will you learn I have eyes in the back of my head?" She handed me a bowl of green beans. "Carry these into the dining room so we can eat."

Grandma Gingersnap lived on the East Side in a giant house on Morningstar Lane. Some might call it a mansion. I'd called it home from the age of seven on after my parents died in a freak sleigh accident. Win grew up in the house next door, and our families were lifelong friends. Not always a good situation, especially after I broke up with him. My grandmother didn't speak to me for a year. I still had to come to dinner once a week, mind you, but those were strange days of staring daggers at each other and trying to communicate our hidden aggressions telepathically. At least now we could do it out loud.

My grandmother had done her best, but I'd been difficult from birth. It only got worse after I lost my parents. My teen years had been rough, and the college years not much better, but now Grandma Gingersnap and I had a sort of truce going on. If I came over for dinner as requested, she'd stop badgering me about my life choices. It worked. Usually.

"Tell me about your day," she said as she sat at the head of the long dining room table, her snowy white curls perfectly coiffed, her maquillage flawless, and her clothing elegant. The only thing marring her impeccable appearance was a red apron with a giant, smiling snowman on it, a gift I'd created in my high school home economics class. It was the only sewing project I'd ever completed successfully, and I was touched she still wore it, especially since I'd purposefully misplaced the carrot to make it look like the snowman had a penis.

"My day? It was...interesting."

I sat next to her, on her right, my usual seat. Grandma Gingersnap paused, fork halfway to her mouth. She put it down and narrowed her eyes at me. They were the same shade of blue as mine. The only difference was mine didn't shoot laser beams when I got mad—at least I didn't think they did.

"Define 'interesting.'"

I held up a finger to indicate I needed to finish chewing the giant bite of roast beef I'd shoved into my mouth. It was delicious, as always, and we also had potatoes, carrots, and fresh rolls. I suspected there might even be cherry pie for dessert. Grandma Gingersnap prided herself on three things. Her family, her cooking, and her ability to always know whenever I kept something from her. It was like her superpower. I didn't even bother trying to hide things from her anymore.

"Well, I have a new job. Kind of."

"Oh, you do?" she asked, going back to her meal. "What is it?"

"I'm acting as a tour guide to a dark elf sent by Elven High Council to spy on us. Could you please pass the butter?"

Her eyes widened, and for a minute, I worried she might choke. She didn't. She dabbed her lips genteelly with a linen napkin and took a sip of wine before responding.

"You're going to have to do better, Tinklebelle. I want details. Now."

"And I want butter."

We had a five-second stare down before she handed me the butter. I thanked her with a flutter of my eyelashes and went on with my story. I told her about Cookie and Jax and the potential job on the naughty list team. She listened carefully. I didn't mention what had happened to Joy. My grandmother tended to freak out over things like people dying in the middle of the sidewalk on a Monday afternoon. It was better to keep it to myself.

After I finished speaking, she took another sip of wine— a longer one this time. Actually, it couldn't qualify as a sip. She drained the glass and poured herself another. She offered me a top off, but I demurred. I'd barely touched my first glass. I still felt icky from the two Grinches I'd indulged in earlier.

Putting her elbows on the table, she folded her hands

ABIGAIL DRAKE

together. "I need to get this straight. The last time we spoke, there were complaints about you from the reindeer, and yet now you are being offered a promotion as long as you act as a tour guide for a dark elf with questionable motives."

"Yes. But it sounds worse when you say it that way. Let's focus on the potential promotion part, okay?"

"Let's not." With a sigh, she took the napkin off her lap and placed it next to her plate, a sign she'd finished eating. Not good. "Why don't you talk to your uncle—"

"Nope."

"But Tinklebelle—"

"No way. We've discussed this before, Grandma. Subject closed." I made a motion like slamming a book shut for emphasis.

She lifted one elegantly arched eyebrow but didn't call me out. The sadness and disappointment in her expression pained me, so I kept my focus on the roast beef. It still tasted amazing, but it was harder to swallow. For some reason, I had a big lump in my throat now. Thanks, Grandma.

"What do you plan to do, oh wise one?" she asked.

"I plan to do my job," I said, getting defensive. This happened every time I came for dinner, right before my grandmother served dessert. "And Jax has been pretty impressed. He even asked for my help on a...special project."

"A special project?"

"Yes."

"A *secret* special project?"

"Um, yes...?"

Now she was the one rolling her eyes. "Never trust a dark elf, Tink. You know better. I lived in Elf Central before I married your grandfather. I know what I'm talking about. They aren't like Christmas elves. They are bad seeds. All of them. I know from personal experience."

My jaw dropped. "Oh, glistening gooey gumdrops. Did you *date* a dark elf when you were younger?"

She pushed back her chair and stood up. "I'm not even going to grace that with an answer," she said as she cleared off the table. I was still eating, so I covered my plate protectively. "Dark elves are wicked, and if he's asking you to help him with something, I'm sure he's up to no good. I suggest you go straight to Cookie Wassail first thing in the morning and tell him what's going on."

"Noelle said the same thing."

"Because Noelle is smart," she said, her voice clipped. "You should listen to her."

"He's not a bad elf. His name is Jax Grayson. He works for the Elven High Council." I was repeating myself. I always did that when I was nervous, and my grandmother knew it.

She let out a bark of laughter. "Oh, honey. That makes things worse, not better." She covered my hand with hers. "You have known this man since this morning, and yet you're willing to put your career on the line for him? Don't do it. I know you're trying to find your path, and I admire you for it, but you need to trust me on this. Jax Grayson is trouble. And he'll get you into trouble, too. Listen to me and do as I say. Please."

I nodded because I knew she was right, and I was also afraid she might withhold cherry pie from me if I didn't agree with her. "I will. I promise."

She leaned back in her chair with a relieved sigh, but her hawk-like eyes still studied me closely. "Is there anything else you wanted to tell me?"

I considered mentioning Joy and the candicocane problem, but that would lead to a whole bunch of additional questions, and right now, I wanted to have cherry pie and go home and sleep.

I slapped a broad smile on my face and tried to erase any modicum of guilt from my eyes. "No, Grandma Gingersnap. Nothing at all. Is it time for pie?"

CHAPTER SIX

I arrived at Cookie Wassail's office at just after eight
the following day. His administrative assistant, Mince
Mingle, tried to lock the office door when she saw me
coming, but I was faster, slipping in before she could locate
which key she needed on a giant ring.

"Good morning, Mince," I said as cheerfully as possible.
"I'm here to see Cookie."

I wore a dark green skirt and a crisp white blouse; my
matching green wool coat tossed over my arm. Even my
shoes, green velvet pumps, matched, but Mince was not
impressed.

"Mr. Wassail is not here."

"I'll wait."

Humming a tune, I plopped onto one of the hard,
wooden chairs lining the wall and sipped my coffee. It was a
large peppermint mocha with extra whipped cream and
candy sprinkles on top—my favorite morning beverage.
That might explain why my skirt currently seemed a little
snug, especially in my butt. And judging by the way my

blouse gaped slightly between buttons, I might have gained some weight there too. Great.

I pulled on my blouse as discreetly as possible, trying to close the gap, but to no avail. I needed to go to the gym, and I should cut down on the peppermint mochas, but I took another sip and sighed. It was delicious. Maybe I'd start tomorrow.

I picked up a copy of *Elf Magazine* from the small table next to me. Flipping through it, I stopped at the society pages. Win was pictured coming out of a charity ball with Candy Holiday on his arm. People often said Candy and I resembled each other, but I disagreed. She was much prettier than I'd ever been and more put together—inside and out. Then again, I was usually a hot mess, so the bar wasn't set terribly high.

Win's parents stood next to them, his father distinguished and his mother classy and well-dressed. Win had been their miracle baby, born after twenty years of trying. They were close friends with Grandma Gingersnap, but they'd never warmed to me. They called me a disaster magnet, which was pretty accurate. Ever since I was small, I'd always been in some form of trouble or another, and they feared I might get their precious Win in trouble, too.

It never happened because Win was a model citizen. A sexy, handsome, good-in-the-sack model citizen who never went along with any of my schemes and kept me out of trouble on more than one occasion. Win was perfect, and the sole thing his parents and I could agree on was he deserved someone far better than me. Maybe Candy was that person. I bet his parents loved her.

I'd heard through the grapevine they'd been dating, but seeing them together, even in a photo, still kind of bothered me. Candy had been my friend until the night a few years ago when I'd caught her kissing Win under the mistletoe. She'd tried to make amends—calling to apologize, sending me flowers, leaving notes at my door—but I'd never been amenable to amending. Instead, in true Tink Holly fashion, I sought revenge. What can I say? My life was falling apart all around me, and Candy was a convenient target for my pent-up anger and spite. Or at least that's what my therapist said. Or maybe I was a horrible person. The jury was still out.

In truth, my revenge plot regarding Candy was pretty simple. I knew where she kept a key to her apartment (under the perfectly decorated fir tree by her front door), so I made a copy of it and let myself inside while she was at work.

I'd intended to play some harmless pranks on her, to mess with her mind, but things escalated quickly. My shenanigans got out of control, but I couldn't stop. It was like years of rage and frustration spilled out of me, and I directed it all at Candy.

I switched her favorite shirt for one that was two sizes too small, so she'd think she was getting fat. I stuck bits of fiber insulation inside all of her bras so her boobs would itch. Using rubber gloves and being careful, I put hot sauce on her vibrator. I felt kind of bad about that one, but not enough for me to stop. At last, I came up with a great plan. I bought something called Liquid Ass and sprayed it all over her apartment. It smelled terrible. I overheard her complaining to friends about it and nearly peed my pants. She kept cleaning, trying to find the source of the smell, but couldn't—mostly because I snuck in while she was at work and sprayed more of it every week.

Best idea ever.

While spraying the Liquid Ass for the third and final

time, I had another brilliant idea—to replace her expensive vodka with water. Not wanting to waste so much perfectly good alcohol, I drank some of it first. Unfortunately, I may have had too much because as I got ready to leave, disaster struck, and I dropped the Liquid Ass.

I'm not sure why the fine people who created Liquid Ass chose to put it in glass bottles. Perhaps it had something to do with the odor leeching through plastic. I'll never know, but when I dropped it, and it shattered, a smell was released upon the world that had never been released before. It was so bad my eyes watered, and my stomach heaved. Up came all the vodka, and the smell of the vomit made it all so much worse.

I ran out of the apartment, covered in Liquid Ass and puke. I couldn't call an Ubersled because no one would want to drive me smelling like this, and I couldn't take the subway or a bus. I had to walk the four miles home, in heels, gagging and crying the whole way.

The police were waiting for me when I reached my apartment. Candy had suspected something was up and installed security cameras. It wasn't the first time I'd been arrested, but hopefully, it would be the last. Candy didn't press charges on the condition I get help, so I went to therapy and anger management classes. Afterward, I never dabbled in revenge crimes again. I'd learned my lesson. Even now, years later, remembering the smell of Liquid Ass made me gag.

Mince shot me a dirty look, probably due to the gagging sound I'd made at the Liquid Ass memory, but I ignored her. I'd gotten pretty good at ignoring strange looks and snide comments. Among the elven community of the North Pole, I was sort of infamous. Either people knew me, or they knew *of* me, and tended to judge me based entirely on rumors—kind of like how I judged Jax. The difference was I knew I was doing the right thing, even if I'd woken up with a sick sensation in the pit of my stomach. My moral compass kept sending off warning beacons, but I ignored it. My moral compass had been wrong before—many times. But Grandma Gingersnap and Noelle had no such problem. Their judgment was right up there with Santa himself, so I had to follow their guidance regarding Jax. I'd be a fool if I didn't.

At half-past eight, Cookie arrived. Mince tilted her head to indicate where I sat, and when he saw me, he closed his eyes and opened them again, almost like he hoped I'd disappear. I stood up and attempted a courteous facial expression. For someone with a resting grinch face, it took effort. Often it made me twitch. Today was one of those days.

"Hi, Mr. Wassail. Do you have a few minutes to chat?"

"Must we?" he asked. "Dealing with you two days in a row is more than I can handle."

My eye was definitely twitching now. "Yes. We must. Sorry to ruin your day."

"Day? You're ruining my week. Maybe even my month." With a resigned sigh, he waved a hand, showing me into his office, and closed the door behind me. I followed him across the room.

"Here's the thing—"

He held up a hand. "Stop. Coffee first."

I waited patiently for him to pour a cup from the machine in the corner of the room. I imagined Mince had made him a fresh pot when she arrived. He was going to need it this morning.

After he took a long sip, he put down his briefcase and glanced through a stack of paperwork before addressing me again. "Please sit." He pointed to a leather chair near his desk. "And tell me what you've done now, Ms. Holly. Because I'm sure it's something. It's always something."

As much as I resented his remarks, he had a point. I opened my mouth, but no words came out at first. I'd been organizing my thoughts since I woke up this morning, but now this all seemed wrong. Very wrong. Still, I had no choice.

I cleared my throat. "I need to talk with you about Jax Grayson."

He narrowed his eyes at me. "What about Jax Grayson?"

"He might not be here to do an audit. He could be spying on us."

He leaned back in his chair and scratched his chin. "For what reason?"

"I don't know." I didn't want to tell him the rest, but I knew I had to do it. "Yesterday, a woman died on the sidewalk in Central City in front of Happypie's Hamburgers."

I decided not to mention I knew the woman who died. That would lead to an entirely different set of questions, and as much as I wanted the naughty list job, I trusted Cookie about as far as I could throw him.

"I heard." He gave me an odd look before going back to shuffling through the papers on his desk.

"We were there."

That got his attention. He froze in mid-shuffle. "What do you mean?"

"Jax and I were having lunch at Happypie's. We saw it happen. He gave her CPR. I...we watched her die." My voice shook, and I steadied myself. "And Jax told me a candicocane overdose killed her. He said candicocane was becoming a big problem amongst all the tribes, even ours. He asked for my help."

Now Cookie's eye had begun to twitch. "What do you think he wants you to do?"

"I'm not sure, but he seemed to know a great deal about the candicocane problem on the North Pole."

Cookie stiffened, something strange passing over his face. Was it guilt? Or fear? Or indigestion? I could never tell with Cookie.

"We don't have a candicocane problem on the North Pole."

I frowned at him. "But I saw a woman die from an overdose yesterday, and I've heard it's happening more and more frequently."

"You 'heard.' From whom?"

Realizing I now risked getting Noelle in trouble, I shrugged. "You know. Around. People talk."

He folded his hands on his desk. "Ms. Holly, are you certain the woman you saw died of a candicocane overdose or is that simply Mr. Grayson's interpretation?"

I faltered. "Well, he said he'd seen it before—at the capitol. And he seemed to know what he was talking about." It was on the tip of my tongue to mention Jax worked for Elf Enforcement, but I didn't. Something held me back. I'd done what Noelle and my grandmother told me to do and decided it was enough. I now regretted coming here at all. "Why would he lie?"

Cookie pointed at me. "Good question. That's the first question you should have asked." He shook his head sadly. "How long have we known each other, Tink?"

I shifted uneasily in my chair. "I graduated from college and got my first job around five years ago. I'm guessing I met you then."

"Yes, and I've watched you go through job after job and mess up every single time. I've tried to be patient. For the sake of your family—"

"My family has nothing to do with this."

"But because of your family, I've given you more chances than you deserve. You understand that don't you?"

It was hard to argue with the truth. "Yes, I do."

"And now you want a big promotion—a job managing the naughty list team. We both know you don't deserve it, but I was willing to give you another chance. I asked this one small favor in return. I wanted you to keep an eye on Jax Grayson, but could you? No. Instead, you come to me with this nonsense and a fictional story about a North Pole drug issue where none exists. You were supposed to keep him from seeing anything we didn't want him to see, and you couldn't even do such a simple task. I'm disappointed in you. And I'm disappointed in myself for thinking you would do as we asked for once in your life."

I swallowed hard. "I'm sorry, Mr. Wassail. I assumed I was doing the right thing by bringing this matter to your attention, but obviously, I was wrong. Perhaps it would be best if I went back to my job in the reindeer division and you find someone else to take Mr. Grayson around."

He let out a laugh. "The reindeer division? Oh, Ms. Holly, you're misunderstanding the gravity of this situation. We're not talking about returning you to your old job. We've already filled your position there."

I shifted in my seat, a dull panic forming in my chest. "What are we talking about exactly?"

"You're looking at a demotion." Cookie leaned closer, folding his hands on his desk, and giving me a menacing look with his beady black eyes. "There is only one job lower than the reindeer division, and you know what it is."

"The coal mines?" The words came out as a whisper, and I panicked. "You can't."

"I can, and I will."

Once an elf went to the coal mines, they could never return to their old life. It was a one-way ticket—a prison sentence. A subterranean nightmare. And the uniforms were even worse than the reindeer division. They were the color of poo.

"You're not being fair."

"Fair?" Cookie laughed. "We both know the truth, and it's at my discretion, isn't it? You, Miss Holly, won't have a choice, but you have one right now."

"What do you mean?"

The gleam in his eyes turned even nastier. "Find out what Jax Grayson is doing. Make him trust you, and report back to me. He's here for a reason, and I need to know what it is. I expect you to do as I ask, Tink. It may be your last chance to redeem yourself."

Redeem myself? I didn't like the sound of that. I also didn't like being threatened.

When I was small, Grandma Gingersnap took me to a psychiatrist. She was at her wit's end. After a barrage of tests, the doctor (who seemed emotionally exhausted herself) came up with a diagnosis of ODD—Oppositional Defiance Disorder. It meant if someone told me to do something, I had a strong and almost uncontrollable urge to do the opposite, despite what impact it might have on my life.

It explained many things, including my inability to hold a job. A lot of my problems came as the result of other people being awful, but I brought some of it upon myself. I realized as much now. I also realized Cookie knew it, and I'd been right with my assessment yesterday when Jax walked into the room. Cookie Wassail had set me up. He wanted me to fail. He wanted to send my slightly-larger-than-normal butt off to the Coal Mines, but what he didn't know was he'd switched on my ODD. Not a good thing, but I maintained my composure. I'm not sure how, but I did.

Cookie didn't have a clue. He sat at his desk with a smug smile on his face. He had me cornered. "I simply want your help, Miss Holly. Is it too much to ask? If so, I can fill out the paperwork and send you to the coal mines right now."

"No. That won't be necessary."

"Good," he said with an even smirkier smirk. "I'm glad you see it my way. You're a smart girl, and you could have a bright future ahead of you. Or not. It's your choice."

My choice? What a joke. "Are we done here?"

"Almost. Mr. Grayson, it seems, is unhappy with the itinerary I kindly provided for him and wants to make his own schedule from now on."

"And you're okay with that?"

"No, but it makes no difference since you'll still be his guide, and you'll report back to me." He gave me an assessing look. "Get closer to him, Tink. Make him trust you. And, most importantly, distract him. It's vital we find out what he's up to as soon as possible. Christmas is, after all, a month away. The last thing we all need is a problem right now with Elven High Council. Are we clear?"

"Crystal."

He must have seen something in my face because he lowered his voice. "Would it hurt you to play nice for a few days?"

What little patience I had was nearly gone. "I'll do what I have to do," I said, forcing the words out of my mouth. I needed to get away from Cookie immediately. I'd reached my breaking point, and I knew it. One more snide comment from him could put me right over the edge. "I repeat, are we done here?"

Cookie let out a derisive snort. "We're done." I got up to leave, but he stopped me. "Remember who you are, Ms. Holly, and where your loyalties lie. I shouldn't have to remind you, but it seems to have slipped your mind."

Elf off you elffing elfhole.

It was a good thing Cookie couldn't read my thoughts. Judging by the nasty gleam in his beady eyes, however, he could take a guess. But I refused to give him another opportunity to demote or fire me.

I managed to answer without killing him. "I could never forget," I said, my face tight. "No one will ever let me."

CHAPTER SEVEN

When I stepped out of Cookie's office, Jax stood there, waiting for me. He'd arrived early. Crap.

I plastered a smile of greeting on my face, hoping it didn't seem too fake. "Good morning. Ready to get started?"

He studied me, and although his expression was unreadable, his eyes were as cold and hard as onyx. "I am." He held open the door for me, and we stepped out into the hallway. "Early morning meeting?" he asked, his voice clipped and precise.

Darn it. He knew I'd blabbed to Cookie. But how?

I struggled for an air of nonchalance, but it may have come across as pissy. "Mr. Wassail wanted to discuss the itinerary. He said you're now calling all the shots, and I'm your..." I frowned. "What was the term you used yesterday? Ah. I remember now—your *cruise director*. Or maybe you're more like a king. Tell me where you want to go, Your Majesty."

I gave him a deep bow, and his expression darkened. "Don't call me that," he said, practically spitting out the words. "And stop acting like the affronted party. I have a job to do and not much time to do it. Rather than meeting your ex-boyfriend and your friends Nippy and Snippy and Sugarplum and being given hamburgers along with the redacted official tour, I'd like to see the places I need to investigate. Are we clear?"

"Yes," I said, clenching my teeth together so hard it hurt. "But the next melf who has the nerve to ask me if I am clear on something is going to get punched in the nose."

I said the last part softly, but not softly enough. I needed to learn how to mutter under my breath better or maybe find a way to keep my mouth shut.

"Melf?" he asked.

"Male elf." I crossed my arms over my chest. "Are we going to get moving, or do you want to stand outside Cookie's office and chat all day?"

I should have played nice but didn't have it in me at the moment. I tried to remember the breathing exercises I'd learned in my anger management classes but couldn't seem to recall a single one.

"I'd prefer to get moving. You're the one holding things up." Jax shoved a brown paper bag at me. "Here. Maybe this will help."

"What is it?" I looked inside the bag and suffered a pang of guilt when I saw a chocolate muffin inside—like the ones Joy used to make. I looked up at Jax, stunned. "Oh, Jiminy Christmas. Why did you have to go and be so nice and thoughtful all of a sudden? Dang it, Jax Grayson."

"You said you needed to be fed regularly. I'm doing as instructed."

It was hard to see since my eyes burned with tears. "Thank you," I said, my voice thick. "You're very kind."

"I'm not kind. I'm practical. Now, where should we go first?"

"You want my opinion?" I lifted one eyebrow. "Why would you give two figgy puddings about my thoughts on the matter?"

"Because I'm a stranger here. I have few contacts and know little about the culture and customs of your people. It would save a great deal of time and effort if you'd help." Pulling a copy of the *North Pole Gazette* out of his briefcase, he handed it to me. "For example, look at this paper. You're having the same spike in candicocane related deaths we're having in Elf Central, and yet no one is reporting on it. Why?"

Noelle had pretty much said the same thing. "I don't know, but someone is trying to hush it up." I glanced up at him. "Are you sure Joy died of an overdose?"

He pulled out his phone. "I am. Remember how her fingers turned so dark and mottled?" He scrolled through his pictures, showing me photo after photo of pale hands with swollen, purple digits. "A candicocane overdose is called *livedo digitus mors.*"

"Blue finger death?"

"Yes, but the blood coming out of her orifices was thanks to the reindeer tranquilizer." He shoved his phone back into his pocket. "I know I'm right, Tink. You have to trust me. That's what killed her, and I'm sure her death was no accident."

I studied his face. He was telling me the truth, or at least what he believed to be the truth. I saw it in his eyes. "Poor Joy," I said, glancing at the paper again. "But why isn't anyone reporting this?"

"Your guess is as good as mine."

My brain still felt foggy. I needed to eat, so I took out

my muffin. I offered some to Jax, but he shook his head. "I don't eat chocolate for breakfast."

"Your loss," I said, handing him the copy of *Elf Magazine* I'd accidentally stolen from Cookie's office as I took a bite. "Hold this for me."

"What is this?" he asked, leafing through the pages. He stopped at the photos of Win and Candy and lifted one dark eyebrow. "Your famous ex-boyfriend?"

I stifled a groan. "And my ex-friend, Candy Holiday."

"Your friendship ended because of Winter Snow III?" He couldn't keep the sneer off his face. He really did not like Win, but he probably didn't like me much, either.

"Yes. Well, that and some minor vandalism on my part. Water under the bridge."

"What kind of 'minor vandalism'?" The sneer had been replaced by what almost qualified as a smile.

With a sigh, I filled him in on the Liquid Ass episode. To his credit, he only laughed once. Maybe twice. It was hard to tell, since Jax was a very controlled sort of elf, but it felt good to make him laugh. And the muffin seemed like a peace offering. Maybe there was hope for this guy yet.

As Jax and I exited the building, we passed a giant poster of Santa riding on his sleigh, and Jax turned to me. "May I ask you a question?" When I nodded, he continued, his face tinged slightly pink with embarrassment. "How does Santa do it?" He indicated the poster with one hand. "Deliver all those gifts in one night?"

"Santa can control time. It's gifted to him when he's elected. And he makes a solemn vow to never use it for anything personal." My heart clenched in my chest, but I pushed away the feeling and all the memories associated with it. "The only other North Pole 'magic' is flying cattle. Yay."

"You sound pretty jaded."

"It would take days for me to tell you all the various reasons I hate this holiday."

"Since we're short on time, will you help me instead with the question at hand?" When I gave him a confused look, he rolled his eyes. "My itinerary, Tink. Where do we start?"

I paused mid-chew, staring at him. I knew I shouldn't help him. I didn't want to risk trouble with Cookie, and I didn't want to hear Grandma Gingersnap and Noelle tell me "I told you so" from now until eternity. But if there was any chance Jax might find out what happened to Joy, I had to point him in the correct direction at least. It was the right thing to do.

"I know just the place," I said.

"The hospital?"

I shook my head. "Nope. We need to go to Joy's parents' house. Today is her wake." I glanced at my watch. "But it's not until noon."

"What should we do until noon?"

"Experience the wonders of Christmas?" I laughed at the look on his face. "I'm kidding. I'll show you around."

"Can we go to the reindeer department?"

"The reindeer department is on the other side of town, and it's a big complex. In the interest of time, we should save it for later. Do you agree?"

"Certainly. Why don't we start at the top? Santa's workshop?"

"No," I said, louder than I intended. I shook my head, lowering my voice. "We shouldn't. They're busy right now."

Jax frowned. "Even more reason why we should visit."

Seeing no way out, I shoved the last of the muffin into my mouth. "Fine. Santa's workshop it is. I won't be able to set up a private meeting on such late notice, but we can take a public tour. They last about an hour, and they're kind of cheesy, but at least you'll get a look at the place."

"Works for me. I'm trying to acclimatize myself. Anything helps."

Santa's workshop was only a few blocks away. As we walked, I pointed out various buildings—the North Pole library, the fire station, the gum drop shop, and the candy cane factory, and watched Jax's face as he took it all in.

"This is the first time you've been here, right?" I asked. "Is it what you expected?"

He looked around at the snow-covered cobblestone streets, the wooden buildings designed to resemble gingerbread houses, and the annoyingly happy Christmas elves meandering up and down the street. They were all smiling and sparkling and wishing us a merry Christmas as they strode past. Most wore red or green. The traditional elf look was hot again, which meant the male elves wore a Christmas take on lederhosen, and the females wore dresses with striped stockings. Hats were popular, too. And fluffy earmuffs. I tried to imagine Jax in bright red lederhosen and matching earmuffs and failed miserably.

"What do you think?" I asked.

He lifted a dark eyebrow. "I find it charming."

Not the answer I expected. "Which part?"

Jax lifted his hands. "All of it. The music, for example. Is it always playing?"

"Yes. Christmas carols. All day every day, but don't worry. You'll learn to tune it out eventually, or you'll go crazy. It's usually one or the other."

He ignored the sarcasm. "And does it always smell like this?" He inhaled deeply. "Like spices and cookies and baking bread?"

"Pretty much."

We reached the center of town, and Santa's workshop loomed in front of us. Dark wood with a bright red roof, it looked like a chalet on steroids. A large clock on the front showed both the time and the number of days until Christmas. As we stood there, it struck nine. A bell sounded and colorful wooden figures of happy elves popped out and danced and twirled on the balcony above the clock.

"What is that?" asked Jax, enthralled.

"You've never seen a cuckoo clock before?" He shook his head. "Oh, you're going to love what's inside."

We walked into the cavernous lobby, with blazing fireplaces at either end, huge Christmas trees lining one wall, and trays of cookies set out for visitors. The tour was given from the safety of a small, colorful train that wound its way through the building. We got our tickets, and strolled around, waiting for the tour to start. When the train pulled up, with a cheerful "choo, choo," we chose a seat in the last car, the caboose, and settled in. Each car was open, like a series of attached wagons, and only large enough for two riders. Jax and I had to sit so close our thighs touched. I tried to ignore the fact he had extremely muscular thighs as the train set off, and the tour began.

"Welcome, welcome, and merry Christmas," said the tour guide, an elf who introduced himself as Lolly Hamhock. "Keep your hands and feet inside the car at all times." He shot me a pointed look. I'd been resting my elbow on the side of the car, so I slipped it guiltily inside. "And also, photography is strictly prohibited. You can take all the elfies you want later, when you're back in the lobby. Now, let's begin."

We rode through a dark tunnel and exited into the middle of Santa's workshop. The train ran on an elevated platform, but below us, happy elves performed happy duties while singing happy songs. It made me want to puke.

The toys were made using a complex production system. The wooden trains, for example were created by machines, but elves painted the details by hand. They also brushed the shiny hair of new dolls and tied the bows around the necks of fluffy teddy bears. Some performed quality control on brightly colored tops and tested yo-yos. It was incredibly well-organized chaos.

"Have you worked here?" asked Jax, watching as an elf tested ping pong balls.

"Uh, no. This is one of the few places I haven't worked."

Jax was so captivated, he didn't question my response. Not that I minded. I enjoyed watching his rapt expression as he took everything in.

"And now," said Lolly, as we neared the end of our tour. "It's time to see you-know-who."

The other passengers on the train tittered excitedly. I did not titter. I slumped in my seat as the train went through another tunnel and popped out next to a brightly illuminated room located behind a glass wall. It had a large desk, a cheery fireplace, and another special element as well.

"There he is!" The shout came from the front of the train. "It's Santa!"

All the elves leaned to the right, hoping to catch a glimpse of the big guy. Santa sat at his desk, looking busy, but he still had time to give the people on the tour a smile and a cheery wave. Jax waved back, grinning. I did not.

As the train pulled away, I glanced over my shoulder. Santa was still there, watching the train leave, but now he had a confused frown on his face. I slumped further in my seat and didn't relax until the tour finally ended, and we stepped out of the train.

After visiting the gift-wrapping department, the letter writing department, and the toffee-making facility, it was time to visit the place I'd been dreading most—Joy's house. The modest ranch with blue siding had a white picket fence and a wreath made of pine boughs on the front door. Someone had covered the wreath in black crepe, customary for a family in mourning, and the strands of red and green twinkle lights hanging on the eaves of the porch remained dark and unlit. Nothing said sorrow like a non-twinkling twinkle light. The sight of them made my heart ache. But when I reached out to open the gate, I realized we'd forgotten one essential detail.

"Hold on. What's our story?" I asked Jax.

"Excuse me?"

"To explain your presence."

"You can't say I'm visiting from Elf Central, and you're showing me around?"

"You're joking, right?" When he seemed confused, I rolled my eyes. "Jax Grayson. I wouldn't bring you to visit people who'd just lost a daughter as part of a tour, would I? It has to be something else." A thought occurred to me. I knew it would likely be a colossal mistake, but it seemed like the only option. "I've got it. You'll be my boyfriend."

"I'll be your what?"

"My boyfriend. You're here for moral support because I'm sad. Boyfriends do that sort of thing, you know."

"One would assume, and yet—"

I held up a hand to stop him. "Do you have a better idea?" He furrowed his brow, and since he did not, I continued. "Trust me, okay? Christmas elves love a love story.

Instead of being a stranger, you'll be the Romeo to my Juliet or whatever."

A tearful middle-aged couple exited the house and came toward us, promptly giving Jax the Christmas elf version of the stink eye. He got that a lot here. It gave me an excellent opportunity to prove my point, so I pulled out a tissue and dabbed my cheeks.

"Pardon me. Is this the Berry house?" I asked them with a sniff.

"Yes," said the woman, her eyes swollen from crying. "Did you know Joy?"

"I did. She was my friend. We worked together." I didn't have to fake the emotion in my voice. It was real. "I'm Tink Holly, and this is my boyfriend, Jax. We were there when it happened. It was terrible. Jax tried to save her, but..."

I honestly couldn't go on, and their entire demeanor changed instantly. "Oh," said the woman. "You poor dears. So sorry for your loss."

After hugging me, she pulled Jax into a hug as well. Her husband did the same. "It's an awful thing," the man said, his mouth wobbling with emotion. "Especially after what happened to her brother."

I frowned. "Her brother?"

Our new friends seemed perplexed, like it was something we should have known about, but I didn't even realize Joy had a brother. She'd never mentioned it.

"Evergreen died a year ago," said the woman. "Of a drug overdose."

I shot Jax a worried look. Joy's brother had died of an overdose, too?

The woman must not have noticed my reaction, because she continued speaking. "It's such a tragedy. That poor family." She let out a sniff. "Joy's parents are inside. I'm sure they'll appreciate the two of you stopping by."

They hugged us again, telling Jax he was "a good boy" and saying they hoped to see us again someday. Meanwhile, we didn't even know their names. Elves were like that—insta-friends who believed in insta-love and got sick of each other insta-fast. Deep emotions were not our forte. We preferred to stick to the more superficial ones.

As soon as they were out of earshot, Jax leaned close. "What just happened?"

"I told you, Christmas elves love a love story, especially a doomed one, and a relationship between us would definitely fall into the 'doomed' category."

"This whole thing still seems like a horrible idea. After we're done here, will we have to go on pretending to be a couple? Because it could get messy."

I considered his question. "It's unlikely we'll know anyone here. Unless you have friends I'm unaware of in the Christmas elf community?"

"Uh, no. I don't. But, still, to pretend to be involved with you seems unprofessional, to say the least."

I lifted an eyebrow at Jax. "Do you or do you not want to know what's going on here?"

He raised his hands in surrender. "Fine. You're right."

I put a hand to my heart. "Wow. You know exactly what to say to make me feel special, honey buns. I'm one lucky lady."

He let out a snort and put his hand on my elbow to guide me into the house. "Let's get this over with. And please don't call me honey buns ever again."

When we entered the small, tidy house, we got some strange looks, but no one said anything. The elves assembled in the tiny space spoke in hushed voices, with the occasional sniff here or there. I glanced around. It was weird being where Joy lived, where she baked her muffins and went about her life. Pictures of her hung on the walls with a boy I could only assume was her brother. Joy and Evergreen as babies. Joy in kindergarten with a missing front tooth and an adorable smile. Joy graduating from high school. They seemed like a normal, happy family, but in the last few photos Evergreen was different—thinner, and with a haunted look in his eyes.

The saddest part about seeing their lives displayed in a series of pictures were all the ones that would be forever missing. Weddings that would never happen. Babies who would never be born. Family trips they'd never take.

"Are you okay?" asked Jax, his dark eyes concerned.

I wasn't but saw no point in discussing it. "Let's talk to her parents. We need to figure this out."

Joy's parents sat side by side on a couch in their living room, surrounded by people who loved and cared for them but alone in their grief. I knew the feeling well. I'd experienced it myself.

"Mr. and Mrs. Berry?" They looked up at me, eyes filled with pain. "I'm Tink Holly. I worked with Joy."

Mrs. Berry's eyes brightened a notch and she stood up to pull me into a hug. "Joy talked about you so often. She loved working with you. I heard you were with her when it happened?"

"Yes. We both were." I indicated Jax.

"And you are...?" asked Mr. Berry, who'd also risen to his feet. I heard no judgment or hostility in his tone. Perhaps for a person who'd been through so much, a minor thing like a dark elf showing up on his doorstep was no big deal.

"I am Tink's boyfriend." The words sounded awkward

on his tongue, or maybe only to my ears. Either way, the Berrys didn't seem to notice.

"Tell us what happened. Please." Mrs. Berry squeezed my hand. "We've gotten so little information from the medical team on the scene."

I paused, gathering my thoughts. "Jax and I were having lunch at Happypie's. We saw someone in distress outside, and I realized it was Joy when we went out to help." The memory of Joy's spasming body, the blood coming from her orifices, and the look of absolute terror in her eyes flashed through my mind, but there was no way I'd share those memories with her grieving parents. "Jax performed CPR, but it was already too late. I was holding her hand when she passed. She wasn't alone."

They listened, absorbing what I'd shared with them. "Thank you for being there with our baby girl," said Mr. Berry. When he put his face in his hands and wept, I had to close my eyes. His pain was so raw. It cut through me like a knife.

Mrs. Berry put a soft hand on my shoulder. "I realize you didn't know my daughter long, but she considered you a friend. And she also told me you were one of the smartest people around."

I let out a laugh. "Well, I don't know about that, but Joy was one of the kindest. And the most thoughtful. She was also an amazing baker."

She lifted a finger, indicating I should wait. "Oh, dear," she said. "I almost forgot. Joy left something for you on her desk. Let me get it."

I looked at Jax, confused. Joy had left something for me?

Mrs. Berry came back a few minutes later. She handed me a stamped envelope with my name and address on it. I recognized the loopy, pretty writing on the front as Joy's.

"I found it in her room," she said.

"Thank you."

"You are most welcome." She pulled me into another fierce hug and whispered in my ear, "I don't believe what they're saying. Joy would never do drugs. I'm sure of it."

"I feel the same way," I said, and she squeezed me even tighter.

"I know you have connections, Tink. Please use them to figure out what happened to my baby."

Her gaze locked on mine, and I saw the unasked question in her eyes. Would I do this for her? When I nodded, she gave me a shaky smile.

"Good. Thank you, Tink. I can't tell you what it means to me." She glanced up at her husband. "To us."

I just promised a grieving mother I'd find out the truth about her daughter's death. Why did I do such a thing? I was a screwup. Everyone knew I was a screwup, but after years of getting passed over and virtually ignored, it seemed my unique skills were suddenly in demand.

Cookie wanted me to spy on Jax. Jax wanted me to help him. Noelle wanted me to stay out of trouble, and Grandma Gingersnap wanted me to be normal. But Mrs. Berry simply wanted the truth. And I planned to find it for her.

CHAPTER EIGHT

I hoped we could make a quick escape, but instead, a group of Mrs. Berry's friends forced us into the kitchen and made us eat plates filled high with ham and an assortment of lukewarm side dishes. They were neighbors and friends of the Berrys, all in shock about Joy, and all wanting to feel useful by bringing desserts and casseroles to Joy's poor parents.

"She was too young," said a woman around my grand-mother's age named Dimples Dollypop. "And their grief is compounded by having lost Ever as well. Both of their beloved children—gone far too soon. But you never know when your time is up. We have to seize the day and live life to its fullest. No one promised us tomorrow, and today is a gift. That's why it's called the present."

Everyone around us nodded at her sage advice. Dimples used to work in the Christmas card department, writing the interior matter, which was why she spoke in clichés and inspirational messages. It wasn't her fault. After doing it for nearly five decades, it likely became a habit.

I'd barely lasted a few weeks in the Christmas card

department. Apparently, there isn't a market for cards reading, *Guess what? Santa doesn't believe in you either.* Or *Stay classy this Christmas. Santa doesn't need another ho.* But the one they fired me over was, *Merry Christmas! Just kidding. Go screw yourself.*

They did not appreciate my gift—their loss.

"What happened to Joy's brother exactly?" I asked. The whole room grew silent. The woman standing next to me leaned close and spoke in a soft voice.

"Evergreen went down a dark path." Her eyes widened as she glanced over at Jax. "No offense."

"None taken." Jax looked like he wished he could be anywhere but here.

"Was it, um, candicocane?" I asked, keeping my voice low, but it carried.

"Yes. Ever was a wild one. He got in with the wrong crowd," said Dimples. "The friends you make are the chances you take. It's a sad thing, and I'm not saying he asked for it, but it does seem like he could have avoided it. It was different with Joy, though. She did nothing wrong. Nothing at all. She didn't party or drink or smoke. She worked hard and volunteered at the senior center. She never caused her parents a moment of worry. It's tragic she died in the same way as her big brother."

When Dimples cried, I pulled a tissue out of my bag and handed it to her. "I'm so sorry. I didn't know Ever, but Joy was my friend, and she was a good elf right to her core."

"She was," said a lady in a bright green hat covered with poinsettia.

"As sweet as her muffins," said the elf cutting up the pies. She handed Jax and me a piece. I was never one to refuse a slice of pie, and this looked like chocolate cream. Lovely.

"So where did the two of you meet?" the pie lady asked, causing Jax to almost drop his plate.

"Yes," said Dimples, glancing back and forth between Jax and me. "We're all curious. Love is a gift that never needs wrapping."

More nodding at Dimples, the bringer of all wisdom. "Or duct tape," said the woman in the green hat, her mouth full of pie. When we all stared at her in confusion, she swallowed her pie and continued. "Love doesn't need duct tape either."

"Back to my question," said Dimples, sending the duct tape lady an odd look. "How did you kids meet?"

My mouth was full of pie at this point, so Jax had to answer for us. "We met at work," he said.

"Have you set a date yet?" asked a woman standing next to Dimples.

"Excuse me?" I asked.

"For your wedding?"

Jax choked on his pie. I patted him firmly on the back. "Not yet." I gave her a bright smile. "But I'm not letting this one get away. He's a keeper." Once he stopped choking, I used the hand that had been patting him on the back to playfully link my arm with his and stared up at him adoringly. He seemed freaked out by the whole experience, but the women in the kitchen let out a collective sigh.

"When did you know he was the one?" asked Dimples.

"I took one look at him and said, 'He's the guy for me.' But it wasn't the same for Jax. He mistook me for a cruise director."

They all laughed. Jax looked ill but recovered quickly. "But it turned out she was not a cruise director, and the rest is history."

I chimed in, "And the rest is history."

There was a long pause and an even longer collective sigh before a woman standing in the corner spoke. "It's nice to see a young couple in love," she said, sipping coffee from a mug covered in snowflakes. "Especially on a sad day like today."

"It certainly is," said a familiar male voice coming from directly behind me. "And so completely unexpected."

I looked up in shock to see Win standing in the kitchen doorway, with Candy by his side. Crap on a cracker. But I was already in too deep. There was no way to get out of it now.

I pasted a smile on my face. "Hi, Win. You've already met Jax." I noticed a muscle working in Win's jaw. I ignored it and indicated the classy blonde on his right. "And this is Candy Holiday."

"Ah, Candy," said Jax, with a smile. "I've heard all about you."

Candy glanced back and forth between us. "You have?"

To my amazement, Jax put an arm around my shoulders and pulled me close. "Oh, yes."

He didn't elaborate, which was kind of hilarious, and I knew he had his arm around me only to get back at me for embarrassing him with the love at first sight comments. I had to give him points for it. It was excellent payback in front of my ex and the woman who'd filed a restraining order against me.

Not that she was the only person who'd ever filed a restraining order against me. Tinsel from accounting had, too. And Reggie from the DMV. And a woman named Scarlet Knickers who was an exotic dancer, but the Scarlet Knickers incident was a total misunderstanding. I got wasted one night and thought I could dance, but it was the alcohol talking. I hadn't meant to bump into her and knock her offstage, nor was it my fault she landed in a snowbank. If it were me, I'd chalk it up to being one of the inherent dangers of her profession.

"The two of you are dating now?" asked Win.

Jax pulled me even closer. "We are. Most definitely."

Dimples nudged him. "Don't be shy, you two."

She pointed up, and of course, we stood right under the mistletoe. Why? Because I'm Tink Holly, and that's how things went for me.

Jax frowned, about to ruin everything. "I don't—"

I cut off his words by going up on my toes, wrapping my arms around his neck, and kissing him solidly. Frankly speaking, I had no choice. It was mistletoe. On the North Pole, that was a mandatory thing. In the old days, refusing to kiss under the mistletoe may have been a punishable offense. Also, I had to admit I felt curious. What would it be like to kiss Jax? I secretly wanted to find out.

At first, Jax stiffened, and I worried he might push me away, but he didn't. Instead, he wrapped his arms around me. Although I'd planned for this to be a quick peck, a brush of my lips against his, something strange happened. Jax kissed me back—and I was lost.

Holy hot cinnamon tarts.

If all dark elves kissed like Jax Grayson, it was no wonder they had a reputation. He held me close, the curves of my body molding perfectly to the hard planes of his. It was such an incredible sensation I may have let out a soft moan. I was making out with Jax in the kitchen of a grieving family, right in front of my ex, but I couldn't seem to stop kissing him. He was intoxicating.

Eventually, Jax ended it. When he did, I stood there staring at him, stunned. He seemed stunned, too, but he came out of it quicker, giving our audience a slightly sheepish grin. "Well, it's easy to see why I fell for her, right?"

I blinked at him in astonishment. For someone who balked at pretending to be my boyfriend, he'd certainly gotten into the spirit of things.

Everyone in the kitchen sighed, except Win. He looked like he wanted to punch Jax right in the face. To make matters worse, Puck and some of the other guys from the reindeer department had arrived, too. So much for our little lie going unnoticed.

"I heard Tink was making out with some dude in the kitchen," Puck said. "I didn't realize it was you, Jax. Well, color me red and call me a cranberry. What great news." He gave me a noisy kiss on the cheek since I was still, technically, standing right under the mistletoe, then he grabbed a plate of food.

"Definitely great news," said Frank, with a mischievous glint in his eyes. The other guys on the reindeer team were harmless, but Frank was audacious when it came to mistletoe. The whole custom was creepy enough, but Frank took it to the next level. Once, at a party, he'd hung a sprig from the belt buckle of his jeans. I'd lost count of how many girls got wasted and kissed him beneath the mistletoe that night, but it was to be expected. Frank was charismatic. If he could charm a dozen girls into kissing his crotch, the man had skills.

I thanked whatever Christmas angels had kept me from sleeping with him, because it would have been a horrible mistake. I may not have many boundaries, but Frank was one of them.

When he made his move, eyes on the mistletoe, I took a quick step to my right, but I needn't have bothered. Both Jax and Win stepped up to block him.

For a long moment, the three of them stared at each other, and I was afraid they might come to blows. Win and Jax had taken an instant disliking to each other, but with Win and Frank, the friction went way back. We'd all been friends growing up, but as far as I knew, those two hadn't spoken in years. A friendship between a rule follower like Win and a rule breaker like Frank could only last so long.

I was a rule breaker, too, which was one reason why Win and I had been doomed from the start.

Frank took another step forward, fists clenched, an angry expression on his normally congenial face. Thankfully, Puck defused the situation nicely.

"Aw, does Frankie want a kiss, too?" he asked, planting a kiss right on Frank's mouth. Puck laughed along with the other guys at the look on Frank's face, but I saw the serious glint in his eyes as he put a hand on Frank's shoulder. "Go get something to eat, kid," he said softly. "This isn't the time or the place."

Frank backed off but kept his gaze locked on Win's. Even though their animosity had nothing to do with me, I felt like this was my fault. I hated everything about this stupid mistletoe tradition, although I hadn't minded kissing Jax. Not one bit.

"We'd better go," I said, tugging on Jax's arm.

"You're right. I'll get our coats."

I went to the foyer to wait for him and wasn't surprised when Win joined me. "Will you tell me what's going on?"

He nearly vibrated with fury. I frowned, not liking his tone. He was with Candy now—he'd been with her for months. And we broke up nearly two years ago.

"What do you mean?"

He leaned closer, his voice a harsh whisper. "You are not dating Jax Grayson."

"What makes you say so?"

"I know you. I've always known you. That's one thing you can't deny or push away or change."

I gave him a sad smile. We were talking about more than my fake engagement with Jax here. "But do you know me? Really?"

He ran a hand through his blond hair. Even when he mussed it, it went right back into place. Win was perfect. And he deserved someone who was at least close to perfect. Sadly, it wasn't me. And as much as I hated seeing the pain in those bright blue eyes, there was nothing I could do to fix it.

"I always assumed we'd end up together," he said, his voice soft. "Eventually."

"Me, too. I'm sorry, Win."

If it took me kissing Jax in the Berry family kitchen for Win to realize we'd never end up together, maybe it was a good thing he saw us. Still, it broke my heart, mostly because I knew I'd broken his once again, and Win didn't deserve it.

Candy didn't deserve it either. She stood in the doorway, listening to us and looking like Win had punched her in the gut. I didn't know what to do or say. Fortunately, Jax showed up with our coats and saved me from any further embarrassment.

"Time to go, honey buns," he said, helping me into my green coat. "I let the Berrys know we were leaving. They said to thank you."

I buttoned my coat, feeling numb. "Bye, Win." I gave him a wave, but he didn't respond. Even now, after all these years, I still cared for him. I didn't know if it would ever stop, but I hoped, with time, it would get easier.

"Jiminy Christmas," I muttered as we walked out the door.

Jax eyed me. "Well, that all went according to plan."

I let out a laugh. Finding out Jax had a sense of humor had been the best thing to happen to me today. "I'm so sorry."

"I'm not." I looked at him in confusion, and he continued. "It was a brilliant idea. Doing any sort of undercover work is tricky here. Dark elves tend to stand out."

"Oh? I didn't notice."

He smiled at me. "But you came up with the perfect solution. If the other Christmas elves think I'm with you, it changes the dynamics. It's an interesting phenomenon."

"Well, I can explain it to you simply. Do you know what the most popular television show is on the North Pole? It's *The Bachelor*. Christmas elves watch it obsessively."

"A human program?"

"Yes, which makes it even funnier. We're the most gullible and trustworthy creatures in existence."

"I've noticed. But gullible isn't the right word for it. There is a certain innocence amongst the people here. It's heartwarming."

I pretended to weigh the options. "Innocent, oblivious. It's hard to tell which."

"What about you?"

I frowned. "What about me?"

He tilted his head and studied me, which made me nervous. It seemed like Jax could see things others couldn't. I didn't like it.

"You aren't oblivious."

"And I'm not innocent either."

My phone pinged with a text from Noelle. *You got a package. It's chocolate. Can I have some?*

"Sorry," I said to Jax. "It's my roommate. Give me a second."

I texted her back. *What? Who sent me chocolate?*

She responded right away. *No idea. The only thing on the note is your name and address. But it's your favorite. Snarkleberry Dingalings. The expensive kind.*

Oh, happy day! Snarkleberry Dingalings weren't the sort of candy I could afford to buy for myself. I hadn't had them since Win got some for me for Valentine's Day a long, long time ago. I was way overdue.

Of course, you can have some, but don't eat the whole box. Those chocolates might be my dinner.

Putting away my phone, I glanced up and down the street. "Our Ubersled should have been here by now. Do you want to walk? It's only a few blocks to the subway station."

Jax walked next to me, matching his long strides to my shorter ones. "You don't have a vehicle?"

"I do. But I can't drive it."

"Why?" he asked, eyes twinkling. "I sense another story here."

I waved away his words. "It was nothing. My license got suspended. I can get it back in a year or so. But we have more pressing things to discuss." I pulled the envelope out of my purse—the one Joy had made out to me. "Like— what's inside this?"

"You're right. I'm curious as well."

"There's a coffee shop not far from here. Want to stop and get a drink?"

"Yes, and while we're walking, you can tell me the story about how your license got suspended."

I shot him a dirty look as we walked. "If you insist."

"I do."

I blew out a long breath. "First of all, let me say it was not my fault."

He had the nerve to laugh. "It never is."

I folded my arms over my chest. The temperature had dropped in the biodome. The engineering crew lowered it occasionally to bring on some snow. One year, they weren't careful and ended up causing a blizzard that resulted in over two feet. I'd been about ten at the time and thought it was terrific. The people who had to clean it up, though, were less than thrilled.

"This time, it truly wasn't. A police officer pulled me over for exceeding the speed limit, but I hadn't been. I was certain of it." I paused, getting annoyed all over again. "When I said as much to the officer, he got mad and broke my rear sled light with his bully stick. Then he gave me a ticket for having a faulty rear light."

"Why?"

"I may have called him names. And threatened him. And I may have thrown a snowball at him and hit him right in the face. That didn't go over well, but I couldn't help it. I was distressed. I was also on my way home from my anger management class, so it did not look good at all."

Jax tossed his head back and laughed, and I couldn't help but laugh, too. It was kind of funny, in retrospect.

"The judge decided to make an example of me, so he suspended my license for two years. Thank goodness for Ubersleds," I said dramatically. "Look. There's the coffee shop."

Once we entered the warm coffee shop, we ordered our coffees and found a quiet table by the window. Jax drank his black. No surprise. I ordered a caramel macchiato with extra whipped cream and caramel chocolate drizzle on top. Jax watched as I got a spoon and ate the whipped cream. It was so delicious I had to stop a second, close my eyes, and I may have moaned a little. When I opened my eyes, he was staring at me. It was disconcerting. And it made me realize I owed him an apology.

"About what happened at the Berry house." I lapped up another spoonful of whipped cream. "I'm sorry I put you in such a compromising position."

"What position?"

I took another spoonful of whipped cream and noticed Jax seemed unusually interested in the way I licked it off the spoon.

I froze in mid-lick. "The 'forcing-you-to-kiss-me-under-the-mistletoe' position."

"Oh. The kiss. Don't worry about it."

"What do you mean?"

He leaned forward, his dark eyes intense and his voice low and sexy. "Tink. You didn't force me to do anything."

"Oh."

He gave me a crooked smile. "Is that all you have to say about it?"

I shrugged. "I guess so. The last thing I want is for someone to accuse me of sexual harassment. Again."

He sat back up. "What? Again?"

Waving a hand, I shook my head. "Never mind. If you're okay, I'm okay."

His gaze was steady. "I'm okay."

I gave him a thumbs up. "Good. We've established we're both okay." I pulled Joy's letter out of my purse. "Let's see what this is about."

Opening it, I pulled out the single page and unfolded it. Once I read what was on it, I frowned. I wasn't sure what I'd expected, but this was not it.

"It's a recipe?" asked Jax.

I turned the page so he could read it, too. "For chocolate muffins." Penned in Joy's rounded, swirling handwriting, she'd taken her time with it, writing in black ink but making specific letters red and others green. It looked festive and Christmas-y, but why would Joy send me this? I didn't bake. She knew I didn't bake. And at the top of the page, she'd written a short note.

Dear Tink,

In case you need this later. I know you can figure it out.

Your friend,

Joy

I read over it several times. If Joy thought I could figure out how to make muffins, she was sadly mistaken. "I don't get it."

"Well, you liked her muffins, right? Is it out of the bounds of reality she would send you her recipe?"

He made a good point, but something still seemed off here. "I guess not."

Picking up the letter, I put it back into the envelope. Jax tilted his head. "What's on the back?"

Confused, I turned it over. Someone had stamped the page with *Property of the North Pole Baking Company.* "What does that mean?"

Jax seemed as confused as I did. "I have no idea, but it tells me where we should go next after you finish your bowl of coffee-flavored caramel cream."

He was right. My coffee never tasted like coffee. I drank it for the caffeine and the sugar mainly. But I didn't follow the rest of what Jax said.

"Huh? Where are we going next?"

He pointed to the back of the page. "If Joy was such a good baker, why was she working in the reindeer department?"

"Good point."

"And the most obvious place to go if we want to find out exactly why Joy wasn't baking professionally is...?"

He paused, and I looked at him, eyebrows raised. Did he need me to say it out loud? Judging by the expectant look on his face, apparently, he did. This man loved his job, maybe too much.

"The North Pole Baking Company?" I asked dutifully.

"Yes, the North Pole Baking Company," he repeated, his eyes gleaming with satisfaction. "Let's go."

CHAPTER NINE

The North Pole Baking Company was easy to find. We simply left the coffee shop, turned right, and followed the scent of sugar cookies and happiness until we reached our destination. I sighed as I breathed it in.

"I love the smell of this place. It's perfection. I used to come here on school field trips when I was small. It was the highlight of my year."

Jax smiled at me. "You do like your sweets."

"I'm a Christmas elf. It comes with the territory. However, the whole thing about Santa requiring cookies on Christmas Eve is a scam. Not even Santa could handle that much sugar."

Jax gazed up at the North Pole Baking Company sign. "What's the plan? Do I get to pretend to be your beau again?" He asked the question with raised eyebrows, and even though I wasn't usually a blusher, his words made my cheeks get hot. And thinking about the kiss in Joy's kitchen made other parts get hot as well.

I lifted my hands, but whether in defeat or in defense, I couldn't tell. "Nope. We're good. It makes sense to bring you here on your fake audit tour. Now let's find out why Joy sent me a muffin recipe."

We walked inside and went straight to reception. The effect Jax had on people was getting old. One elf fainted. Another ran into a wall when she saw him. We had to revive the man who'd swooned and get some ice for the woman with the bruised nose, but once the excitement died down, the receptionist finally took us to see Mr. Butters Crumpet, the head of the North Pole Baking Company.

A short man with a big belly, he had on a green velvet suit with white fur lapels. He was hurriedly shoving files into a desk as we walked in, an expression of pure panic on his face. As soon as he saw Jax, he slammed the drawer shut. "Hello. Nice to meet you. To what do I owe this pleasure?"

Photos of Mr. Crumpet with a plump, pleasant-looking woman and a bunch of plump, pleasant-looking children adorned his desk. I counted at least six children—a whole herd of Crumpets.

He indicated we should sit, and his secretary, an elf named Chad (short for Chadiwinkles), brought us cookies and cocoa. Handsome and trim, Chad wore an outfit similar in style and color to his boss. When he asked if we wanted mini-marshmallows, Jax declined. Not to be rude, I took his share. Who didn't like mini marshmallows? Jax didn't take any cookies either.

"Oh, well," I said when he declined the beautifully decorated confections. "More for me."

"Your capacity for sugar astonishes me," he said softly as Chad poured cocoa for his boss. Like me, Mr. Crumpet took several heaping spoonfuls of marshmallows. He was obviously a wise man.

After Chad left, Mr. Crumpet turned to us. "Now, what can I help you with?"

"Mr. Grayson is here on behalf of the Elven High Council," I said. "He's doing an audit, and we're visiting several different departments. The baking company is one of the places on our list."

"And we're also investigating the death of one of your former employees. Joy Berry."

I kept my gaze on Mr. Crumpet, but Jax's comment startled me. It seemed to startle Mr. Crumpet as well. He accidentally inhaled one of his mini marshmallows with an odd popping sound and nearly choked on it. He had to take a drink of water to stop coughing.

"Excuse me?" he asked, eyes still watering. "Are you saying Joy Berry is dead?"

"I'm afraid so. Mr. Grayson and I were there when it happened."

"But she was so young and such a nice kid." Mr. Crumpet appeared genuinely shocked by the news. "And she had great potential. How sad."

This wasn't what I'd expected. Mr. Crumpet had tears in his eyes, and not because he'd inhaled a mini marshmallow. He seemed genuinely fond of Joy. I'd assumed she'd left this job on bad terms—because that's how I'd left most of my jobs. "Can you tell us why she was let go?"

He frowned in confusion. "Let go? She wasn't let go. Joy Berry quit."

I dropped the cookie I was eating onto the floor. It shattered, but I didn't even glance at it. I was too shocked by what Mr. Crumpet had revealed to us.

"Why would she quit?" I asked.

"I have no idea." He folded his hands on his desk and twiddled his thumbs. "One day, she came in, apologized, and gave her two-week's notice. I was shocked to tell you the truth. She'd just gotten a promotion. She was the assistant to the Director of Secret Ingredient Acquisitions." Mr. Crumpet's pale blue eyes grew misty. "And now she's gone. Poor kid."

Jax put his untouched cocoa onto a side table and leaned forward. "And she never explained why she left?"

I bent over to clean up my cookie, not wanting to leave a mess on Mr. Crumpet's floor. But as I gathered the crumbs, I spied a photograph lying under the desk. It must have fallen there when Mr. Crumpet was shoving things into the drawer.

Thinking it might be a clue, I grabbed it as discreetly as possible. As soon as I glanced at it, though, I knew why Mr. Crumpet had seemed so nervous when we first came in, and it had nothing to do with Joy. Trying not to be too obvious, I shoved the photo into my purse, tossed the cookie crumbs into the wastebasket, and brushed off my hands before returning to my chair.

"Joy gave her notice a few months ago, right after our director, Mr. Slippers, retired. It was a tough time for all of us. Mr. Slippers was also a great person to work with, and he left big shoes to fill." He cleared his throat. "No pun intended."

"Could you tell me more about Joy's employment history?" asked Jax, taking a notebook out of his inside jacket pocket. "Like any issues she may have had?"

"There weren't any, but let me get her file." He pulled it out, and read over his notes to us, but like he said, there wasn't much to tell. Joy was a model employee.

As Jax recorded the information, I watched him. The more time we spent together, the more convinced I became Jax might be on the up and up, no matter what Noelle and Grandma Gingersnap said. But if Jax was telling the truth, who was the liar? It didn't take me long to get to the answer.

Cookie Wassail.

But why?

We showed Mr. Crumpet the muffin recipe, but he shook his head. "We don't produce muffins here. We make those at our breakfast plant on the other side of town. I'm awfully sorry."

Jax jotted down that info as well. "No, this has been informative," he said. He gave Mr. Crumpet his card. "If you think of anything else, will you let me know?"

"Certainly. I wish I could be of more help, but we keep limited personnel files on site, particularly for former employees. Most are stored at elven resources."

"Could you give me permission to look at those files? If I could find out more about why Joy left, it might be beneficial."

"Sorry, but I don't have that kind of authority. No one does. Other than the people who work in elven resources, and they aren't inclined to share personal information. Well, and the big guy, but no one wants to bother him this close to Christmas." Mr. Crumpet paused, his gaze falling on me. "Wait a second. Did you say your name is Tink Holly? As in Tinklebelle Holly—?"

"Yes." I jumped to my feet, extending my hand to the startled Mr. Crumpet. "And we should let you get back to work. Thank you for your time."

Jax shot me a curious look as we left the office but waited until we were walking down the steps to the sidewalk to say anything. "Why did you rush out of there?"

"No reason," I said, which was a total lie, but I put on my best I'm-being-totally-and-completely-honest face. "I thought we'd finished."

He shoved his hands into the pockets of his jacket. "I

would like to know why he was hiding files when we walked in. He was up to something. I sensed it."

"He most certainly was up to something," I said, handing him the photo I'd found under Mr. Crumpet's desk. "But it's not what you think."

"Oh," said Jax, studying the photo of Mr. Crumpet and Chad in a compromising position. "I see. Okay. Nothing to do with our investigation, I guess."

"Nope. But we nearly gave him a heart attack. Poor Mr. Crumpet."

"Poor Mrs. Crumpet."

"True," I said with a laugh. "You never know what's going on behind closed doors, now do you?"

My phone pinged with a text from an unfamiliar number. As soon as I read it, all the air left my lungs in a whoosh.

"No, no, no, no."

"What's the matter?" asked Jax, placing a hand on my arm.

"It's my roommate," I said, pulling away from him. "I have to go."

Glancing around to get my bearings, I took off at a jog, heading straight toward North Pole General Hospital. Jax ran along with me.

"What's the matter?" he asked. "What happened to your roommate?"

"They took her to the emergency room," I said. "For a candicocane overdose."

Jax muttered something. It sounded like a curse, but I didn't speak Dark Elvish. "Should we call for an Ubersled?"

"No." I was out of breath already, and I'd barely run half a block. I needed to work on my cardio. "We can get there faster on foot."

When we arrived at the emergency room, my heart pounded and not only from exertion. I was terrified. I kept picturing Noelle dying like Joy had and couldn't take it. I couldn't lose two friends in two days.

I'd known Noelle my whole life, and she'd been my one constant, my rock. I didn't want to imagine the world without her in it.

The ER was busy, and I had to fight my way to the reception desk. I got dirty looks from several people, including the woman working there, an exhausted-looking nurse named Faith Pine. Nurse Pine opened her mouth, about to tell me to move to the back of the line, but she closed it when I spoke.

"Please. I'm here for Noelle Toffee."

As soon as I mentioned Noelle's name, the nurse's demeanor changed. "You must be Tink. I'm the one who sent you the text. You were listed as her emergency contact."

"Thank you." I could barely speak. "Can I see her?"

Faith gave me a sympathetic look. "She's in room three. You can go right back." She pushed the button to open the doors to the treatment rooms, and Jax and I went through. We found the room quickly, but to my surprise, two police officers stood outside the door.

"I'm her roommate," I said, shaking from head to toe. "May I see her, please?"

One of the officers, a big guy with kind eyes, spoke to me. "You must be Tink Holly," he said. "I'm Officer Pudding, and this is my partner, Officer Bing. Head on in. She's been waiting for you."

I stared at him blankly because I'd been expecting the worst. "Waiting for me?" If she was waiting for me, it was an excellent sign. It meant she was still alive. My knees went weak.

Officer Pudding must have noticed my distress. "She's going to be okay," he said, patting my arm. "Don't be scared."

I wasn't scared. I was terrified.

As Jax spoke with the officers, I stepped into the room, dread filling my chest. I knew it was a flashback to the time I'd been here many years ago, as a seven-year-old orphan. But this time, there was no blood. There was also no shouting, no crying, and no pitying looks from strangers. There was only quiet, and my best friend lying all alone in a big hospital bed.

I sat in the chair next to the bed and took Noelle's cold hand in mine. Pale and silent, she was attached to several beeping monitors, and she looked awful. But at least she was alive.

"Tink?" Noelle's voice was soft and raspy, like they'd intubated her or maybe pumped her stomach.

"I'm here," I said, brushing her dark hair away from her face. As soon as I touched her, her eyes fluttered open.

"Are you okay?" she asked, her gaze unfocused.

"I'm fine," I said, trying and failing to hold back tears. "It's you we're worried about."

She closed her eyes again, almost as if the effort to keep them open was too much for her. Jax came into the room and sat in the chair next to mine.

"I spoke with the policemen," he said, his voice soft.

"Did you find out what happened?" My hands shook, and I folded them together on my lap.

"I did." He paused, his gaze locking with mine as he took one of my hands in his. "Your roommate overdosed on candicocane, the kind that killed Joy. The kind laced with telazol."

I stared at him in shock, pulling my hand out of his grasp. "Noelle would never, ever use drugs," I said with a sniff. "No way."

"You're right. She didn't do it on purpose, Tink. She ingested it by accident."

My jaw dropped. "Ingested it? You're kidding, right?"

"No, I'm not. Fortunately, she understood what was going on right away, and she had narzipan with her at the time. She called for help and gave herself the injection. It saved her life."

"Thank goodness." Tears fell steadily down my cheeks. I wiped them away. "Poor Noelle."

"That's not everything." Jax gave me a steady look. "The drugs were in a box of chocolate delivered to your apartment earlier today."

Was this all my fault? Had I caused this? I steadied myself.

"Are you talking about the Snarkleberry Dingalings? Are you saying someone was trying to hurt me?"

Jax shook his head, his expression grave "No, Tink. Someone was trying to kill you."

CHAPTER TEN

O fficers Bing and Pudding let me know my apartment was now a crime scene. They suggested I find somewhere else to stay. Somewhere safe. And they promised to get in touch with Noelle's parents.

Mr. and Mrs. Toffee had moved to Florida when they retired, and now lived in an adults-only elven village near Sarasota. Water elves owned large swathes of land there, and in addition to having quite a few fancy resorts (some for elves and others for human tourists), they also built several retirement communities. Most were populated by Christmas elves tired of the cold and hoping to enjoy their days riding around in golf carts, swimming, and relaxing in the sun. Poor Mr. and Mrs. Toffee. This would be a huge shock.

"Do you have a place?" asked Officer Pudding.

"Yes. My grandmother lives on Morningstar Lane. She's out of town, so I'll let her know I'll be staying there."

I sent Grandma Gingersnap a quick text saying our apartment building was being fumigated for cockroaches and asked if I could stay at her house. She immediately told me I could and let me know there was a lasagna in the freezer if I was hungry.

But please don't bring any of those roaches to my house. Or anything else.

I frowned, wondering what she meant by the last part. Maybe I should have told her there had been a fire, and we had smoke damage. Then again, she would have replied with something like, *Make sure you don't bring any fire into my house, young lady.* She was pretty predictable.

"I'll stay with Tink." Jax shoved his hands into his pockets before shooting me an apologetic look. "If that's all right with you."

"I'd be grateful."

"Good, because if someone was brazen enough to send you those tainted chocolates, they might be willing to do something even more reckless." His words made an icy chill wash over me.

"Are you serious?"

"Yes," said Jax. "You could be in danger, Tink."

"I agree," said Officer Pudding. "We'll keep a sled out front, too."

I immediately imagined the calls my grandmother would get about a police sled in front of her house. "Can it be unmarked? Please?"

"For an address on Morningstar Lane, I promise we'll be as discreet as possible."

When he walked away, Jax turned to me. "What did he mean? What's on Morningstar Lane?"

I ducked my head. "Oh, you'll see."

While Jax grabbed a few things from his hotel room, Officer Pudding pulled me aside. "We'll have to let your uncle know what happened," he said.

Folding my arms over my chest, I stared at a spot on the floor. "I figured. But, hey, when you speak with him, can you ask him not to tell my grandmother? I don't want her to worry."

"Sure," he said, giving me a curious look. He didn't ask why I wouldn't tell my uncle myself, however, and I didn't volunteer an answer, but there was something I needed to know.

"I heard about the chocolates. Jax said someone intended them for me. Is that true?"

"Unfortunately, it is." Officer Pudding led me to a row of chairs in the hallway next to Noelle's room. "The box was delivered this afternoon. We asked your roommate about it right after they stabilized her. She didn't see who left it. She heard a knock on the door and found it sitting there. There was no note, only your name and address on the box, and as soon as she ate one, she knew something was wrong. We're lucky she's seen enough people overdose on candicocane that she immediately suspected what was happening. And we're also lucky she was able to give herself a shot of narzipan."

"Narzipan is the only thing that can stop an overdose like this, right?"

"Yes," he said. "Although when it comes to drugs tainted with telazol, narzipan doesn't always work, especially if it's given too late. Your roommate is lucky to be alive."

After thanking Officer Pudding, I joined Officer Bing in Noelle's room and sat next to her until Jax returned with an overnight bag. She slept the whole time.

"Are you ready?" Jax asked, keeping his voice low.

"Yes." Kissing Noelle on the forehead, I made Officer Bing promise he would not leave her side. A few years younger than Officer Pudding, he was good-looking and sincere. I felt safe leaving Noelle with him. Also, there were worse things than waking up to a face as handsome as Officer Bing's. Maybe Noelle would thank me later.

Officer Pudding drove us to my grandmother's house. If Jax was impressed by the row of mansions or at all intimidated when we pulled up in front of the biggest one on the street, he didn't show it.

"Will you need anything from your place?" asked Officer Pudding.

I shook my head. "I'm fine."

Knowing my grandmother, she had held onto all my clothing from high school and college. I could almost guarantee my prom dress was hanging in the closet, too. "Thank you, Officer Pudding."

"You're welcome, Ms. Holly. Be safe." A sled pulled up with two men inside. Officer Pudding gave them a nod. "Your security detail is here. I'm leaving you in good hands."

"Thank you, Officer Pudding," said Jax, getting out of the car. "We'll be in touch."

We waved goodbye and stepped inside the spacious foyer. Taking off my coat, I hung it in the closet near the door and slipped out of my shoes. Jax wore a black wool coat over his suit. When he shrugged out of it and handed it to me, I was surprised by the softness of it. It was cashmere and expensive. I knew my textiles. Better yet, it smelled like him.

As Jax stuck his head in the front living room and flicked on the lights, I took a good long whiff. The coat carried his scent, a combination of soap and some sort of spice, but it wasn't the cinnamon or nutmeg that was popular here. This was different. Unusual, sexy, and a little mysterious—like Jax himself.

When I finished smelling his coat like a weirdo, I hung it up and followed him into the living room. "Can I give you a tour?"

"Yes, please," he said. As he stared around the room, he wasn't admiring the décor or impressed with the grandeur. He eyed each window, door, and point of entry obviously considering our safety. He needn't have worried. Grandma Gingersnap had a state-of-the-art security system, as did everyone else on Morningstar Lane. It went with the territory.

After showing him the panel and explaining how it worked, I guided him through the rest of the house. "This is the kitchen," I said, waving a hand to indicate the massive room. "Where the magic happens."

He smiled. "Considering how much you like to eat it doesn't shock me you'd look at it that way."

"You're right," I said. "Also because my grandmother is an amazing cook." I opened the door to show him all the frozen meals inside, gesturing like someone displaying the grand prize on a TV game show. "Tada. We will not starve, which is good news indeed."

I pulled out a tray of lasagna and stuck it into the oven, setting the timer for an hour. After showing him the rest of the first floor, including the den and the outdoor patio (complete with a fire pit and hot tub), I took him upstairs.

"There are several guest bedrooms. Choose whichever one you'd like."

"Which one is closest to yours?" he asked, peeking into the rooms, his overnight bag in one hand.

"Um, this one." I pointed to the door of the bedroom next to mine.

He gave me a strange look. "I'm not going to steal your virtue, Tink. You don't have to be worried."

"Who's worried?" I asked, my cheeks getting hot again. I seemed to blush a lot lately. I cleared my throat. "And I won't steal your virtue either. I swear." I held up my hand, imitating the Elf Scout promise.

His lips quirked. "As long as we're clear on neither of us stealing the other's virtue, will you be comfortable with me sleeping next door?"

"Most definitely," I lied. I wondered if I'd sleep at all, knowing he was so close. I also wondered if he wore pajamas. Jax seemed like the kind of guy who would sleep naked—an intriguing thought.

I opened the door to the room, showing him the en suite bathroom, and checking if he had fresh towels and supplies. Not that I needed to. My grandmother employed several housekeepers who made sure her home was always perfect. But they were off while she was on vacation.

"I'm going to take a bath and freshen up," I said. "Do you want to meet downstairs in an hour or so for dinner?"

He nodded. "Would you mind if I checked the perimeter of the house? I want to make sure I've got a handle on everything before we turn in for the night."

"Okay. Check away."

I went into my room and shut the door behind me with a frown. *Checking the perimeter?* What did he expect to find? The episode with Noelle was scary, but Jax acted paranoid. Did he think someone would dare attack us in my grandmother's house? Anyone foolish enough to even contemplate it had clearly not met my grandmother.

Unbuttoning my blouse, I ran water in the tub. As expected, my grandmother kept the place stocked with all sorts of bubble bath, shampoo, and other toiletry items. She even had the kind of perfume I used back in college when I thought smelling like patchouli was a good thing.

I bypassed the patchouli and went with lavender-scented bath salts. According to the promise on the bottle, the lavender would help me relax enough to sleep. I might need more than lavender this evening, especially if I kept picturing Jax naked. And he was even sexier when he talked all special ops and said things like "checking the perimeter."

"You can check my perimeter any time you want, baby," I said to myself with a giggle. But as I sank into the warm water, my giggling soon turned to tears, and those tears morphed into huge, silent sobs.

My best friend almost died today—because of me. And the fact that I'd gone to Cookie, even though my gut told me to trust Jax, made it so much worse. Somehow, even when trying to do the right thing, even when attempting to follow the advice of Noelle and my grandmother, I'd screwed up once again. It was bad enough when it affected me. This time, it had almost cost Noelle her life.

It seemed even more important that I help Jax figure out what was going on. It was far too late to back out now. I was in this for the long haul.

With a sigh, I leaned back into the water, inhaling the floral scent of the bubble bath. It was soothing, but the lavender on its own wasn't going to cut it. I also planned to raid Grandma Gingersnap's wine cellar this evening.

After washing my hair and having a long soak, I dressed in a pair of yoga pants, warm socks, and a soft hoody. Pulling my hair up into a messy bun, I didn't bother with makeup. I planned to eat dinner and go straight to bed alone. Definitely alone. Without Jax. Even though every time I thought about the kiss we'd shared, I seriously reconsidered the promise I'd made about not stealing his virtue.

The smell of lasagna wafted up the stairs, calling to me with its spicy, sausage-y siren's song. I went to the basement to grab a bottle of red wine, and when I entered the kitchen, I noticed Jax had taken off his shoes and his jacket. He'd also rolled up his shirt sleeves and appeared to be making a salad, which somehow seemed very sexy all of a sudden.

He looked up at me when I came in and stopped right in the middle of chopping a cucumber to stare at me. It went on so long it got uncomfortable.

"What?" I asked, looking at my outfit. "Is something wrong?"

"No," he said. "Not at all. You sparkle, a lot. It takes some getting used to, I guess."

"Well, I am a Christmas elf," I said, giving him a slight bow.

"Yes, you are." He gifted me with one of his rare smiles. "Feeling better?"

"I am," I said, opening the bottle of red wine and pouring two generous glasses. "And this will help even more." I handed him one, and we clinked glasses together.

"Cheers." He took a long sip. "Oh, this is nice."

"Only the best for Grandma Gingersnap." I lifted my glass in a mock salute. "What are you working on here?"

He waved a hand to indicate the vegetables. "Salad. I found these things in your grandmother's refrigerator. I hope it's okay to use them."

"Of course. She always leaves food here in case I'm starving, homeless, destitute, intoxicated, on the lam, in trouble with the law, or have nowhere else to go."

"Like tonight?"

I laughed, but there was no humor in it. "Yes. Like tonight. Which means she'll be able to say, 'I told you so' forever and ever. Lucky me."

"Are you and your grandmother close?"

"Tricky question. My parents died in a sleigh accident

when I was seven. She raised me, and I love her, but we're different people. I did not turn into the granddaughter she'd always hoped for, and I understand her disappointment. It was hard for her to accept who I was, but eventually, she did, and our relationship is better than it used to be. High school was rough, though."

"Ah, your rebellious teenaged years."

"Yes. And those turned into my rebellious college years. And my rebellious post-college years. I was a handful. It took me a long time to grow up."

I sat on the kitchen island and watched him work. He had a dishtowel over one shoulder, a focused expression on his face, and a lock of hair falling out of his ponytail. He seemed at home here, both in the kitchen and in this house. I'd never considered salad-making a turn on, but Jax made it seem oddly sexy. And although I barely knew this man, I was so at ease with him— a disconcerting sensation.

He caught me studying him and lifted one dark eyebrow. In this light, his eyes weren't black but a deep, rich brown.

"You look serious all of a sudden," he said.

I knew little about this guy, and yet I already trusted him with my life. I'd never been the queen of making good decisions, but I knew I could count on Jax, no matter who may advise me otherwise. It made no sense at all, and yet it was the truth.

I answered him honestly. "I was thinking how strange it is I only met you yesterday morning. A lot has happened."

"It has been a busy week."

I smiled at the understatement and swallowed hard. "I trust you, Jax. And I don't trust a lot of people. Try not to disappoint me, okay?" He seemed surprised by my words, but I continued talking, embarrassed by my revelation. "What's on our schedule tomorrow?"

"We need to go to the reindeer department. It was one of the first places on my list, but I got sidetracked with everything that has happened."

"Death, drugs, and drinking. A typical week in Christmasland," I said with a snort. "But you're right. We should check out the reindeer department. Since Joy worked there, it's the most logical place."

"I agree." He gave me a long, steady look. "And I trust you, too, by the way. You aren't what you seem, Tink, and you deserve more credit than you're given." He paused, as if he was embarrassed, too, quickly amending, "From what I've seen so far, at least. If you hold up this well under pressure, it says a great deal about your character."

His words pleased me, more than I cared to admit. "So, I'm not a spoiled rich kid with too much time on my hands who lives to embarrass her family?"

Something odd flickered across his eyes. It vanished before I could identify it. "Do you think that's who you are?"

"No," I said, taking a sip of wine. "I'm just me, flaws and all, and I can't be anyone else. I've tried, truly I have, but I've concluded I'd only be happy if I was able to live my own life." I rolled my eyes. "And, wow, that does sound entitled of me. I know. I'll shut up now."

"Not entitled," he said, making dressing by squeezing a lemon over the salad and adding olive oil and balsamic vinegar. "You're honest. It's refreshing. And I admire you for it. Not everyone has the same openness."

"Candor is my middle name." When he looked up at me in astonishment, I laughed. "I'm kidding."

The timer dinged on the oven, and he pulled out the

lasagna. He'd made garlic bread, too, clever man, and it smelled delicious. As we sat at the kitchen island and ate our dinner, he tried to guess my middle name.

"Is it Ivy?"

"No."

"Fruitcake?"

I burst out laughing. "Maybe it should have been Fruitcake, but no."

We finished one bottle of wine with our dinner and opened another. "Do you want to sit outside?" I asked. "By the firepit? It's nice out there, and so peaceful."

He paused gazing out the window as if assessing any possible dangers. "Sure," he said, but I heard the unease in his voice.

"Don't be such a worrywart." I grabbed blankets from a stash Grandma Gingersnap kept by the back door and handed them to Jax. "We're at my grandmother's house. The safest place on the whole North Pole. What could possibly go wrong here?"

"And that is why I worry," he said, his expression stern. "The 'safest' places are usually where the worst things tend to happen."

His words made me pause. What things had he seen? What had caused him to say something like that? It must have been awful, and the idea of it made me sad for him.

"Not tonight," I said, putting a hand on his arm. "Not here."

While Jax made a fire, I went back into the house to get some other essential supplies. Soon we had a blazing fire, and Jax looked pleased with himself. I pulled a blanket around my shoulders and sat on one of the padded chairs around the fire pit. Jax sat in the one next to me.

"This is lovely," he said, leaning back in his chair and

staring up at the sky. The aurora borealis lit up the night with bands of bright green, blue, pink, and purple. I'd grown up seeing it all the time, but it never got old. For Jax, it was something new and different. "It's so beautiful here. I never expected the North Pole to be like this."

"What did you expect?"

He shrugged. "I don't know. I thought it was all about toys and Christmas."

I gave him a wry look. "It *is* all about toys and Christmas."

He chuckled. "Yes, but it's so much more. It's not what I expected." He turned, and his gaze met mine. "And you're not what I expected either, Tinklebelle Mossypot Holly."

I laughed so hard I snorted. "It's not Mossypot. Ew. But speaking of unexpected..." I pulled out a bag of marshmallows, graham crackers, and chocolate, doing a happy dance in my seat as I showed them to him. "Look what I found in the pantry."

"More sweets?"

I stared at him, dumbfounded. "You've never had s'mores before?"

"S'mores?"

I reached out and grabbed his hand in a gesture of sympathy. "You poor, poor man. We'll remedy this right now."

I taught Jax how to make a s'more. He seemed to enjoy it, but he didn't want more than one. He did, however, like making them so much he kept feeding them to me.

"No. Stop. I can't believe I'm saying this, but I'm so full."

"One more," said Jax, putting it together and feeding it to me. I'm not sure how it happened. I may have licked one of his fingers as he gave me the s'more, which led to me licking another finger and another. That made his eyes get all hot and unfocused, and before I knew what was happening, we were kissing. Again. And this time, there wasn't any mistletoe.

"Mmmmm," he said, sighing into my mouth. "You taste so good."

"It's the marshmallow. And the chocolate," I said between kisses.

"No, it's you, Tink Holly. Just you."

As he explored my mouth with slow sweeps of his tongue, his hair fell out of his ponytail and brushed against my cheek. It felt like silk, and he tasted like sin. Jax Grayson was trouble, and I loved trouble, but this was a terrible idea.

"We should stop," he said, his voice unsteady.

"We should," I said, kissing him some more. Why did everything bad have to feel so good?

"Tink. You're killing me."

"It seems like a great way to go," I said, moving closer to him. I'd planned to climb onto his lap and have my wicked way with him, but unfortunately, he stopped me.

"No," he said, his voice soft and his breathing unsteady. "We've been drinking. And you're in a vulnerable position right now."

"I'm not *that* vulnerable," I said, sounding so irritated he laughed.

"Yes, you are. Look at what happened to your friend, Joy, and to your roommate. It would be enough to throw anyone into a spiral."

He brought my hand up to his lips and kissed my fingers one by one. I sighed. I liked this guy—what a revelation. "You're right, I guess. But can I have a rain check?"

"Yes, you may. Tinklebelle Cuddlehug."

I snorted. "Nope. Not it."

"Tinklebelle Stocking Stuffer?" he asked. I gave him a dirty look. "Tinklebelle Jinglebug?"

I groaned, rising to my feet, and offering him a hand. "It's late," I said, helping him up. "We both need to rest. And you are never going to guess my middle name."

"I like a challenge." He moved closer to me, cupping my face in his hands, and brushing my lips with his. "I will figure it out, Tink. And I'll figure you out, too."

"Good luck." When something wet and cold hit my face, I looked up. "Oh, great. It's snowing."

Jax lifted his face to the sky. "I've never seen snow before."

His joy made him seem younger and even more handsome than usual. For a moment, I stood there and watched him, wondering what it felt like to experience snow for the first time. I had no idea, but, to my amazement, I enjoyed seeing my world through his eyes. And when he smiled at me, I couldn't help but grin back. Snow swirled around him as stars twinkled in the dark sky, and the aurora borealis seemed especially dramatic and magical this evening.

"Goodnight, Jax," I said, going up on my tiptoes to kiss his cold cheek. "See you in the morning."

"Goodnight, Tink."

Somehow, I'd become blind to the beauty all around me. It seemed like poetic justice a dark elf would be the one to help me see it again.

CHAPTER ELEVEN

The following day, I woke up with joy in my heart. First of all, Noelle was doing much better, and the nurse I spoke with was convinced the hospital would discharge her in a few days. I'd called several times during the night, and talked to the same nurse, Awreatha Feelgood, each time. By the end of her shift, we'd bonded. I hadn't been able to speak with Noelle yet, since she was sleeping, but Awreatha assured me she was in good hands. Noelle, as a fellow nurse, was one of them, and they took care of their own.

The second thought I had was kissing Jax the night before and the way he'd looked as the snow fell. That gave me joy in my heart, too, and I jumped out of bed, eager to see him.

Also, I smelled coffee. I was eager for coffee as well.

Unfortunately, when I reached the kitchen, I let out a startled squawk. Jax was sitting there drinking a cup of coffee, looking all big and sexy and delicious—no problem there. But sitting right next to him was none other than my uncle, Kris.

Jiminy Christmas.

"Tink Holly. Watch your language." Uncle Kris lifted an eyebrow as if amused.

I covered my mouth with one hand. "Crap on a cracker. Did I say that out loud?"

My uncle's lips twitched. "You didn't have to say it out loud. I saw it on your face."

"Oh, great. You're reading minds now?" I rolled my eyes. "Is that one of your new tricks?"

I heard a smothered laugh behind me and turned to see Topper Twinkle, my uncle's assistant, standing in the doorway. "Your uncle's newest trick is using kanban and kaizen to increase productivity at work," he said, helpful as ever. "We've figured out there is a thing or two we can learn from humans." When I gave him a dirty look, too, he grinned at me in pretty much the same way my uncle had. "Not that you asked."

Topper was about the same age as my uncle and used to be a professional skier and a wild reindeer wrangler. He had the body of an athlete, a kind heart, and he'd always been good to me.

"Nice to see you, Topper," I said.

"You, too, sunshine." Topper had always called me that, ever since I was a girl. Well, when he wasn't calling me a pain in the ass.

Topper knew me well. We shared a long history, and he'd gotten me out of more than one problem of my own making. I called him my uncle's "fixer," which always made him smile. He said the only things he'd ever had to fix for my uncle were problems created by me. He wasn't lying.

When Topper stepped outside to make a phone call, I avoided my uncle's gaze and went straight to the cupboard and pulled out a coffee mug.

"I take it you met Jax?" I asked, trying to sound nonchalant about the whole thing.

He nodded in Jax's direction, eyes twinkling. "I've had the pleasure."

"Good."

He laughed—a hopelessly jolly sound. It made everyone around him laugh as well. Except for me. I was immune. And so, apparently, was Jax, who didn't look happy. He looked uncomfortable.

"Would you like some privacy?" Jax asked, obviously eager to get as far away from us as possible. "I can go check on things out front."

My uncle shook his head. "No, Jax. I prefer that you stay here. I find when Tink is involved, it's always good to have witnesses."

"Hey—"

He shushed me. "Stop being all prickly and come over here. I haven't seen you in a month of Sundays." He tapped a finger to his rosy cheek, indicating he wanted a kiss. I obliged because I love my uncle. I truly do. But I don't like spending much time with him.

I poured myself half a cup of coffee and filled it the rest of the way with eggnog flavored creamer. The perfect ratio of sweetness to caffeine. "How is Auntie Clarice?"

"She's well, thank you."

"And the boys?"

"They're all as right as rain. But I'm not here to talk about them. I'm here to talk about you. What's going on, sweetness?"

I took a long sip of coffee-flavored eggnog. The combination of sugar and caffeine hit my brain with a welcome zing. "I'm not sure, Uncle Kris. I guess someone tried to, uh, kill me or something yesterday."

"In other words, a typical Tuesday?"

"Yes," I said, with a smile. I'd missed him. As hard as it was to be around him, I should have made more of an effort. "You didn't tell Grandma, did you?"

"Oh, heavens no. The last thing we need right now is to make her worry. Let's allow her to enjoy her cruise." I heaved a sigh of relief, but it was short-lived. "If, however, anything else happens, I will call her."

"Snitch," I muttered.

"Brat," he said without any malice, almost like an endearment. Jax watched our interaction with a curious eye, like he wasn't sure what to make of it.

"I came over to check on you," said Uncle Kris, folding his hands over his belly as he leaned back in the chair. "I heard about Noelle."

I swallowed hard. It gutted me to picture my friend in that hospital bed, especially knowing it was sort of my fault. "She's going to be discharged soon. She'll be fine."

"But will you?"

There was a long pause before I answered, and when I did, my voice sounded unsteady, even to my own ears. "Yes. I will."

He stared at me, as if assessing the situation carefully. "From what I hear, this seems like a random act. Normally, I'd insist you come and stay with us—" When I opened my mouth to protest, he held up a hand to silence me. "But since Mr. Grayson is here, I feel comfortable leaving you in his care."

"Like a babysitter?" I asked, putting down my coffee and folding my arms over my chest.

"Exactly." Reaching inside his double-breasted suit, Uncle Kris pulled out his pocket watch and checked the time. "I have to get going. I'm trusting you to behave Tink. To be safe. Are you sure you're okay?"

"I'm fine. I swear."

He handed Jax a business card. "This is my direct line. If she isn't fine, at any point and for any reason, I ask that you please contact me immediately. I hope you don't mind."

Jax took the card. "Of course not. I will, sir."

"Good," he said, tilting his head to study Jax's face. He did the same thing to me all the time. In a disconcerting way, it was like he could see right into a person's soul. It made me extremely uncomfortable. Jax, however, seemed as utterly unaffected by it as he had been to my uncle's laugh.

The doorbell rang, and before I could answer it, the door flew open, and in came Win's mother, Angel Snow, followed closely by Topper. He gave me an apologetic look, but we both knew there was no stopping Mrs. Snow when she was on a mission.

"Kris," she said, hugging my uncle. "I saw your sleigh out front and came over to see you."

"It's been too long, Angel. I'm checking on my niece. She'll be staying here for a few days."

Mrs. Snow wrinkled her nose like she'd smelled something dirty. "Oh, will she? How nice." Her gaze shot to Jax, and her expression turned even uglier. "This must be the new boyfriend we've heard so much about."

There was a moment of silence, during which Uncle Kris's eyes locked on mine, and he did the weird soul-searching thing again. I tried to communicate with him telepathically to let him know what was going on. I didn't know if he'd understood or not, but he gave Mrs. Snow a warm smile.

"Yes, but I only stopped by to visit. Jax's father is an old friend of mine. They're keeping an eye on my mother's house while she's away."

"Oh, really?" said Mrs. Snow, with an excited gleam in her eye. I knew she was burning to tell everyone I was living in sin with a dark elf in my grandmother's house. Mrs. Snow loved gossip and hated me. It was a bad combination.

I wondered, not for the first time, if Uncle Kris knew what he was doing. But the thing was, he always, always did. I needed to sit back and trust him for once.

Mrs. Snow left, practically running out the door, and my uncle sighed. "You know Angel can't keep a secret to save her life, right?"

"I do," I said. "How long before Grandma finds out?"

He glanced at his watch. "I'm guessing about an hour at most. Good luck."

"Thanks, Uncle Kris."

He tilted my chin up with one finger and looked deeply into my eyes. "Well, Tink. What can I say? Life is never boring when you're around."

I let out a laugh. "Understatement."

"I suppose it is." He kissed me goodbye, and Jax and I stood at the door, watching him go.

"See you later, Tink," said Topper.

"Not if I see you first."

It was our standard farewell, and it made Topper chuckle. Some things never got old.

Uncle Kris made it a point to chat with the policemen in the unmarked car before he left. He may have signed autographs for them, too. He did that a lot. As soon as he was gone, I closed the door and headed back into the kitchen. Jax followed me, stomping rather than walking. The stress of the last few days had taken its toll on both of us, and I knew he was about to explode.

"What a delightful surprise," he said, his words dripping with sarcasm.

"Wasn't it?" I sat at the island, hoping to resume my coffee drinking in peace, but Jax refused to let it happen. He stood on the opposite side of the room, giving me the stink eye.

"I find it odd you forgot to mention your uncle was Santa Claus."

I folded my arms over my chest. "Nor did I mention anyone else in my family. Just like you've told me nothing about yours. And besides, the clues were all there, *detective*. You never asked."

He lifted his brows so high they nearly touched his hairline. "Oh. Is that what people do here?" A sarcastic and irritating smile formed on his face. "Hello, Tink. Nice to meet you. Is your uncle Father Christmas, by any chance?"

Turning away from him, I went to the pot for another cup of coffee. It was empty, which made me even more irritated. "Don't be a jerky-jerk face."

"Nice, Tink. You're full of fun and surprises this morning."

"What do you want from me, Jax? Because I can't figure it out."

As I clattered around, putting dishes into the sink and swearing under my breath, Jax watched. When he finally spoke, his words stunned me.

"I want to trust you."

When my eyes met his, I glimpsed something there, something vulnerable and sad. All my anger left me in an instant, and I felt deflated, like a popped balloon.

"I'm sorry. You aren't a jerky-jerk face. I was crabby."

"Thank you, but this changes everything. We need to talk."

As I made another pot of coffee, he shoved his hands into the pockets of his pants. He must have found an iron in the spare bedroom because they were perfectly pressed. I, on the other hand, had rolled out of bed, brushed my teeth, and come straight downstairs, still in my wrinkled jammies. I hadn't even brushed my hair.

"Talk? About what?"

Tilting his head to one side, he studied me. Last night, his eyes had seemed such a warm brown. Today they looked like cold, hard, onyx.

"Hmmm. Let me see. Do you not understand how this is so much more complicated because you are the niece of one of the most powerful men in the entire elven world? Do you honestly not comprehend the intertribal implications of this entire situation? But instead of focusing on the candico-cane crisis or about how you were nearly assassinated, we must, instead, come up with a story for your grandmother. We have to explain why we lied and pretended to be romantically involved when we've only known each other," he glanced at his watch. "Exactly forty-seven hours and twenty minutes."

I waved away his words. "Oh, don't worry. I'll tell her the truth. She can see right through my lies. It's like she has psychic powers. Seriously. There is no point in trying to deceive her."

"And what about Cookie Wassail? Will you tell him the truth, too?"

I hadn't thought about Cookie. "I'm not sure. I'll cross that bridge when we come to it."

"Avoidance. Good answer. And it seems to be your modus operandi."

Maybe he was a jerky-jerk face. "I'm sorry I didn't tell you Santa Claus was my uncle. It's not always easy being the imperfect niece of a perfect man. I don't talk about it much because people treat me differently as soon as they know. They expect me to be remarkable or amazing. Something I am most definitely not. But I am the same person I was yesterday, so please don't treat me any differently because I have a few famous relatives."

"A few—?"

My phone rang. It was Grandma Gingersnap. Already. Fudgity fudge cake.

"Oh, snap. And now I have to deal with this, the person I disappoint most of all—my grandmother. But I'll take care of it. I always do. So you can cross it off your list or you can continue to be angry about it. I don't care. I'll be back when I'm done."

Sending him a dirty look, I stomped up the steps to my room, answering my phone on the way. "Hi, Grandma," I said in the sweetest voice possible. "Are you having a nice trip?"

"Are you kidding? I leave you alone for one day. One day. And the neighbors are already calling to tell me you're involved with a dark—"

I interrupted her. "It's not true. We're not involved. I'm helping him with the investigation I told you about."

"The one I advised you not to do?"

"Yes. That one. And I pretended Jax was my boyfriend so people would feel more comfortable opening up around him. There is nothing to worry about."

"Oh. Lovely. Except people now think you're fooling around with a dark elf. Didn't you hear me when I told you they are dangerous?"

I put a hand to my head. "Jiminy Christmas. Are you racist much, Grandma?"

"Watch your language." She let out an exasperated

noise. "I'm not racist. I'm honest. Do you know this man at all? Or his family? These are not the sort of elves you should mess around with, Tink, even in jest. Trust me. I learned the hard way."

"The hard way?"

She lowered her voice. "When I was your age and working at Elf Central, I dated a dark elf."

I dropped my phone. When I picked it up, it was upside down, and I had to turn it around in order to hear her. "Wait. You had a *thing* with a dark elf? What was his name?"

"Zakar of Neslos. It was fifty years ago, and it ended badly. He broke my heart, but not long afterward I met your grandfather and lived happily ever after." Her voice got emotional. My grandfather died when I was small, but I knew my grandmother missed him every day. It still didn't explain the whole dark elf story.

"Um, back to Zakar of Neslos. When you say you dated him, do you mean you—"

"Don't even finish your question. I'd rather talk about how you ended up in a fake relationship. Explain that one to me and be quick about it. I have a belly dancing class in twenty minutes."

Explaining the situation to her without mentioning Joy's death or Noelle's near-death was tricky. Fortunately, she'd been chiefly concerned about my secret love affair, so when I rattled off something about an audit, I lost her attention immediately.

"And were you upfront with Cookie Wassail like I told you?"

"Yes," I said. "I took your advice."

I didn't add that I regretted it now. It seemed irrelevant and would make her late for her class.

"Good. It's about time." I heard strains of music coming from over a loudspeaker. It sounded like something out of *Scheherazade*. "I've got to go. Call me if anything else happens, like you get married or pregnant." She paused. "I was joking about the last one. Please, dear God. Do *not* get pregnant."

"Grandma. Stop."

"Fine. Be safe. Make good choices. Use your brain. I love you."

"Love you, too."

Hanging up the phone, I flopped back onto my bed with a groan. "This day could not get worse."

The words no sooner had left my mouth when my phone rang again. "Fudge, fudge, fudge," I said, thinking it might be my grandmother again. It wasn't. It was Nippy Nibblewrap.

"Tink?" His voice was a whisper. "I heard about your roommate. Are you okay?"

It sounded like Nippy was in a closet. Weird. "I'm fine. Thanks for asking. What's up?"

He didn't answer for a second, and when he did, his voice was an octave higher than usual, like someone had him by the jingle balls. "I need to talk with you and your friend, Jax. It's about his audit. Can you meet me later? It's important."

"Sure." I grabbed a pen from my old desk and wrote the address on a slip of paper. A photo of a young Win sat there, gleaming at me with his megawatt smile. I put it face down on the desk. I couldn't look at Win right now. "Are you okay?"

He didn't answer my question. "See you tonight. And be careful Tink. Watch who you trust."

He hung up before I could ask him anything else. I sat

there a moment, stunned when I realized precisely what I'd heard in Nippy's voice. It was fear. Nippy was terrified, and to tell the truth, now so was I.

CHAPTER TWELVE

After a long argument about whether or not I should leave the house at all, Jax finally agreed I could go out as long as I wasn't alone. Meaning, if I was with him. I agreed to it, albeit grudgingly, because I was afraid he might handcuff me to the bed. And not in a good way.

We had a bunch of stuff to do today, but I'd wanted to see Noelle first. He seemed to get it, but one thing bothered him as we stepped out of the Ubersled in front of North Pole General.

"What did Nippy say exactly? Other than he wants to meet us tonight in an abandoned warehouse in the middle of nowhere?"

"It wasn't so much what he said. It was how he said it." I chewed on my lower lip. "And the warehouse isn't in the middle of nowhere. It's only a few blocks away from Happypie's. Speaking of which..."

He shot me a skeptical look. "You can't be serious. We ate breakfast less than an hour ago."

I placed a hand on my belly. "It was small. I can't help it if I'm still hungry."

"Small? We had bacon and eggs and potatoes and toast. And you had cookies for dessert, which is odd in itself. I didn't want to say anything at the time, but there is no such thing as having dessert after breakfast. Dessert is served after dinner, if at all."

I turned my nose up at him. "That may be true where you come from, but here dessert is the most important meal of the day."

He let out a frustrated groan. "Dessert is not a meal."

"Says who?"

"Says me. Says everyone."

"Well, I say it is. So there."

"Did you just tell me, 'So there'? What are you? Twelve?" he asked, getting annoyed.

We were marching down the long corridor of the hospital side by side. He wore black. Again. And to counteract all his darkness, I'd dressed in winter white. It was an outfit I'd snatched from my grandmother's closet, a snug-fitting, sleeveless turtleneck dress with a matching swing coat and heels. With my blond hair up in a bun, my makeup understated and classy, and a pair of pearl earrings I'd also borrowed from my gran, I looked pretty darned good, if I did say so myself. And I carried a bouquet of red roses for Noelle, which added to the effect.

I came to a stop because his words irritated me. "Do I look twelve?" I waved a hand, indicating my body. His dark eyes scanned me from head to toe, almost like a visual caress.

"No." A lock of hair had slipped out of my bun. He reached up to tuck it behind my ear. "You do not look twelve."

For a second, I thought he might kiss me, but he didn't. Such a disappointment. He did, however, change his tone.

"You've been through a lot these last few days. If a Happypie's hamburger and a double chocolate shake with extra whipped cream will help, I will provide it for you."

"You will?" I asked, putting a hand over my heart.

"I will," he said, rolling his eyes. "What was it Joy said? If you don't eat regularly, you get kind of grumpy. She was right."

I gave him a shaky smile. "She was a good friend. And so are you." I kissed his cheek. "Thank you, Jax."

He rocked back on his heels as if shocked by both my gesture and my words. "You're, uh, welcome...?"

I linked my arm in his, and we continued to walk toward Noelle's room. "Don't phrase it like it's a question. You should respond like it's a statement. Like you believe what you're saying. Be confident about it." When he didn't say anything, I nudged him. "Go ahead."

He looked at me out of the corner of his eye. "You're seriously going to make me say it?"

"Yes. Let's practice. Thank you for being my friend, Jax."

"You are welcome, Tinklebelle Bunnykins."

I guffawed, a sound so loud one of the nurses shushed me. After apologizing to her, I looked up at Jax, who was grinning. "That is *not* my middle name," I said, keeping my voice low and unable to stop a giggle from escaping my lips. He seemed so pleased with himself.

"I'll figure it out eventually. How many names can there possibly be?"

When we got to Noelle's room, two police officers stood outside, guarding her door, but they let us in after we showed them the proper ID. I was pleased to find Noelle sitting by the window in a wheelchair and gazing outside. She turned and smiled when she saw us. "Hey, there."

"You look better." I handed her the roses and kissed her cheek. "I thought about getting you chocolates, but..."

She let out a laugh, which was what I'd hoped to achieve. "Ha. Good one."

I perched on the edge of her bed. "Sorry. Too soon?"

"Definitely too soon." Her eyes went to Jax. "You must be Mr. Grayson. Thanks for babysitting Tink for me."

"It's a hard job, but someone has to do it."

"Hey—" I began, but they both laughed.

"You're telling me," said Noelle. "You know about the food thing, right? If you don't feed her, she gets crazy." She made a swirling motion with one finger next to her ear.

"Oh, I've noticed. Do you know she has dessert after breakfast?"

"Yes," said Noelle with a laugh. "Dessert is her favorite meal of the day."

"Okay, okay," I said. "I'm glad you're having fun at my expense. You're both hilarious."

"We're both serious," said Jax.

Noelle pointed at him. "I like you. You see through her nonsense."

He pointed right back at her. "I like you, too. And please call me Jax."

I scowled at them. "If you're done bonding now, can we move on?"

"Not quite," said Noelle. "There is something I need to say."

"Do not tell him about my bra collection."

She let out an exasperated breath. "Why would I tell him about that? And hundreds of bras is not a collection. It's a hoard. You're a bra hoarder."

"They'll be worth something someday."

"No, they will not." She shook her head in disbelief. "Please be quiet for two seconds. I need to apologize." She looked appraisingly at Jax. "I was wrong about you. I told Tink not to trust you. I'm sorry." She turned back to me. "And I should never have told you to go to Cookie with my concerns, Tink. It was a mistake. I hope you didn't listen."

Before I could respond, Jax jumped in. "Oh, she listened to your advice. She went straight to Cookie." When I opened my mouth to protest, he held up a hand to stop me. "And I understand why. I fully expected it, and I planned accordingly. I don't blame either of you. I do think Tink trusts me now, though."

"I do," I said, confused. "Hold on. You knew I spoke with him yesterday morning about you?"

"You aren't as sneaky as you think you are, or maybe I have the same lie-detecting ability as Grandma Gingersnap."

Noelle's eyes got big in her pale face. "You met Grandma Gingersnap?"

"Not yet, but I met Uncle Kris."

"Oh, wow," said Nicole.

"Exactly," said Jax. "Now *that* was unexpected."

After we left Noelle's room, I knew I should apologize to Jax about Cookie but wasn't sure how. I decided to blurt it out.

"I'm so sorry."

"I told you I understand. To be honest, I didn't trust you, either. I'd only known you for a day. It takes at least two or three to earn my complete loyalty." He smiled at me, giving me a gentle bump with his elbow. "And I trust you now. Even if you did betray me to Cookie."

"I didn't tell him you were a dark narc," I said, keeping my voice low. "Don't worry."

"What did you tell him exactly?"

"I said I didn't think you were here to do an audit. And he asked me to spy on you."

Jax paused, staring at me. "*Have* you spied on me?"

"I haven't spoken with Cookie since yesterday morning. I might be wrong, but part of spying is sharing information with the person you're spying for. I haven't done any of that, so I guess we can add spying to the list of jobs I'm not good at."

We stepped into the elevator. Jax pressed the button for the lobby, and leaned against the wall, studying me. "Thanks for not being a good spy, Tink."

"You're welcome."

"But why did you agree to do it in the first place?"

I focused on my shoes, so I didn't have to look at Jax. "Cookie oversees job assignments. I thought the reindeer department was as low as I could go, but he so kindly reminded me hell has a basement, and the basement is called the coal mines."

A muscle worked in Jax's jaw. "He threatened Santa's niece with the coal mines? Surely, he couldn't—"

"Oh, yes, he could. It's a meritocracy here, Jax, and the last thing I'd ever do is ask my uncle for help. Cookie knows that which is why he's threatening me with the coal mines if I don't do as he asks." It was hard even to admit it, but there was more. "And supposedly I'm up for a job on the naughty list team if I do what he wants."

"Why 'supposedly'? I think you'd be good at the whole naughty list thing."

"Thanks. So do I, mostly because I have so much experience with being naughty." The words came out sounding sadder than I'd intended. "Anyway, Cookie told me I could have it if I did what he wanted, but I'm pretty sure he was lying. And I'm pretty sure he's using me."

When the elevator doors opened, we walked out into the bright and sunny hospital lobby. A skylight in the ceiling bathed the area in natural light, and a sparkling Christmas tree sat in the middle, blinking merrily.

"Can you give me a second?" Jax pulled me aside, leading me to a bench in a quiet nook near the wall. He sat next to me. "I have to stop by the police department next. I need to talk to the officers who were on the scene yesterday."

"Oooh. 'On the scene.' You make it sound so official."

"It is official." He leaned forward, resting his elbows on his knees. "There are some things you need to know about me."

"Oh, yeah? Please say it's something kinky."

That got a laugh out of him, which was my goal. "No, it's not kinky. Sorry to disappoint you. Although I am curious about your bra collection."

"It's extensive."

"I'm sure it is. It's about why I'm here. I told you I've been investigating the recent uptick in candicocane related deaths, but there is more to it. Someone is secretly transporting large amounts of the telazol-laced candicocane all over the elven world. They're employing some sort of magic to do it, but it doesn't show up on our radar, so we can't track it. This is a volatile situation, and it's escalating fast. I must be getting close, but I never meant to put you into any danger."

I covered his hand with mine. "I believe you, Jax."

"And I never thought I'd be pulling Santa Claus's niece into the middle of this."

"Oh. I see. That's why you freaked out when you met Uncle Kris."

"Yes," he said and ducked his head. "Well, that and the fact he is Santa Claus. Come on, Tink. Even you have to admit it's pretty cool."

I gave him a sad smile. "If you say so."

He frowned, and I knew he was about to ask me what I meant, but my phone buzzed with a text. After glancing at it, I handed my phone to him.

"It's Cookie. He wants an update. What should I tell him?"

He handed my phone back to me. "Nothing. I suggest you tell him nothing until after we talk to the police."

I shoved my phone back into my purse. "Okay. Let's go."

"That's it?"

"Yep."

He stood and reached out a hand to help me to my feet. "You do trust me, don't you, Tink?"

"I do," I said as we stepped out into the cold. "Please don't make me regret it."

Officer Pudding waited for us at the North Pole Police Department headquarters. Watching Jax interact with him, I couldn't believe I didn't immediately pin him as a cop. While Officer Pudding stepped away from his desk to get a file for us, I leaned closer to Jax.

"More about this 'dark narc' stuff. Do you have handcuffs?"

"No."

"Do you like to frisk people?"

"No," he said, with a twitch of his lips.

"Do you carry a concealed weapon?" I asked, tilting my head discreetly to indicate his crotch.

"Tink. Stop it."

"Sorry. I find all this undercover detective stuff extremely hot. When you say, 'undercover,' do you mean—"

He placed a finger against my lips. "Please be quiet," he said, but I saw the twinkle in his eyes, even if he tried to act all serious.

"Fine. I'll shut up." My silence lasted about five seconds. "Why are we here exactly?"

"To find out what the police know about Joy's death. We were waiting on toxicology reports. They came in this morning."

"You've been working with the NPPD this whole time?"

"Yes, I have."

"Why did you need me?"

"Because an audit is the best way to have unfettered access to paperwork, but it wouldn't look authentic unless I went through company headquarters." He turned his chair slightly to face me. We were so close our knees knocked together. "I wanted to stir the pot. When you do that, strange things bubble to the surface. I never meant for you to be involved. For you to be a target. When they killed Joy —and yes, I'm even more certain she was murdered after what happened to Noelle—things went in a direction I never intended. Someone must have found out she was talking to me. They must have thought she had information, but I don't know who is behind it, and I also don't know why they're going after you now."

"What are we going to do?"

He took my hand in his, lacing his fingers with mine. "You aren't going to do anything. I'll find a way to keep you safe and figure out who is behind this."

"But you said I could help you. I want to help."

"This is different, and you are helping—by staying safe. It was bad enough involving an innocent elf in this whole mess, but involving Santa's niece? Sorry, Tink. We can't do it."

Officer Pudding came back to his desk while Jax was still speaking. He held a red file in his hands. "He's right, you know. If something happened to you, the repercussions would be severe. We can't risk it. Speaking of which..." He gave Jax the red file and handed me a box with a narzipan injection kit inside. It was a glorified EpiPen. I knew how to use it because Uncle Kris's middle son was allergic to tree nuts, and I used to babysit him when he was little.

"I have to carry this around with me?" I asked.

Officer Pudding nodded, his expression serious. "You need to have it with you at all times. Until we figure out who is behind this, you're at risk."

I tapped my foot impatiently. "I'm a damsel in distress, waiting around for the bad guy to get me?"

Jax answered for Officer Pudding. "No, you're a smart, responsible person who has the good sense to listen to the people who are trying to keep her safe. This isn't sexism. It's not misogyny. You are not a police officer, Tink. We don't want you to end up like this."

He slammed the file on the desk in front of me and opened it. I flinched at the sight of Joy's body. "Jax. Please."

"No. You need to see this. It could have been you. Do you have any idea how close you came to dying? If Noelle hadn't eaten one of those chocolates, you would be on this slab right now." He jabbed a finger at the lab results. "Cause of death: Overdose. Candicocane laced with telazol. And look at the amount in her bloodstream. It's off the charts. This was no accident. Someone killed her, and they tried to kill you, too."

I was quiet the whole way to company headquarters. Seeing those photos of Joy had frightened me, and I knew Jax was right. I knew I should listen to him. I knew I should play it safe, but something inside me felt unsettled. I'd never been an exceptionally patient person, and instead of waiting for something else to happen and counting on someone else to save me, I would much rather have gone on the offensive. But it looked like I didn't have any choice in the matter. Jax Grayson had made the choice for me.

Yes, I was pissed.

"I'd like to meet with my friend who works on the naughty list team before I decide how to handle Cookie. It should only take a few minutes. Also, it'll give you a chance to see that department as well, and ask questions, if you have any."

Jax didn't argue. Apparently, he knew picking a fight right now would be like playing with fire. I was on the verge of losing elf-control.

The office for the naughty list team was in the basement of company headquarters. It looked like a dungeon, which sort of fit.

A bored receptionist with pink hair barely glanced at us as we walked in. When I asked to see my old friend, Blitz Goody, she paged him twice with her nasal voice and went back to playing Candy Smash on her phone. Blitz showed up a few minutes later, a big smile on his round, ruddy face.

"Tink. Long time no see. What have you been up to? No good, I'm guessing." He pulled me into a hug. "You look amazing. You haven't changed since high school."

It was a lie, and we both knew it, but Blitz was a nice guy. "You haven't changed either," I said—another lie. Blitz had put on about forty pounds and lost most of his hair. The poor guy wasn't even thirty yet.

"What can I do you for?" he asked, giving me a wink. His flirty, joyful expression changed when he noticed Jax standing behind me. "Hello and whoa ho ho. Who is this?"

"Jax Grayson, Blitz Goody. Jax is here from Elven High Council. He's doing a surprise audit."

"Of the naughty list?" asked Blitz, confused.

"Well, we're visiting a bunch of different departments. Can we ask you a couple of quick questions?"

"Sure." Poor Blitz looked nervous.

"It's routine. Calm down, Blitzy."

He took a deep breath and exhaled loudly. "Okay. I'm calm now. Ask away."

"How does the naughty list work?" asked Jax.

"Oh, it's easy. We used to employ magic to do it, but now we use video surveillance combined with new audio technology. We created a device humans keep in their homes so we can listen to every word they say. It's made our job a lot easier, I'll tell you what. And the humans pay us to get the machines we use to spy on them. It's brilliant." When Jax responded with a slightly judgmental stare, Blitz's face turned even ruddier than usual. "Er, and invasive. And sneaky, but it is brilliant. We call it The Listener. The humans call it something else, though. I can't remember the name."

"Interesting," I said, pretending to take notes. "And how many people work in this department?"

"Oh, geez. Let me see. Fifty employees total, I guess."

"How many managers?"

Blitz counted in his head. "Three. No, wait. Four. Flurry Jitters started here last week. I almost forgot about her." He leaned closer. "She's the new team manager, and she's a real piece of work. I can't believe Cookie Wassail stuck us with her. Sometimes I wonder about him."

"Me, too." I tried not to let my disappointment show. That was my job, the one Cookie had dangled in front of me like a carrot, and I'd wanted it so badly. I should have known better. "Well, I guess we're done here."

Blitz looked disappointed. "That's it?"

"Yes, thanks, buddy. Tell Bootsy and the kids I send my love."

I waved goodbye, keeping my chin up. It wasn't until we turned the corner, and I was away from prying eyes that I lowered my guard. My shoulders slumped, and I ducked my head. Without saying a word, Jax pulled me close, wrapping his big, strong arms around my shoulders and pressing his cheek against my hair.

"I'm sorry, Tink."

"It's okay. I always knew it was too good to be true." I kept my face in the crook of his neck as I willed myself not to cry. "I didn't realize how much I'd been counting on that job until now."

"I get it. I do." He gently brushed his fingers over my hair, soothing me.

"Thanks, Jax, but do you know what yanks my chain?" I didn't wait for him to answer. "I thought if I played by the rules and did what society expected me to do, things would finally work out for me, but they didn't. They got worse."

Jax lowered his hands to my waist and leaned back so he could see my face. "Tink Holly. Since when have you ever followed the rules?"

"Until now, I haven't. Which is why I never fit in here. It's my biggest problem," I sniffed.

He shook his head. "No, it's your biggest strength."

I stared at him for a second before going up on my toes and kissing him firmly on the lips. "That is the nicest thing anyone has ever said to me."

"I'm happy to oblige," he said. "Hey, I have an idea. What do you say we skip the visit to Cookie's office?"

"Fine. I have nothing to say to him at this point." I glanced at the clock on the wall behind Jax. "But we're not meeting Nippy for a few hours. What should we do in the meantime?"

He gave me a crooked smile. "I believe I owe you a hamburger."

CHAPTER THIRTEEN

"I know why Cookie assigned you as my tour guide," said Jax as we sat at Happypie's munching on burgers and drinking shakes. After some encouragement from Sugar, Jax had gone crazy and ordered a banana shake to go with his meal. He was living on the edge now, but to me, a banana shake was pretty much just fruit.

"So do I. He figured he could bribe me with the promise of a better job. He thought I'd fall for it, and he was right. It almost worked."

Jax shook his head after having another taste of his milkshake. "That's not why," he said. "Cookie assigned you to be my tour guide for one reason. He chose the prettiest elf he could think of because he wanted to distract me."

Jax continued eating, oblivious to the fact he'd once again found a way to warm my prickly old heart. I stepped around the table, climbed onto the booth seat next to him, and planted my lips on his. When I finished, he seemed dazed.

"What was that for?" he asked.

"You called me pretty," I said, pulling my plate and

milkshake across the table, so they now sat in front of me. "I may as well stay here. Chances are you're going to say something nice again, and I'll have to kiss you again, and it'll be annoying if I have to get up and down and up and down."

"Well, I don't want to cause you any inconvenience," he said, blinking. "But getting back to Cookie. He's hiding something, and I want to know what it is."

"Want me to make a list?"

Grabbing a napkin, I pulled a pen out of my purse and wrote every shady thing I'd ever heard involving Cookie. It was a long list. I had to use both sides of the napkin.

"Why didn't you threaten him with this when he threatened you with the coal mines? You're Santa's niece. Surely your word carries some weight around here."

"First of all, I don't play that way. Secondly, most of this is speculation. I have no proof. Also, I'm saving it for the day he tries to send me to the coal mines. I'm not a woman of threats. I'm a woman of action. Kind of. I wait first, and then I act later."

"I don't understand—"

I shoved a French fry in his mouth. "It's easy. It's about not stooping to his level unless I'm forced to do so. Do you know what I mean?"

When he tried to answer, I shoved another French fry into his mouth. "Here's the thing. As bad as this is, and as angry as I am he promised me a job he'd already given to someone else, in retrospect, I'm relieved. Now he has nothing to hold over me. I no longer have to grovel because I have nothing left to grovel for. It's sort of liberating. Or maybe this is what hitting rock bottom feels like. I'm not sure which."

I glanced at Jax, waiting for a response. He stared at me.

"Can I speak now, or will you try to stick another French fry in my mouth?"

"Hey, you looked hungry. And you're so pale."

"All dark elves are pale."

"And you don't see the irony in that?"

This time Jax was the one who kissed me, and he did so even more thoroughly than I had. The boy had skills. But before I could ask him why he'd kissed me, I looked up to see Win and Candy standing right at our table. Win was glaring at Jax with such intensity, I worried his head might explode.

Win's head. Not Jax's.

"Hey, guys," I said, giving them a weird wave.

"May we join you?" asked Win.

Candy murmured something, tugging on his arm, but he ignored her. I was going to tell them we were finishing up, but Jax answered for me. It seemed we had a pissing contest going on.

"It's always nice to spend time with Tink's old friends," said Jax. "You've known each other since..."

"Since the day she was born."

"Ah. You go way back. What about you, Ms. Holiday?"

She flicked her long blond hair over her shoulder. She had on a blue dress and looked amazing. I was thrilled I wasn't wearing sweats today. Or, even worse, my RAT uniform. "Tink and I were close in high school. After we graduated from college, we sort of drifted apart."

A generous way to describe it. "Yeah, I was kind of a pain in the *ass*."

Jax's lips quirked. Neither Candy nor Win found me amusing.

"I came to warn you about something," said Win, his blue eyes sincere. "There is talk in elven resources. If you're not careful, you're going to end up in the coal mines. It's no laughing matter, Tink. I want to help. Let me pull a few strings."

"No, but thank you, Win."

He lifted his hands, a defeated look in his eyes. "Fine. If you won't accept my help, at least call your uncle—"

I stood up. I couldn't listen anymore, and I was out of French fries. "Not an option, but thanks for the suggestion." I turned to Jax. "Are you ready, Jaxy?"

He narrowed his eyes at the use of this new endearment. "I'm always ready, Tinky."

When he got up and wrapped an arm around my shoulders, I leaned into him, even though it caused a spark of pain in Win's eyes.

"Do you always have to be so stubborn?" Win asked.

I gave him a sad smile. "Yes, I do. It's all I have left. It's the only thing in my life I can control." I shot Candy an apologetic look. "I don't know if I ever thanked you for not pressing charges. I'm sorry I was such a jerk. You didn't deserve it. Neither of you did. But maybe you do deserve each other because you're both truly good elves."

Candy's eyes filled with tears. She blinked them away. "Thanks, Tink."

"You're welcome."

As we walked out the door of the restaurant, Jax gave me a funny look. "Why are you looking at me like that, Jaxy?"

"First of all, stop calling me Jaxy. Secondly, that was mature of you. And kind."

I stopped in the middle of the sidewalk, not far from where Joy had died only a few days ago. Unintentionally, my gaze went to the spot where it had happened, and I swallowed hard. "Life is too short. And, regarding the nickname, I like calling you Jaxy. It's super cute, and you're going to have to live with it."

He looked skyward, as if praying for patience. I got that a lot.

Sugar followed us outside. "Can I talk with you for a second, Tink?"

"Sure," I said, and turned to Jax. "As long as you don't mind."

He shook his head. "Not at all. I have a few calls to make. Take your time."

Jax pulled out his phone as Sugar and I walked to a more secluded area on the side of her restaurant. "What's up?" I asked.

She cupped one of my cheeks in her hand. "I wanted to touch base. I've been worried about you, kiddo. Seeing your friend die must have been a shock. I know my nephew Frankie was devastated. And after what happened to Noelle..." Her voice trailed off. "Do you have any idea who might be behind it?"

I tucked a lock of hair behind my ear. "I wish I knew."

"And sending your favorite chocolates in order to hurt you. Whoever it is must be a monster." She tilted her head to indicate where Jax stood. "Is that why he's here? To investigate?" When I gaped at her, she laughed. "Honey, I know a cop when I see one. Trust me. Is there anything I can do to help?"

"No but thank you."

She kissed my cheek. "Don't mention it. Your mother was one of my best friends in the whole world. A real peach. And as much as I love Win, I have to admit I was glad when you broke up. He's a good guy, but his parents are awful. Can you imagine having Angel as your mother-in-law?" She shuddered and I laughed.

"That would have been a nightmare, for Angel and for me. I'm sure she's much happier with Candy."

"You deserve better." Sugar studied my face. "You know, your mom and I hoped you might end up with Frank someday." When I opened my mouth to respond, she waved it away. "Oh, it was a pipe dream. I understand why it didn't happen, sweetness. Frank will never grow up, and he could never make you happy, but this guy." She indicated Jax again. "Well, when I see you with him, you seem happier than you've been in a long time. Maybe forever. And it warms my heart."

I kissed her cheek. "Thanks, Sugar."

"Don't mention it." She paused, as if weighing her words. "But be careful, okay? What happened might be a random thing, but perhaps you should leave town for a little while. Maybe go on a vacation somewhere nice and warm? They have great prices right now on tickets to Florida. Go see Noelle. I heard she'll be heading there soon to stay with her parents for the holidays as she recovers. It would be a great chance for you to soak up some sun, drink cocktails on the beach, and get away from this place for a while. Whatever's going on here isn't worth the risk."

I said goodbye to Sugar, knowing she was right. Florida did sound awfully nice right now, but I couldn't go. Not until I helped Jax figure out what was going on.

When Jax saw me approach, he hung up his phone. "All done?"

"Yes,' I said. He grabbed me by the hand and led me toward a waiting Ubersled.

"Where are we going?" I asked.

"Back to your grandmother's house."

"Good idea," I said as we got into the sled. "I have to get

changed. I can't go to the warehouse in this." I indicated my white dress. "I need ninja clothes."

His lips quirked at the phrase 'ninja clothes,' but he seemed serious when he responded, "You are not going to the warehouse."

I gave him a skeptical look. "Excuse me?"

He kept his eyes locked on a point somewhere out the window. "It's too much of a risk."

I poked his arm. "But Nippy called *me*. He wants to meet with *me*. How do you know he'll even talk to you?"

"He asked to meet with us, Tink, not you."

"Do you think it's about Joy?"

"I don't know, but something seems off here. I don't want you involved."

Folding my arms over my chest, I leaned back in my seat. "And what am I supposed to do all night?"

Jax lifted one shoulder in an utterly nonchalant way. "I don't know. Knit?"

I did not kill Jax in the Ubersled. My skills at elf-control were impressive. And when he left to meet Officer Pudding, I waved goodbye to him.

"Have a great night at the office, honey," I said.

He eyed me suspiciously but didn't respond, and I knew he assumed I would listen to him. Jax was a guy used to giving commands and having those commands followed. I was a girl used to doing things my own way. Not a good combo. So I did what I do best. I ignored him. He wanted me to remain at home all night, under the watchful eye of the police officers out front. Little did he know, I had years of experience sneaking out of my grandmother's house.

After dressing in black from head to toe, my ninja garb, I grabbed a black jacket and baseball cap. My tennis shoes were red, but hopefully, it wouldn't matter. I went into the pantry and selected a few snacks. Even ninjas got hungry, and I had no idea how long I'd have to wait for Nippy. It could be hours. Without snacks, I might die.

I shoved some beef jerky bites into one pocket and stuck chewy chocolate candy in the other. I wanted all the bases covered. I turned on the television, with the volume up a notch higher than usual, made sure I kept the lights on in the family room, the hallway, and my bedroom, and snuck out the back door.

The path I'd used as an escape route in my misspent youth had grown over slightly, but I still made it. I cut into the Snows' backyard. Win and I played there when we were small, and later, when we were older, we used to sneak out there to mess around. I was a terrible influence on Win. No wonder his parents hated me.

At the sound of his mother's voice, I jumped into the shadows. Apparently, she'd opened the door to let the dog out. Since their dog, a psychotic Yorkie with delusions of grandeur, hated me, this was not good. The dog was creatively named the Duke of Yorkie, which I long ago suggested they shorten to "Dorkie." The Snows had not been amused. They called him Duke, and, as if he knew I'd mocked him, the dog had despised me from day one. Mrs. Snow took this as a sign.

"Dogs and babies always know," she said, insinuating I was a bad person. She may have been right. Babies didn't seem excessively fond of me either.

The last thing I needed was for the rat dog to bark at me, so I hid in the bushes a few feet away from the back door. I had to cross through the yard and past the back door to get to my Ubersled, so hanging out here was my only option. The bonus? I got to listen to Mr. and Mrs. Snow talk, and they seemed to be in the middle of an argument as they stood in their kitchen and waited, back door wide open, for Duke to do his business.

"I told you we should never have agreed to this," said Mr. Snow. "No matter the consequences. If Win finds out—"

"Win is not going to find out, silly."

I heard Mr. Snow mutter a curse word. "Are you certain, Angel?"

"Yes, I am. I don't know why you're upset. We did nothing wrong."

Mr. Snow made a noise of pure frustration. "But if anyone finds out, how will it make us look? Sometimes you forget who you are, Angel Snow."

There was a pause, and Mrs. Snow murmured something I didn't catch, even though I was leaning so close I was almost in the room with them. "...and we had no choice in the matter. In all honesty, Winnie, after what she did to our son, she deserves what she gets."

I frowned. Wait a second. Were they talking about me? I leaned even closer.

"It's ancient history, Angel. Let it go."

"I can never let it go. You know it's about more than what happened. It's also about her mother. Or have you forgotten—"

The sound of barking cut off their argument. Duke had found me, the little monster.

Fudgity fudge cakes.

I tried to quiet him but to no avail. He barked and growled and refused to give up. I stuck my hands into my pockets, remembering I had snacks but forgetting which side held the chocolate and which held the beef jerky. They were roughly the same size and wrapped in similar packaging.

"What is Duke barking at?" asked Mr. Snow.

"Oh, dear. It isn't a coyote, is it?" Mrs. Snow sounded worried. I didn't even realize we had coyotes in this neighborhood. I doubted they could afford the HOA fees. "Go check, Winnie. I'm scared."

Left without any other options, I tossed snack items from both pockets straight at Duke. He was small enough the chocolate could make him sick, but hopefully, he'd opt for the beef jerky instead. Either way, he stopped barking, grabbed one of the things I'd thrown at him, and marched back into the house. He seemed pleased with himself, but as soon as he got inside, Mrs. Snow screamed. "Duke has chocolate. Get it from him. Now."

While they were wrestling with Duke, I took advantage of the opportunity and ran across the backyard as quickly as possible. I may have dropped a few more snacks along the way, but I made it to the other side as my Ubersled showed up.

I pondered the conversation I'd overheard the whole way to the warehouse district but couldn't figure it out. I knew the Snows hated me, but why bring up my mom? Between Duke barking and my hovering behind a bush, I hadn't caught all their conversation. And the bits and pieces I had heard didn't seem to connect to anything.

After asking the Ubersled driver to drop me off a few blocks away from my actual destination, I walked the rest of the way to the warehouse where I was supposed to meet Nippy. It seemed quiet there, but I was almost an hour early.

Nippy had told me the back door would be open, so I

slipped inside the cavernous building. It was dark, but the streetlights cast some light in through the large windows. Once my eyes adjusted, I could at least see enough not to trip over things.

Hearing the soft murmur of voices, I followed the sound, careful not to bump into anything. One of the voices was Nippy's. The other person sounded vaguely familiar, but it wasn't Jax.

I edged closer. I was in some kind of loading dock, with metal barrels all around me. Large and black, I could hide behind them without even ducking. They were stamped with dark ink on the side, and the light was enough for me to make out the words *Biohazardous and Medical Waste*. Lovely. Glancing down, I noticed something white on the floor. Picking it up, I stared at it in confusion. It looked an awful lot like an arm from a Mr. Potato Head toy. I shoved it into the pocket of my jacket and peeked around the side of one of the barrels. A single bulb hanging from the ceiling illuminated the area in front of me. I recognized Nippy's tall, slim form immediately, and saw the frightened look on his pale face.

"Stop." He stood only a few yards in front of me on my right, but he wasn't looking in my direction. He stared at something I couldn't see, something coming from my left. He lifted his hands slowly into the air. "Please don't."

Uh, oh. Was Nippy being robbed? And Jax wasn't due to arrive for at least another twenty minutes or so. Not good.

I pulled out my cell phone and made sure the volume was off. The last thing I needed was to get a phone call right now. My ringtone was *Grandma Got Run Over By a Reindeer*. I chose it mainly to annoy Grandma Gingersnap, but also because I liked the song. I was about to send Jax a quick text when Nippy spoke again.

"You don't have to—" The sound of a gunshot cut off Nippy's words. He flew back into a row of barrels, knocking several of them over. I flinched, stumbling into the barrel behind me. Heavy and probably filled with something gross, it didn't fall over, but I dropped my cell phone onto the cement floor, and it made a loud clattering noise.

Scooping it up, I edged farther into the shadows, my body shaking from head to toe. From here, all I could see was one of Nippy's long legs. His shoe had fallen off when he'd gotten shot. He had on rainbow-colored socks.

Poor Nippy. He was the sweetest and most gentle person I knew. I couldn't see from here where the bullet had hit him, but his body was so terrifyingly still. I choked back a sob.

"Is someone there?" A voice came from the area near Nippy, and the person spoke in a strange, husky whisper. Once again, it sounded vaguely familiar, but I couldn't place it. For a moment, there was silence, and all I could hear was the pounding of my heart, but then I heard something else. The sound of footfalls as whoever shot Nippy moved closer and closer to me.

My back was against a wall. I lowered myself to the floor as quietly as possible and slipped off my bright red tennis shoes. I was afraid whoever had shot Nippy might see them, and I wasn't taking any chances, so I shoved them deep into my dark jacket. I held back a whimper as I zipped it up. So much for being a ninja. Why had I worn red shoes? And why had I come here alone? I was in serious trouble now.

Something scuttled in front of me, running to my right. It stopped and stared at me, and I realized it was a rat. A big, fat rat that ate biohazardous medical waste material for a snack.

Remembering I still had a few snacks left in my pocket, I pulled out what I hoped was a beef jerky stick and tossed it over the rat's head and as far away from me as I could. He must have immediately smelled the tantalizing aroma because he took off, running toward it. When another shot was fired, this time the rat got hit.

"Fecking rat." The voice, and it was definitely a male voice, was low and irritated.

I held my arms tightly around myself, too scared to move. But after a long, silent moment, the footfalls moved away from me, and I heard the distinct sound of one of the exterior doors opening and slamming shut.

Glancing around to make sure the coast was clear, I crawled on all fours past the rat. "Sorry," I said softly. The bullet had practically blown it apart. I'd caused the poor rat's death. Even though it was a rat and possibly full of nasty biohazardous medical waste and Mr. Potato Head parts, I still felt guilty. I understood the lure of beef jerky all too well.

I passed the rat and turned to look at my friend. Nippy still hadn't moved. The single overhead light shone on him. Even though there were still a lot of scary shadows, it was bright enough I could see the room was now empty, and we were alone.

Taking a deep breath, I got off my hands and knees and ran toward him as fast as I could while crouched. I was still in my socks, my shoes tucked into my jacket. When I stepped on something warm and wet and it seeped into my sock, I knew it was Nippy's blood.

I knelt next to him, trying to assess the damage, and it did not look good. He'd been shot on the upper left side of his chest. Tossing my shoes aside, I dug my phone out of my jacket pocket. Nippy opened his eyes and let out a moan.

"Tink. You shouldn't be here. You need to hide."

For a second, I considered doing what he said and hiding behind the barrels again. Or, better yet, getting out of here altogether. Even the old me, the one who seemed to seek out trouble, would have run away. She would have left in a heartbeat. But I wasn't the same girl anymore. Joy's death, and the scare with Noelle, and Cookie's deceit...they all had changed me, perhaps forever.

I straightened my spine. "I'm not leaving you, Nippy."

Picking up my phone, I tried to call 911, but my hands were wet from Nippy's blood. After swearing and wiping them furiously on my legs, I managed to make the call.

"Ho, ho hello—"

I cut the dispatcher off in mid-sentence. "Someone has been shot. We need immediate assistance." I put down the phone but kept it on speaker, so I could use both hands to help Nippy. "He's a forty-year-old male. He's breathing, but he's losing a lot of blood. He has a gunshot wound to the upper left quadrant of his chest."

I pulled off my jacket and covered him with it as I tried to apply pressure to the wound. It didn't seem to help. The good news was that I now knew what to expect from emergency services. I answered their questions before they even had time to ask.

"Okay, miss. Help is on its way." The voice on the line sounded so calm and reassuring, like a kindly grandfather.

"I'm applying pressure, but I can't get the bleeding to stop."

"Keep at it. You're doing great. Is he breathing?

Nippy's eyes were closed, his skin gray. "He is," I said. "But it seems shallow."

"Can you feel his pulse?"

"No," I said, sending my phone a sarcastic scowl. "I'm using both hands to apply pressure."

"Good. You're doing so well. The ambulance is almost there. I'll stay on the phone with you until it arrives."

"Thank you."

"You're welcome, sweet pea. Hold on."

Sweet pea. What my dad used to call me when I was small. I had to hold back the tears threatening to fall. It was like a sign of some sort, but I needed to stay calm if there was any chance of keeping Nippy alive.

A few seconds later, I heard the distant wail of a siren. "The ambulance is almost here, Nippy," I said. "You're going to be okay."

His eyes fluttered open. "It's too late. I tried to stop them—"

He gasped, inhaling deeply, and as he let his breath out, it made a strange, sad sound. A death rattle. "No, no, no. Don't you dare die on me, Nippy."

Removing my hands from his wound, I put them in the center of his chest, about to do CPR, when I heard a sound that made my blood run cold. I recognized the sound from human television programs. It was the click of a safety being disengaged from a gun.

"Freeze. Put your hands up."

I lifted my arms in the air, turning toward the sound of the voice, and saw Jax standing there, feet wide, his expression cold and hard. He held a gun with both hands and pointed it right at my heart.

CHAPTER FOURTEEN

"Cripes, Jax. Put the gun away. Nippy needs your help." When he didn't move, I tried again. "*I need your help, Jax. Please.*"

I'm guessing the note of panic in my voice snapped him out of whatever zone he was in and finally got his attention. He holstered the gun and hurried over. Between the two of us, we managed to keep Nippy alive until the EMTs arrived, but barely. They rushed him to North Pole General, and we followed in Jax's undercover police sled. He didn't say a single word to me during the ride. I didn't blame him. He was mad about what I'd done, and maybe upset at himself for nearly shooting me.

Or at least I hoped he was upset with himself. Maybe he wished he had shot me. I couldn't be certain. It had been a stressful couple of seconds.

We waited on hard, plastic chairs in a silent hallway as Nippy underwent surgery. When the doctor came out to tell us Nippy had been moved into the intensive care unit, I heaved a sigh of relief, but our friend wasn't out of the woods yet. He'd lost a lot of blood and hadn't regained consciousness since the incident, so it was still touch and go. Jax and I remained in a sort of stunned state as we listened to the doctor talk about possible brain damage from lack of oxygen and a blood transfusion. He also told us how close the bullet had come to Nippy's heart and lungs.

"It was millimeters away from ending his life. Your friend is a lucky man."

Lucky? Poor Nippy. He didn't deserve any of this. Even when lying on the cold floor of the warehouse, with his lifeblood pouring out of his body, he'd used his last bit of strength to tell me to hide. To try to protect me.

After the doctor left, we didn't move. We didn't talk either. I stared at my hands. They were still covered in Nippy's blood. It was the second time this week I had a friend's blood on my hands. My clothes were covered in it, too, and my socks had soaked it up like sponges. They squished inside my red tennis shoes. It was Jax who finally broke the silence.

"I could have shot you," he said, pulling me out of my thoughts about my blood-soaked socks. He sat, staring straight ahead and not looking at me. "I could have killed you."

"I know."

"What were you thinking?"

I was about to tell him I hadn't been thinking, but it wasn't true. I turned to face him.

"I had to go, and I'm glad I did. If I hadn't, Nippy might be dead right now. Or are you forgetting that part?"

"Well, you conveniently forgot Nippy was at the warehouse because of you."

I gaped at him. "Because of *us*. He wanted to meet with us. You're the one conveniently forgetting things."

When I got to my feet, Jax stopped me with the touch of one hand. "I'm sorry. You're right."

The events of the night caught up with me and my shoulders slumped. Jax stood and pulled me close. I pressed my face against his chest and breathed him in. I didn't wrap my arms around him, though, and I didn't lean into him. After a few seconds, I gently disengaged.

"I should check on Noelle."

He brushed a lock of hair away from my cheek and tucked it behind my ear. I'd lost my black hat at some point, and my hair was falling out of its ponytail.

"It's late. Noelle will be asleep, and I doubt she'd want to see you like this." He waved a hand to indicate the blood. "I should take you back to your grandmother's place."

"Will you stay there with me?"

"Yes, because with each passing moment, I get more and more concerned with your safety. But if you don't want me to stay—"

"I want you to stay," I said, the words bursting out of me. "Please."

"Then I'll stay." He lifted my chin with his fingers until I was looking directly into his eyes. "You were brave tonight. You did well. You should be proud of yourself."

His words made me feel worse instead of better. "Not well enough. We still don't know what's going on."

"We will," he said, his expression grim. "I only hope we figure it out soon. Before someone else gets hurt."

Standing in the shower, letting the hot water run over my body, I watched as Nippy's blood went down the drain in a swirl of pale pink. Grabbing a washcloth and a bar of soap, I scrubbed and scrubbed, my movements angry and rough. I wanted every last vestige of the evening removed from my skin. After I'd washed my hair twice, and the water ran clear, I sank to the floor of the marble-tiled shower, curled up in a ball, and cried, my face pressed against my knees.

I had no idea how long I stayed there, but eventually, I stopped crying, got up, turned off the water, and reached for my robe. As I tied the belt, I heard a soft knock.

"Is everything okay?" I opened the door, and Jax stood on the other side.

"I'm fine," I said. "I think."

My wet hair hung heavy on my back, and long strands clung to my face. Jax grabbed a fluffy white towel from the pile on a shelf, instructed me to sit on the small stool in front of my vanity, and proceeded to pat my hair dry.

"It's normal to be shaken up by what you saw," he said. "I feel the same myself."

"Is that something you see a lot?" I asked. "Because it's been a long week, and it's only Wednesday. At this rate, I'm dreading what tomorrow will bring, Jax."

"Me, too." He lowered the towel and bunched it up in his hands. I didn't like the raw emotion I saw on his face. I didn't like anything about this entire situation.

Grabbing the brush from my vanity, I proceeded to brush out my hair. He backed away and hung the towel on the knob of the bathroom door. The clothing I'd been wearing lay in a heap on the floor. Jax pointed at the pile.

"What do you want me to do with these?"

I wrinkled my nose. "Throw them away, please."

I thought I'd cried myself out in the shower, but I found I wanted to put my face in my hands and cry yet again. I felt off-kilter and almost numb. Maybe I was in shock. When I'd set out from the house tonight, I'd almost looked at it as a game. Nothing about it seemed entertaining now.

As Jax gathered the clothes, something small fell out of my jacket pocket and landed on the floor. He picked it up and stared at it with a confused expression on his face. "What is this?"

"I'm pretty sure it's a Mr. Potato Head arm."

His confusion deepened. "Excuse me?'

I made a round shape with my hands. "You know. Mr. Potato Head. The toy?"

"I do not know, nor do I understand why it was in here," he said, digging into the pocket on the other side of the jacket. He pulled out the contents with a perplexed frown. "Along with beef jerky and chocolate?"

"Oh. Those are snacks," I said. "Well, what is left of them, at least. I brought them in case of an emergency."

He didn't question why I'd need an emergency snack stash, which meant he now knew me better than I'd realized. "And this?" he asked, lifting the Mr. Potato Head arm again.

"*That* I found on the floor of the warehouse when I was hiding behind a barrel. It seemed out of place."

He studied the piece of plastic with interest. "It may not mean anything, but you were smart to pick it up. You have good instincts, Tink."

I ducked my head, oddly embarrassed by his praise. "No one has ever said anything like that to me before. I usually hear the opposite."

"You do tend to get yourself into some unusual situations."

"Like letting a dark elf I've just met hang out in my bathroom with me?"

"Like that." He gave me a crooked smile.

My shoulders sagged with fatigue, but I wasn't sure I could sleep. Images of blood and rats and Nippy on the floor of the warehouse kept playing over and over in my head. I didn't want to be alone.

"Is there any way you'd be willing to sleep here tonight?" I asked, tilting my head to indicate my bed. "I don't mean to sound so weak and needy, and I'm not trying to get into your Christmas package or anything, but—"

"It's fine," he said. "You've been through a great deal this evening. I would not mind staying with you...if it would make you more comfortable."

"It would. Thanks."

I climbed into bed, turning off the bedside lamp. The moon was bright and full, providing enough light to see. It made me feel better somehow, as did having Jax nearby, although I felt like I'd taken advantage of the situation. He was far too nice, and too much of a gentleman, to refuse me, even if I was acting like an elfling.

Jax didn't call me names, though, or make fun of my fear. He climbed in next to me, his body stiff. As soon as I curled up on my side next to him, though, resting my cheek against his shoulder, he seemed to relax. He sighed and pulled me gently into his arms.

"It's going to be okay, Tink," he said, his voice low and soft in the dark room. "I know I've said this before, but you were brave tonight. You should be proud."

"Oh, I don't know," I said. "There were several less than spectacular moments."

"We all have those." He stroked my hair, soothing me with his touch. "You have to power through. You'll be fine. I promise."

"Thanks, Jax."

"You're welcome, but can I ask you one question?"

When I nodded, he continued. "What did you mean about my package?"

I let out a groan. "Shut up, Jax. Forget I mentioned your package. Please"

"Fine," he chuckled. "Try to get some rest, Tink. It's been a long day."

And as I lay in his arms, listening to the steady beat of his heart, my eyes closed and, at last, with a tiny smile on my lips, I finally fell asleep.

Unfortunately, my happy falling-asleep-in-Jax's-arms euphoria did not last long. I slept poorly and woke up grumpy. I got grumpier when I realized Jax had already taken off. He left a note on the counter demanding I stay put and telling me he'd instructed the guards out front to shoot first and ask questions later if I tried to leave again. I assumed he was joking about the last part. Either way, I didn't take kindly to him ordering me around, nor did I like being stuck in my grandmother's house. It felt too much like when Grandma Gingersnap had grounded me as a teenager. Worse, because this time, I didn't deserve it.

I called the hospital to check on Nippy. He was still unconscious and in critical condition. The nurse had nothing new to report, but at least he remained alive. That was pretty big in my book.

Noelle had already been released from the hospital. Some-how, I'd missed a text from her while I'd been canoodling with Jax. Her parents had come back to take care of her, and as Sugar had predicted, Noelle planned to go back to Florida with them for an extended visit once she recovered enough to fly.

I sat back in my chair with a sigh. This was not the way I'd pictured the week ending, for Noelle or for me. Maybe Sugar was right. Maybe I should go to Florida with Noelle and her parents and get out of here for a while. After all, it wasn't like I had a job to deal with—not anymore, at least. And anything was better than being under lock and key in my childhood home.

My phone rang with a Facetime call from my uncle. Great. Cringing, I accepted it, but only because I'd never hear the end of it if I declined.

"Hey, Uncle Kris. How are things going?" I asked, as his face came into view.

He lifted one silvery-white eyebrow at my question. "Oh, I'm dandy. Especially after I heard my only niece was involved in a shooting last night." He was walking through his workshop, which bustled with activity as everyone got ready for the impending holiday. "What happened, Tink? Are you okay?"

The concern in his voice, so genuine and sincere, made tears well up in my eyes. "I'm fine. I was in the wrong place at the wrong time. You know how it is."

He let out a sigh. I'd heard that sigh before. It was the sigh of disappointment. "We're going to need to talk about this. There will be repercussions—" The sound of an alarm going off in the workshop cut him off. "Fiddlesticks. The stocking stuffer got jammed again. Look, Tink, I have to go, but we need to talk face to face, and soon. Okay?"

He stared at me through the phone, his blue eyes latching onto mine with laser-like focus. "Fine. Yes. Of course. Love you, Uncle Kris."

"You, too," he said, but I could tell his mind was already back on the stocking stuffer machine—as it should be. Uncle

Kris had a lot to worry about right now. I didn't want to add to his problems.

My phone buzzed. It was Jax the Jailor. "I'm on my way back to pick you up. I've hit another dead end. We need to confront Cookie Wassail and find out what he knows. Can you be dressed and ready in five minutes or so?"

I glanced at my flannel jammies with frolicking space kittens on them. "Sure. I'll be ready," I said as I bounded up the steps and headed to my room.

"And Tink," he said. "Make sure you grab something to eat. This might take a while.

I dressed in Grandma Gingersnap's clothing again, an icy blue blouse that matched my eyes and a soft gray pantsuit. My grandmother seemed to collect clothing the way I collected bras, but it worked in my favor. Her style was elegant and sophisticated. I was neither of those, but when I put on her things, I could at least pretend to have some of her polish and flair. It would come in handy when dealing with an elf like Cookie.

Jax had acquired an unmarked police sled for our transport, which was much more convenient than using Uber-sleds all the time. I slid into the front seat.

"Wow. I've never sat in the front seat of a police sled before."

He snorted, pulling out of Grandma Gingersnap's driveway. "How many times have you ridden in the back?"

"Hold on," I said, lifting one finger. I tried to count in my head, but it took a while.

Jax shot me a nervous look. "Are you still counting? Seriously?"

"Yes, I am," I said as I came up with a total. "Twelve times."

He nearly rear-ended the sled in front of us. "How is that possible?"

"Well, the first time was when I was seven. After the accident."

His expression softened. "The one that killed your parents? You were there?"

"Yes." Images of twisted metal flashed in my head, along with the sound of screaming. For years I thought it was my mother's voice I'd heard, but when I learned both she and my father died on impact, I understood the screams were likely my own. "The policeman on the scene drove me to the hospital. Topper was with them."

"You didn't require an ambulance?" he asked, his voice soft.

I shook my head. "Nope. I didn't have a scratch on me. It was a Christmas Eve miracle," I said with a bitter laugh. "Although I didn't see it as miraculous at the time. I blamed myself for years. They were in that sleigh because of me. I'd...I'd snuck out to see my dad at work. It was late, and they were tired, but they had to haul me home. They argued about something on the way back, and I blamed myself for that, too. They never argued." I swallowed hard, glancing out the window. I hated talking about the night my parents died. I hated even thinking about it. "Anyway, I lost both of my parents that night. And it was my first time as the passenger in a police sled."

He gave a slow nod as he digested this information. "I'm sorry for your loss, Tink. What about the other eleven?"

I shot him a smile; grateful he didn't dwell on the first part. "Five were attempts to run away at various times in my childhood. The farthest I ever got was a reindeer camp up north. That one also involved Topper. He found me there and brought me home."

"He did?"

"Yes." Memories of our adventures there still made me smile. "We rode a reindeer back. A flying reindeer. It was amazing. Unfortunately, the police were waiting for me when we arrived at the stables. Police sled ride number six. The other five were normal stuff. Public intoxication, public nudity—a total accident," I clarified. "Assault. That was Tinsel McFly. I regret nothing. And the night of the Liquid Ass bomb, which was the last one. I learned my lesson." I lifted a finger. "Oh. And the time Officer Pudding drove us home, but I don't count that one since I wasn't actually in any trouble."

Not for the first time in my presence, Jax seemed incapable of speech.

"Oh, look," I said, pointing at the brightly lit building coming up on our right. "It's a Fast and Friendly Restaurant. Can you pull into the drive-through? I'm starving."

"I told you to eat," he said but put on his turn signal and pulled into the parking lot.

"You barely gave me time to dress. Also, Fast and Friendly breakfast sandwiches are my favorite."

I ordered two sausage biscuits, two fried potato patties, and a large coffee with six sugars and extra cream. "What do you want?" I asked Jax. Rolling his eyes, he ordered a plain black coffee. I refused to allow such an oversight, so I ordered one more sausage biscuit for him. I think he was secretly grateful. Breakfast from Fast and Friendly always hit the spot.

With my belly full of sausage, biscuits, and deep-fried potato patties, I was armed and ready when we arrived at North Pole company headquarters and went to Cookie's office. What I didn't expect was to find his secretary, Mince Mingle, sobbing at her desk.

"Poor, poor Cookie. He didn't deserve this," she said. People I recognized from other offices on this floor surrounded her, but I didn't know any of their names. When she saw us, she stiffened. "What are you doing here?"

I shot Jax a confused look. "We're here to see Cookie."

There was a moment of stunned silence. "Well, you can't," she said, blowing her nose loudly into a tissue.

She wore her usual prim skirt and a blouse buttoned to her neck, her dark hair neatly pulled into a bun. Mince had squinty eyes and a prominent nose, one she liked to look down on me from whenever possible. She was doing it right now. I had no idea what made her hate me so much, but I also didn't have time to deal with it at the moment.

"Why can't we see him?" I asked

"Because he's disappeared," she said, letting out a wail. "No one knows where he went, and his office is a mess. The police suspect foul play. And when they asked me if anyone might have it in for Mr. Wassail, you were first on my list, Tinklebelle Holly. You made that poor man's life a living nightmare."

She sobbed so hard she almost hyperventilated. One of the administrative assistants from down the hall gave me a dirty look as she patted Mince's back. "Please, Mincie. Calm yourself. You can't help Mr. Wassail in this state, now can you? Breathe with me. In through the nose, out through the mouth."

I inhaled and exhaled along with her. I couldn't help it. And after six or so deep breaths, I felt much calmer, too. Mince went to wash her face in the ladies' room. Her friends returned to their respective offices. When Mince came back, she seemed to be back in control but even more irritated we were still there. I tried a different approach. Buttering her up.

"Can you tell us what happened? We want to help."

"Ha. What a joke. You know what you've done to poor Cookie. Leave me alone. I don't have to tell you anything."

"I apologize for your distress, and for pursuing this at what is plainly a difficult time, but I'm afraid you do," said Jax, flashing his badge.

She blinked in surprise, her dark eyes owlish behind black-framed glasses. "You work for Elf Enforcement?"

He put back his badge. "I do, and I need you to answer a few questions." He took out his notebook. "I will contact the officer in charge, but in the interest of saving time, can you tell me why the police suspect foul play?"

"Why?" she asked, incredulous. "Well, I'll show you why."

She flung open the door to Cookie's office. It looked like it had been ransacked. Files covered the floor, a cabinet rested on its side, and several pictures on the wall were either askew, or the glass had been shattered.

"Jiminy Christmas," I said, keeping my voice soft as I stared around at the carnage.

"Truer words were never spoken," said Jax, taking two pairs of rubber gloves out of his briefcase. He handed me a pair and surveyed the floor littered in files. Total chaos.

"And what are we looking for exactly?" I asked.

"Anything," he said.

M ince Mingle had left as soon as we began opening files. She grabbed the photo of Cookie she kept on her desk, along with her spider plant, and hustled out of the office like someone had shouted "fire." That didn't strike me as odd. It was pretty evident at this point Cookie was hiding something big, and his number one fan, Mince, likely knew all about it.

Jax was at Cookie's desk, rifling through stacks and stacks of unrelated documents. There were insurance papers for nearly every person working at the North Pole, as well as other benefit info and job histories. None of it seemed connected to the candicocane, or Joy, or to a coverup of any kind.

"Whoever did this was looking for something particular," said Jax, slamming a ledger closed in frustration. "They must have found it and taken off. That's the only plausible explanation. I don't know what else we can do."

I sat on the rug in front of Cookie's desk, surrounded by piles of documents I was trying to separate and put into some sort of logical order. Needing sugar to think, I took a snack break and pulled out a bag of malted milk balls. They weren't my favorite, but they'd been on sale at our local grocery store, so I'd gone for it. When I opened the bag, malted milk balls flew all over the floor.

"Come to mama, baby," I said, crawling around on my knees to chase the small chocolate balls and plop them into my mouth. One had rolled under Cookie's desk, but I wasn't about to let it go to waste. I crawled under, grabbed the malted milk ball, and bumped my head on the underside of the desk on the way out. To my astonishment, the bottom of the desk opened, smacking me in the face.

"Ow," I said, covering my nose with my hand. It didn't

seem broken or bleeding, which was a plus, but I saw stars for a moment. When they cleared, I saw something else entirely. "Oh, holy night."

"Are you okay?" asked Jax, leaning over to peer under the desk.

"Yes, but you are not going to believe this." Inside the secret compartment was a thick file with my name on it. I grabbed it and crawled under the desk toward Jax, popping up between his legs.

He took my face in his hands, eyes worried. "What happened? Your nose is red. We'd better get some ice on it, or you're going to end up with a black eye."

I waved away his words. "It's fine. That's why I own concealer."

He frowned. "How often have you had black eyes, Tink?"

"Unimportant. Jax. Pay attention." Still on my knees next to him, I held the file in front of his face. When he took it from me, the room spun, so I placed my hands on his thighs for balance. I must have gotten smacked harder than I realized.

"How did you find this?"

I picked up one of the rogue malted milk balls and showed it to him before popping it into my mouth. "My snack escaped. As I was chasing it, I bumped my head and accidentally found a hidden compartment under Cookie's desk. Is there anything useful in the file?"

"Yes, there is," he said. "And it makes total sense you were chasing candy. Was there anything else in there?"

I glanced back at the open compartment under the desk. It looked empty. "Nope." When I turned back to face Jax, the room swirled around me like I'd drunk too much and had the spins. "Whoa."

Still gripping his thighs, I lowered my head and closed my eyes. He put down the file and gently placed his hands in my hair. My face was in an unusual position, resting between his thighs, but I couldn't help it. I was going to be sick.

"Sorry," I said. "I'm woozy. The drawer smacked me right in the face."

"Take a minute to steady yourself," he said. "I'll get you some water."

"No. Don't move. Give me a second." I let out a moan. Maybe I had broken my nose after all.

"Good girl," Jax said, his hands twined in my hair. "That's perfect. You're doing great."

"What the holy holly heck is going on here?" asked a shocked voice coming from the doorway. I popped my head up to see Win standing there, a furious expression on his face.

"Jiminy Christmas," I said, woozy once again.

Jax, his hands still wrapped in my hair, concurred with my opinion. "My thoughts exactly."

CHAPTER FIFTEEN

W in's shock at finding me with my head in Jax's lap quickly morphed to anger when he caught a glimpse of my bruised and battered face. He exploded, coming toward Jax like a raging bull. I let out a squeak and got to my feet, using Jax's body for leverage to lift myself. In better circumstances, I would have enjoyed having my hands all over him, but not like this. Not when Win was about to kill him.

"What did you do to her?" Win asked, blue eyes blazing. "Did you *hit* her?"

Jax opened his mouth to speak, but I put a hand on his chest to stop him. "Jax did not hit me," I said. "Don't be ridiculous, Win. I banged my head crawling under Cookie's desk. A hidden compartment opened and smacked me in the face." I pointed to the spot under the desk. "Check it if you want to. It's still open."

Casually, Jax stood up, acting as if he didn't have a care in the world, and made way for my ex to lean over and peek under the desk. Win's blond brows drew together in a frown. He still wasn't convinced.

"What were you doing under Cookie's desk?"

"Chasing a malted milk ball."

At my words, Win relaxed visibly. He may not have been fully convinced Jax hadn't taken advantage of me, but he'd know me too long to doubt the lure of chocolate covered anything.

When I swayed on my feet, Jax took me by the shoulders and gently pushed me into Cookie's chair. He lifted my chin to study my face.

"She needs an icepack."

Win looked at me and sighed. "There's a machine nearby. I'll be right back."

When he left, I looked up at Jax. "Be honest. How bad is it?"

"Your face, the file, or the fact Win wants to kill me?"

I laughed, but it hurt. "Ow. My face."

"Do you bruise easily?" he asked.

"Not really."

"Then it's pretty bad. No wonder Win thought I punched you in the nose."

I closed my eyes. "Great."

To my surprise, Jax gave me a soft kiss on my forehead, his hands cupping my face. "You'll be fine. The ice will help."

Win came through the door carrying an ice pack and pushed Jax out of the way to place it carefully over my nose. "Put your head back and rest a moment," he said. "Do you need to go to the hospital?"

"No, but I'd like a Chrismartini."

Win laughed, a soft chuckle, a sound so familiar it made my heart ache. "I bet we could arrange that." He grabbed my hand and squeezed it. "Are you going to tell me what's happening? One of the secretaries said she saw you come in here earlier. She heard from Mince Mingle it had something to do with Cookie, and his disappearance. I don't see how these things could be connected, but with you, anything is possible, so please tell me the truth this time. I know when you're lying."

I peeked at him from behind the ice pack. He was right. He did know when I was lying. I shot Jax a questioning look, and he frowned, folding his arms over his chest, and studying Win with a critical eye.

"Do you trust him?"

"Yes. Win is one of the good guys," I said, hoping I had it right. "You are still one of the good guys, aren't you?"

"You know I am," said Win, a perplexed scowl on his face. "What is going on here?"

I readjusted the ice pack. I'd grown comfortably numb in the sorest spots, which came as a welcome relief. "It's a long story. It's going to take a while."

"And I'd rather not talk about it here," said Jax. "If you're certain you do not require medical attention, shall we move this party back to your grandmother's house?"

"Will there be a Chrismartini involved?"

"Yes," they both said at once.

I slowly got to my feet, the ice pack still pressed against my nose. "Let's go."

Win and Jax argued as we left Cookie's office. "Tink will be riding with me," said Win, taking my elbow as if it had already been decided.

"Absolutely not. She's going with me." Jax took my other arm. "We came here together, and we're leaving together. It only makes sense since I'm staying at her place."

It seemed like Jax had thrown the last, frankly irrelevant, part in to annoy Win. I narrowed my eyes at him, and turned to speak to my ex. "Both of you need to quit it. I'll go with Jax." When Win opened his mouth to protest, I held up a hand to stop him. "I'm not playing favorites. Jax and I have to talk. Don't take it personally, for Santa's sake."

"Fine." Win spoke in a clipped tone. I saw the sorrow in his eyes, but there were things Jax and I needed to discuss in private. He must have felt the same way. He held the door of the sled open for me and even helped me with my seatbelt. He was adorable and attentive, especially while Win was watching, but he started in on me as soon as he slipped into the driver's seat.

"What were you thinking? The last thing we need is for someone like Winter Snow III to be involved." He said Winter's name with a sneer, and I shot him a curious glance. Was Jax jealous? The idea made me oddly happy, but I didn't have time for it right now.

Ignoring the undertones, I focused on setting him straight. "Wrong. This is the best thing that could have happened. We aren't getting anywhere on our own. Win has a lot of contacts, and everyone likes and respects him. He might be just the right person to help us."

Jax remained unconvinced. "How do you know he isn't involved?"

I snorted. "You don't know him. He's as clean as the driven...well, you get the picture."

Remembering the conversation I'd overheard involving his parents, I frowned. Win might be clean, but I couldn't say the same for the rest of his family.

"And yet, you don't seem convinced. You have that worried look again. The one that makes your eyes get all squinty."

193

ABIGAIL DRAKE

I tried to make my eyes appear less squinty. It was harder than it sounded. "I have a worried look?"

"You do. What's wrong?" he asked as we pulled up in front of Grandma Gingersnap's house.

"Nothing. Follow my lead. If anything feels weird regarding Win, I'll tell you, okay?"

Win had already arrived, driving a luxury sleigh. It was red and sleek and shiny, and Win leaned against it as he waited in front of the house. Jax glared at him, but his furious whisper was directed at me.

"How exactly do you plan on telling me whether or not something is weird if Win is sitting right there?"

"I'll do this." I showed him an exaggerated wink, which I'm sure looked ridiculous with my swollen face. "Sound good?"

"No, but—"

I cut off his words by stepping out of the car. I knew getting Win involved was the right thing to do. I couldn't explain it to Jax, but a lifetime of shared experiences made me confident.

In all the chaos, swirling around my mistakes and poor decisions and failures, Win had been my constant. My North Star. Although we hadn't been romantically involved in a long time, I still had feelings for him. And I trusted him completely.

As we walked into Grandma Gingersnap's house, Win and Jax kept shooting each other dirty looks. I could almost smell the testosterone seeping from their pores.

"Will the two of you stop glaring at each other, please? I'm going upstairs to change. I expect both of you to be alive —" Jax got a dangerous twinkle in his eye. I pointed a finger at him, "—and *unhurt* when I get back. Are we clear?"

They both nodded grudgingly, so I stomped upstairs to

my room. As soon as I saw my reflection in the bathroom mirror, I got a shock. My nose was indeed red and swollen, and faint purple marks blossomed under my eyes. Great. I would have not one, but two, black eyes tomorrow. That would teach me to chase a malted milk ball under some-one's desk.

After washing my face as gently as I could and pulling my hair up into a ponytail, I stripped out of my clothing and put on the softest pajamas I could find. The pants had colorful images of cupcakes on them, and the long-sleeved T-shirt read, "Stressed is Desserts Spelled Backward." My mantra.

When I got downstairs, Win and Jax were still glaring at each other, but they each had a drink in their hands, and the tension between them had lowered a notch. Well, until I asked if one of them would make me a drink, too. That turned into another spitting contest, so I finally told them to cease and desist.

"Stop acting like kindergarteners. Jax got to drive me home, so Win can make my drink."

"What would you like? A Chrismartini?" he asked through clenched teeth. He still stared at Jax with murder in his eyes.

"Actually, I'm in the mood for a caramel appletini. Do you mind? There is apple cider in the fridge and caramel vodka where Grandma Gingersnap keeps her—"

Win held up a hand. "I know where your grandmother keeps her liquor, Tink. Have you forgotten how many times we got into it growing up?"

I smiled at him fondly. "*I* got into it, Win. You were always the one trying to make me behave."

"Some things never change."

After he went into the kitchen to mix my drink, Jax

checked out my face, wincing at the damage. "It's even worse than I thought."

"I'll be fine. I hope the file was worth it."

When Win came back with my drink, we went into the family room to talk. Win made a fire in the hearth, and I curled up in the chair closest to the fire. Jax sat in the seat next to me. Win sat directly across, and between us was a coffee table. Win and I had played about a million board games at this table and even played strip poker once when we were older, while Grandma Gingersnap was at her monthly Daughters of the First Five meeting. As an Ivy who married a Holly, my grandmother took her genealogy seriously. I took my strip poker seriously. Win and I got to third base that night.

Win swirled his drink in his glass as he stared at the contents. He'd loosened his tie, and his hair looked like he'd been running his hands through it. It was odd, but as long as I'd known Win, I'd never fully gotten used to how beautiful he was. In terms of sheer gorgeousness, I'd never in a million years thought any other elf could come close, but Jax truly was Win-level pretty. He'd taken off his suit jacket and tie and rolled up the sleeves of his shirt. His dark, silky hair hung loose and brushed against his shoulders. I was sitting in a room with two of the best-looking elves I'd ever seen but comparing them was pointless. It was like comparing apples to oranges.

If fruit were super sexy. Which it wasn't.

Maybe the drawer had hit my head harder than I realized.

"Now would be the time to tell me what's going on," said Win, taking a sip of his drink.

Win listened as Jax explained, and I was impressed both because Jax was thorough, and because he didn't hide anything. He explained he was an Elf Enforcement agent investigating drug-related issues on the North Pole and finished his tale with our trip to Cookie's office. Win leaned forward as he listened, his elbows on his knees.

"What was in the file?" he asked.

"That's what we're about to find out." Jax put the file on the table in front of us. Close to two inches thick, Cookie had written my name on it in his impeccable handwriting. I had no idea what might be inside but imagined it wasn't good. I also didn't know why Cookie would keep my personnel file locked in a secret compartment under his desk. It made no sense at all.

Jax opened the file, and Win tilted his head to read. "Your aptitude tests from high school?" he asked with a frown. "Hardly sensitive documents, but they don't usually keep this kind of stuff, and not as a hard copy."

I picked up the results of my aptitude tests. I'd never seen them before and was amazed to find I scored off the charts in every subject, even math. "I suck at math. That can't be right."

Win rolled his eyes. "You don't suck at math. You never sucked at math. You lacked confidence."

Jax sifted through my college transcripts, before he got to the paperwork regarding my first job, a coveted position working directly under the CEO of marketing for the entire corporation. I'd loved that job, and things were going so well up until the moment I got called into Cookie's office, and he told me Mr. Lumpkins had fired me.

I bit my lip as I studied the report from my old boss, Sprinkle Lumpkins. He'd been a nice old guy, and he seemed to like me, but he didn't have a single good thing to say about me in this report.

I swallowed hard, picking up the next page inside the

file, and froze. This was also an evaluation from Sprinkle, but the answers were different. They were glowing.

Ms. Holly is a hard worker with a brilliant mind for marketing and great potential in the company. I have to say I'm disappointed she's being reassigned already, but I wish her the best.

Setting the pages side by side on the table, I studied them. Both looked official, but which one was true?

"Reassigned? I thought you got fired," said Win.

"So did I."

Jax lifted both to the light. "This is the real one," he said, pointing to the page full of kind words from my ex-boss.

"How can you tell?" I asked.

"It's the signatures, isn't it?" Win studied them, too. "One is signed with a pen. The other is stamped."

Jax nodded in agreement. "And you know what that means, right?" When we both shook our heads, he continued. "No one fired you from your job, Tink, but someone wanted you to think that was the case."

I glanced up at him, confused. "Why?"

Win looked confused, too. "You never confronted Sprinkle Lumpkins about your performance review?"

I shook my head. "I was too ashamed. Cookie inferred I'd only gotten the job because of family connections. I felt like a total failure. An imposter. And afterward, I refused to use my connections or my uncle's name. I wanted to earn success on my own. But I never did."

"You should have," said Win, his face tight with anger on my behalf.

"I have to agree with Win," said Jax, leafing through page after page in the file. "Someone did this to you on purpose. And that isn't all." He pulled out the results of several drug tests, all of them saying I'd been high or intoxicated at work.

I stared at him in shock. "It never happened."

"I believe you, but someone has been working hard to set you up, and they are playing a long game."

"But who?" asked Win. "Because not just anyone can go into a file and falsify reports. It has to be someone way up on the corporate ladder."

"How far up?" asked Jax.

Win's eyes met mine. "At the top...or close to it."

We spent the next hour looking through the file, and with each page, my heart sank lower and lower. I caused many problems on my own, but some of the things were clearly not my fault. Why had Cookie so painstakingly assembled all of this? It seemed highly irregular. And the fact he saved the glowing reports, as well as the negative ones, made me even more suspicious. When I found a sweet note inside from Nippy praising my efforts, even though he said I had no aptitude for collections, I got teary.

Poor Nippy.

Something niggled in my brain, something Nippy had said about incorrect weights and missing documents. Could that have been what he wanted to talk with us about? Was that what had gotten him shot? We might never know. Nippy might never wake up. It made me want to weep.

As if sensing my distress, Win absentmindedly patted my hand. "None of this makes sense, but we're going to get to the bottom of it."

"This goes much deeper than I expected," said Jax, getting to his feet. "Excuse me a moment. I have to make a phone call."

As soon as Jax left the room, Win caught my gaze. "He's

right. This is serious, Tink. We need to talk to your uncle Kris. We have to tell him what's going on."

I shook my head. "No." When Win opened his mouth to protest, I stopped him. "Trust me."

Jax got off the phone. "I've called in a security team from Elf Central. They should arrive in a few hours. Until we figure out exactly who is involved, I don't want to take any chances with Nippy, Noelle, or with you," he said, giving me a nod, his face tense. Seeing Jax worried made me worried. It seemed to bother Win, too.

"You don't trust the North Pole police?" asked Win.

"Pudding and Bing seem like good cops, but at this point, I don't trust anyone," said Jax.

"Neither do I." I shot Win a pleading look. "Which is why I can't go to my uncle with this."

Win sat back in his chair, shocked. "You honestly think your Uncle Kris could be involved?"

"No. I don't want to put him in danger. I don't know how high up this goes," I said, my eyes meeting Win's and Jax's. "But I intend to find out."

CHAPTER SIXTEEN

I t took some convincing to get Win to leave. If it weren't for the repeated calls from Candy, he probably would have insisted on camping out in Grandma Gingersnap's living room. But apparently, they had plans. To be honest, I needed some Win-free time myself. I had a lot to process. After he left, I grabbed a bottle of red wine and a blanket and went outside to sit next to the fire pit. Jax stayed inside to do some paperwork. By the time he joined me outside, the fire crackled merrily, and the bottle was almost empty.

"Are you okay?" he asked.

"No, I'm not." I stared into the flames, comfortably numb from the combination of wine, getting smacked in the face, and a shocked sort of grief. I'd spent the last five years convinced I was a failure. Useless. A person who messed up every single good thing that came her way, but in truth, someone had tried to destroy my life, and I'd nearly let them. "Why would someone do this? It's so purposeful. So mean."

He sat next to me. When I offered him the remainder of

the bottle of wine, he demurred. With a shrug, I poured the rest into my glass and took another long sip. Without commenting on how much I'd had to drink, Jax took the now-empty bottle and set it aside.

"The child of a wealthy and powerful family can be a target for many reasons. Sometimes it's jealousy. Sometimes it's a way to manipulate someone else. Sometimes it's out of spite, over some real or imagined sin committed against them."

He sounded like he knew from personal experience, but I was too drunk to try to figure out what it meant exactly. Instead, I focused on what he was trying to tell me. "This is because of my family? Because I'm a Holly?"

"And because of your uncle. A powerful man has powerful enemies."

I let out a laugh. "Enemies? My uncle has no enemies. He's the most beloved Santa of all time. His popularity rating is through the roof." I pointed in the general direction of my grandmother's roof.

"Even more of a reason for someone to want to destroy him. To get to him through you." Jax didn't have a jacket on, so I shared my blanket, wrapping it around his shoulders and snuggling closer to him, pressing my cheek against his arm. He laced his fingers with mine, a comforting gesture. "Let's look at this one piece at a time, Tink. What exactly do we know?"

"We know someone killed Joy. We know someone drugged Noelle. We know the person who drugged her was targeting me. And we know someone shot Nippy." I ticked off my fingers one by one. "Oh, and we know someone was setting me up. Why did Cookie hide the file?"

"I suspect he planned to use it as backup, in case he ever needed proof. A negotiating tool."

"Or a blackmailing tool. Whoever was behind this doesn't want it to get out."

He rubbed his jaw as he considered my words. "Most of Cookie's personnel files were online. He didn't keep hard copies in his office."

"No, they went online a few years ago. Right before I started working there. I remember because Cookie pitched a fit about it. He doesn't like change." I frowned, remembering the many heated exchanges I'd had with him in the past. "He's also a misogynist. And a bully. And a jerk. But everyone kisses his bum because he has a lot of power."

"I assumed it might be Cookie at first, but that doesn't feel right. Whoever is behind this has a lot more power than Cookie Wassail. Or they have something on him—a secret he doesn't want anyone to know."

"It could be. Cookie seems like the type."

"This is all connected, but I can't figure it out."

"Me, either." I let out a yawn. "You get a tip from Joy, and she ends up dead. We investigate Joy's death, and—kaboom—Noelle nearly dies because someone wants to kill me. Nippy wants to tell us something, and he gets shot. And right after Nippy gets shot, Cookie disappears. Yeah, I'd say it's connected."

He gazed down at me, his expression grave. "And I seem to be the common denominator in this equation. I'm sorry, Tink."

"Uh, not where I was going with my line of reasoning, so please don't apologize. If anything, I'm the common denominator. My point is things have escalated quickly, and another connection is still unclear."

"What connection?"

My eyelids were heavy, but I forced them to stay open. "Evergreen Berry. Joy's brother. We know he also died of an

203

overdose, but how does his death connect with Joy leaving the job she loved to go and shovel reindeer poo? It makes no sense."

"But you're right. That's where the puzzle begins."

I woke up the following day with a pounding head and a heavy heart. Someone had been using me for years, controlling me for years, and I'd been blind to it.

I glanced at the clock on my nightstand. It was still early, but I knew I couldn't go back to sleep. Jax had kindly left some painkillers and a large glass of water at my bedside table. I took them and flopped back onto my bed with a groan. The wine may not have been the best idea, but I'd needed it at the time.

Forcing myself out of bed, I hopped into the shower, feeling more awake as the hot water pelted my skin. My mind swirled with all the possible scenarios of who might be involved and why, but it was so frustrating. I still had no clear answers, but I thought about Joy Berry and the words Jax said last night.

That's where the puzzle begins.

"Puzzle. It's a puzzle." Jumping out of the shower, I wrapped one fluffy, white towel around my body and dried my hair with another as I ran out to my room. Digging through my bag, I found the envelope Mrs. Berry had given me with the recipe inside. Joy had made certain letters red and others green for a reason.

I spread the page out on my desk, grabbed a pen and some scratch paper, and set to work. In minutes, I had my answer. The red and green letters spelled out *Look in the reindeer feed.*

"Jiminy Christmas."

I shot out of my room and went in search of Jax. I found him in the kitchen sipping coffee and making breakfast. He'd cooked bacon, and it smelled amazing. He may have been the perfect man.

"Tink? What's wrong? Why aren't you dressed?"

Glancing at my body, I became conscious of the fact I only had a towel on, but this was too important to wait. "Never mind. Look what I figured out."

I held up the recipe and showed him what the words spelled out. His face brightened. "Look in the reindeer feed? Oh, Tink. You clever, clever elf."

He lifted me and spun me around. I squealed and wrapped my arms around his neck. But somewhere in the middle of the spinning and squealing, I ended up kissing him. And the next thing I knew, Jax was kissing me back.

He pushed me against the wall, threading his fingers through my damp hair with a groan. "Tink. What are you doing to me?"

I didn't answer. I was too busy kissing him, my legs wrapped around his waist.

Somehow the towel covering my body disappeared, although I was uncertain whether he'd ripped it off or if I'd let it drop. Either way, I was naked. And I wanted him. Badly.

"Jax," I said, the sound coming out as a pant as he kissed his way down my neck, one hand squeezing my bottom as the other found my breast.

I was currently in a state of intense and powerful need, which may have been why I didn't hear the front door open. Nor did I hear Win walk into the kitchen. He cleared his throat, and I opened my eyes to see him standing right behind Jax.

I let out a yelp. "Win. Fudgity fudge cakes. What are you doing here?"

Jax muttered a curse, lowered me to the ground, and handed me the towel. He turned, blocking my body with his and giving me time to cover myself.

Win stared at us. "I can't believe this is happening. Are you sleeping together?"

"No, we aren't sleeping together," I said, shifting Jax gently aside so I could face Win directly. Also, I thought I could provide a nice buffer if Win once again decided to kill him. I shot Jax a look over my shoulder and almost laughed at his stormy expression. "Well, not yet, at least."

Apparently, Jax was not a guy who liked to be inter-rupted. I was the same way. I leaned against him, and he put his hands on my bare shoulders, his touch warm and comforting on my skin.

"Why are you here, Win? And how did you get in?" I scowled at him. "Did you use the key at your parents' house? If so, it's a totally inappropriate use of an emergency key."

The Snows kept a spare key at their house in case Grandma Gingersnap ever needed it, and we did the same. Win and I had used those keys for years to sneak into each other's house for late night booty calls. Those were the days before both houses had alarms. The only alarm back then was Duke, which was why Win normally came here.

He seemed affronted. "The front door was unlocked."

"No way. I locked it before I went to bed."

Jax lifted a finger. "Uh, I stepped outside to grab the paper and check on the officers out front. I may not have locked it when I came back."

"Oh," I said, still mad. I turned back to Win. "And you let yourself in?"

His face reddened. "I knocked, but you must not have heard me, since you were otherwise..." He didn't finish his sentence, but I saw the raw pain in his eyes. "Anyway, the officers told me to go inside."

I had trouble letting go of my anger, because it was mixed so thoroughly with guilt and embarrassment. "What was so urgent?"

"I have information," said Win, sounding as snippy as I did. "Can we talk?"

Pulling the towel tighter around my body, I glanced at Jax. He nodded, albeit grudgingly. "Fine," I said. "But let me get dressed first."

After running to my room as quickly as possible and putting on sweats and a T-shirt, I headed back downstairs. Win and Jax sat at the kitchen table, drinking coffee and refusing to look at each other. I rolled my eyes, grabbed a cup, and joined them.

"So, Win, what did you have to tell us?"

He took a sip of coffee. "As you know, I oversee logistics, which includes shipping. When I checked my email this morning, I found something." He held up his phone. "An email from Nippy Nibblewrap. He'd sent it to me Wednesday morning."

"And he got shot Wednesday night," I said, covering my mouth with one hand. "What did it say?"

"He wanted to let me know he'd noticed some discrepancies in shipping documents. He asked if he could discuss them with me."

Jax perked up. "He mentioned the same thing when we spoke with him in collections."

"He was onto something." Win handed me his phone. "According to the documents Nippy sent me, several large shipments of toys went out, but Nippy noticed right away something was off. The weights were too heavy for that type of toy. He's a details guy and has a memory for numbers like no one I've ever met. I'm not sure anyone else would have even caught something like this."

I drank more coffee, trying to wake up my poor, hungover brain. "And he went to collections to see who paid for the shipment, right?" I asked, giving the phone to Jax. He read the attachment before handing it back to Win.

"Exactly," said Win. "But collections has no record of it at all. He found shipment after shipment, always the same toy, always over the normal weight, and none had been paid for or received. Anywhere."

I locked eyes with Jax as I asked Win, "And this toy you mentioned, by any chance, was it Mr. Potato Head?"

With a frown, Win scrolled through the email. "Let me see..." He glanced up at me in surprise. "Yes, it was. How did you know?"

"I found part of a Mr. Potato Head toy the night someone shot Nippy. It was only a few feet away from him, in the middle of a warehouse."

Resting my face in my hands, I tried to put the pieces together, but we were still missing significant parts—like a Mr. Potato Head minus the potato. We had all the arms and legs and googly eyes but nothing on which to build them.

Win pulled down my hands. "What kind of warehouse?"

I told him the address and described all the barrels with the words *Biohazardous and Medical Waste* painted on them in white letters. "The barrels were huge, and I found the Mr. Potato Head arm right next to them."

Win scratched the golden stubble on his jaw. "It makes no sense. We don't store any hazardous waste so close to town. We store it outside city limits and dispose of it at the outlier communities."

"What are the outlier communities?" asked Jax.

"There are Christmas elves who choose, for one reason or another, not to live within the confines of the biodome," said Win. "They call us 'domers' and we call them 'outliers.' They are the reindeer ranchers—the elves who gather and train wild reindeer, or those who simply want more space and freedom."

It was a nice way to paint the picture. I wondered if Win believed it. Judging by the sincerity in his blue eyes, I figured he did.

"That's not all there is to it," I said. "The jail is out there too, as well as the coal mines. And elves born in outlying communities face a lot of judgment from domers. Sometimes they're even compared to South Polers. They have their own customs, food, and even their language is..."

I frowned, remembering something. I didn't know why it hadn't occurred to me before.

"What is it, Tink?" asked Jax, his hand on my forearm. Win shot him a death glare, but he had zero right to be jealous of Jax. And he had no right to make me feel guilty either. I had more important things to focus on right now.

"The elf who shot Nippy. Did I tell you he also shot a rat?"

"You didn't," said Jax. "But we found the remains."

I wrinkled my nose, remembering how the poor rat had practically exploded from the impact of the bullet. "After he shot Nippy, I dropped my cell phone. The shooter heard it. He looked for me, but thankfully the rat showed up and saved my life." I snorted. "A rat saved a RAT. Reindeer Assistance Team. Get it?"

"I get it, but what does it have to do with the elf who

shot Nippy?" From the way he clenched his jaw, I could tell Jax struggled to stay patient. Not an easy task.

"It was what he said. 'Fecking rat.' It's an outlier word."

There was a moment of silence as they absorbed that information. "It figures," said Win.

"What do you mean?" asked Jax.

"Whenever there is a problem, it's usually an outlier behind it. Sad, but true."

I gaped at him. "Seriously, Win? Outliers face enough prejudice without you adding to it."

Had Win always held those views? I had no idea. It bothered me that a person I'd known my whole life could feel like a stranger to me at times, while Jax, who I'd known a total of five days, did not.

Five days. Holy cow. And I'd almost had sex with him in my grandmother's kitchen.

"Oh, fracken frackleberries," I said. "My grandmother is coming back a week from Monday."

"Have you told her what's going on?" asked Win.

I gave him an incredulous look. "No way. And don't you dare tell your mom about it either. You know she'll go straight to Grandma Gingersnap. Well, if Uncle Kris hasn't already. But your mom will tell her, so keep a lid on it, okay?"

"No problem, since I'm currently not speaking to my parents anyway."

His words unsettled me. "Wait. What? Why aren't you speaking to them?"

"Long story." He turned to Jax. "What do we do now?"

Jax considered it. "Tink and I need to go to the reindeer department. Maybe you could look into the warehouse situation for us. I'm sure it ties into all of this, but I haven't figured out how yet."

"Will do. I have a meeting in an hour, but I'll check it out when I finish."

"Be careful," warned Jax grudgingly. "We don't know what we're dealing with yet, but we know they're violent. And they're desperate. It's not a good combination, so don't play the hero."

Jax left the room to take a phone call. The security team he'd requested from Elf Central had arrived, and they were checking in. I gave Win a hard look, hoping he would listen to Jax's advice. My ex annoyed me at times, but I couldn't handle the thought of him getting hurt.

"Take his warning seriously, Win."

"I'll be fine," he said, rising to his feet. "Don't worry."

I grabbed his arm. "I'm not kidding. If anything happened to you, I'd never forgive myself."

He brushed his knuckles across my cheek. "I didn't realize you still cared."

"Of course I care, stupid."

"Good to know."

"And, well, since you mentioned your parents, there is something I need to tell you."

I conveyed as best as I could what I'd overheard while lurking right outside their door with pockets full of beef jerky and chewy chocolate. Win reassured me the dog was fine. As much as I hated Duke, I was relieved I hadn't killed him.

"Any idea what your parents were discussing?" I asked, almost afraid to hear the answer.

"I'm not sure," said Win, with a sigh. "But I'm already angry with them."

"Why?"

He ran a hand through his hair. "I got a call yesterday,

right before I encountered you and Jax in Cookie's office. It was Snooky Snookums from the *North Pole Gazette*."

"The one who does the society pages?"

"Yes. Apparently, my mother told her Candy and I were getting engaged."

I wasn't sure what I'd expected, but that wasn't it. "Oh," I said, oddly pained by the announcement. "Congratulations...?"

He shook his head, his gaze glued to my face. "It isn't true. Fortunately, I was able to correct it before the story got out, but Candy was somewhat dismayed by my reaction."

I toyed with the hem of my shirt. "What was your reaction?"

"I was furious. Not at Candy, of course, but at the situation. It led to a long and painful discussion between Candy and me about where our relationship was going. She seems to think I'm not over you yet." He ducked his head. "And I seem to think she's right."

"Oh, Win—"

"Don't say anything. Please. You'll make it worse. Because I'll never get over you, Tink, but I'm going to have to learn to live with it."

His words battered me like physical blows, but I knew he was right. There was nothing I could say to make things any better. "I'm so sorry, Win."

He rolled his eyes. "Stop. I should be the one apologizing."

"For what?"

He placed a gentle hand on my face. "For my parents. For not trying harder to help when things fell apart for you years ago. For, well, for everything."

"Win Snow. Listen to me now. You were the best boyfriend and the best friend any girl could ever have."

"But I kissed Candy—"

I lifted a hand. "I hurt you badly, too. And you didn't deserve it."

"Maybe you didn't deserve what happened to you, either. Did you ever consider that?" He kissed my cheek and left. I watched him go, wondering what I'd pulled him into, but knowing I'd spoken the truth.

If anything happened to Win, I'd never forgive myself. He still had a piece of my heart, and maybe he always would.

CHAPTER SEVENTEEN

J ax and I arrived at the reindeer department right before ten. The facility—which was primarily outdoors—boasted a small office building, a giant barn, some storage sheds, and an enormous paddock surrounded by a wooden fence. Since the reindeer could fly, the fence may have seemed unnecessary, but it was a little-known fact we clipped all their ears with an anti-flying device. It was our nasty secret. It made me sick, and lots of other elves felt the same way, which was why the reindeer department kept it quiet. If they didn't, reindeer rights activists, as well as elves all over the world, would have had a cow (no pun intended).

As much as I hated the whole concept, I understood why the tags were necessary. They were for the safety of the reindeer as well as everyone else. Rogue reindeer roaming through the North Pole could cause all sorts of chaos. They tended to drink a lot and make poor decisions. And flying rogue reindeer? Even worse.

Not long before the clips were approved, a reindeer flew right into a speeding train. It was killed instantly.

Unfortunately, the train was full of school children on a field trip, and they all witnessed the animal's gruesome demise. It was not a stellar moment for the reindeer department, and thus, the tags—and the fences. Now the department had strict protocols in place to avoid any further catastrophes.

First of all, only a RAT could remove the tags, and only with prior authorization. Also, the tags only came off once a RAT saddled the reindeer for training or hooked them to Santa's sleigh for the big night. Otherwise, they were grounded. Literally. And with the anti-flying devices, they were no more magical than a herd of Holsteins.

Well, if Holsteins were smelly jerks. And the reindeer were winners in the odor department. It was so bad I smelled them before I saw them and wrinkled my nose in disgust.

"I hate this place."

Jax looked around at the fluffy white snow, the paddock full of frolicking reindeer, and the elves in their neon green coveralls. "How can you feel that way? It's amazing," he said with a grin.

He was such a kid about all this stuff. I found it surprising a dark elf could be so jacked up about Christmas.

"Amazingly repulsive, maybe," I said, trying not to smile back at him. "It smells like horny reindeer and lost dreams. Speaking of which..."

"Hey, Tinklebelle. Long time no see," said Comet, who stood inside the paddock, only a few yards away from us.

"Jerkface," I muttered under my breath before giving the large buck a nod in an attempt to play nice. "Hello, Comet."

"Mmmmm," he said, his brown cow-like gaze turning into a leer as it flickered over my body. I'd put on yoga pants and sneakers. This wasn't the place to wear anything nice, but I'd forgotten how much Comet liked yoga pants. He liked them almost as much as he liked insulting me. "Oh, you are one hot sprite, Tinklebelle. But did you gain weight? Not that I'm complaining. I like a doe with some meat on her bones."

I gave him the finger. "Suck it, Comet."

Jax let out a snort, as if trying to hold back his laugher, but it died when Comet lifted a leg. "Hey, is he going to—"

Whatever Jax meant to say was cut short when Comet urinated.

"No, you suck it," said the giant reindeer. I jumped back a millisecond too late. "Got you."

Comet tossed his head back with a loud laugh as I stared at my damp tennis shoes. Jax watched on, horrified. Apparently, he'd never gotten up close and personal with a reindeer before. Sadly, I had. Many times. And this reindeer seemed to take special joy in torturing me.

I scowled at him. "I hate you, Comet."

His eyes met mine, and I saw something so cold and mean there it made me flinch. "The feeling is mutual, you stuck-up—"

"Hey, Tink." I turned to see Rudolph approach. He was one of the few reindeer I actually liked. "Who's your friend?"

"This is Jax," I said, as Comet skulked away. "How have you been, Rudy?"

He looked over his shoulder, ears twitching, as he watched Comet's retreating form. "Oh, you know. The same."

I understood what he meant. Rudolph had come out a few years ago and suffered pretty much constant torment since. Homosexuality was not generally accepted in the reindeer community. Well, publicly, at least. They liked to put on a big show about their masculinity. They were a bunch of homophobes.

Jax stared at Rudolph, eyes wide. "Hold on. This is Rudolph? *The* Rudolph? The one from the song?" He hummed a few lines before leaning closer with a questioning frown. "But your nose isn't red."

Rudolph and I glanced at each other and burst out laughing. "Common misconception," I said at last.

"The reindeer department recycles our names," Rudolph explained. "The first Rudolph had a kind of reindeer rosacea. It made his nose look red and bulbous, but it didn't glow. The name was passed on to others, usually the outsider on the team. When the last Rudolph died, I took over. And when I die, I'll be replaced, too. Same name, different reindeer."

"But this Rudolph is the best Rudolph," I said, patting him.

Rudolph licked my hand. "Thanks, sweetness. I bet that's what you tell all of us."

"I do not." I glanced around the paddock. Comet was off trying to hump one of the does. "I don't tell Comet he's the best. Not by a long shot."

"Agreed," said Rudolph. "The last Comet was much nicer—other than that minor tax fraud issue."

"Oh. I forgot about that. Is he still in jail?"

"He gets out in a few weeks."

I glanced at the clock on the main building. The rest of the workers were on their ten o'clock coffee break. We'd timed our visit perfectly. I glanced at Rudolph.

"Jax and I have to take a look at something in the barn. Do you mind?"

"Of course not. Can I help?"

I shot a look at Comet. "Would you mind giving a shout if one of the other reindeer approaches? It's almost time for your reindeer games, so I doubt it'll be an issue, but just in case?"

"Sure," he said, a sad look in his eyes. He hated reindeer games. I didn't blame him. He was always the last one picked, and the other reindeer, led by Comet the jerkface, loved harassing him.

I moved closer to the small deer. "Jax is here to do an audit for the Elven High Council. Do you want to be our guide this morning? Instead of playing all those stupid games?"

He smiled at me in the reindeer way, which meant he opened his mouth extra big. "Thanks, Tink."

He stood outside the doorway as Jax and I slipped into the barn. I showed Jax straight to the barrels of reindeer feed. He peeked inside. "What's in this exactly?"

"A mix of oats, grains, and some plant-based protein. It always comes in these barrels." I tapped the one next to him with my finger. "Barrels that look exactly like the ones I saw in the warehouse the night someone shot Nippy."

"I agree." Jax went up to one of the barrels and looked inside. "Where do they keep the empty ones?"

I showed him to an area behind the barn, a large metal structure with a curved roof. "The food comes in through that door, and the empty barrels ship out through the other door. Deliveries are made on Mondays. The reindeer go through about a hundred barrels of feed a week."

"Why are there so many barrels stored here?"

I frowned. He was right. There were a lot more than a hundred. We did a quick count but stopped when we recognized there were closer to two hundred empty barrels. "I have no idea," I said. "I was a RAT, which meant I took care of the reindeer themselves. I fed them, but I didn't move the barrels around, mostly because I wasn't certified to use a forklift."

"Let's check these out," he said, nodding toward a barrel.

"Okay, but you'll have to be quick about it. The RAT coffee break ends at 10:15." I glanced at my watch. It was already 10:08. "We only have seven minutes."

"Got it." Jax opened one of the empty barrels and looked inside. He studied the outside of the barrel and seemed confused about something.

"What is it?" I asked.

"The barrel is larger on the outside than it is on the inside."

I looked harder. Jax was right. I couldn't believe I'd never noticed it before. He pushed the barrel onto its side and pressed on the base. To my astonishment, it popped open.

"Whoa. A hidden compartment?"

He nodded. "With a false bottom." He ran his hand along the inside. When he removed it, his fingers were covered in the same fine white powder I'd been constantly coated in when I worked in the reindeer division.

"RAT dust," I said. "I came home every day covered in the stuff. It's a byproduct of their feed or their fur or something."

He gave me a strange look as he set the barrel carefully back in place, making sure it was lined up precisely with the others. "This isn't dust, Tink."

"What is it?"

Before he could answer, the door opened, and someone stepped inside. When I saw it was none other than Frank

Yummy, I relaxed and shot him a bright smile. "Frank. You scared me."

He didn't return my smile. "What are the two of you doing in here? This is a restricted area."

His reaction bothered me. Frank was an even bigger rule-breaker than me. "Sorry. We were—"

"It's my fault," said Jax, pulling me close so he could discreetly wipe the reindeer dust on my white hoody. "I wanted a moment alone with her."

Frank eyed us closely. "Is he serious, Tink?"

"Well, you know me," I said, snuggling closer to Jax. "No impulse control."

Frank did know that about me. His shoulders relaxed a notch. "You didn't touch anything, did you?" His green-eyed gaze traveled around the room as if assessing every inch.

"No. We walked in a second before you got here. Rudolph is giving us a tour."

I couldn't tell if my old pal bought it or not. Fortunately, Rudolph saved the day. "Horny humans," he said, sticking his head in the door and pretending not to see Frank. "If you two are done in there, can we continue our tour, please? I have a massage at eleven, and I don't want to miss it."

After getting Puck's permission, we enjoyed a brief tour of the reindeer department with Rudolph himself. Jax was enthralled. Rudolph was a great source of information. And gossip.

"You know how Vixen was messing around with Dancer's wife, Gertrude? Well, now she's preggers. She's expecting a calf this spring. And Dancer was snipped. The offspring can't possibly be his."

"Oh, yikes. Poor Dancer."

Dancer was one of the nicer reindeer, especially compared to Comet, Vixen, and Prancer. But Jax didn't seem incredibly interested in the tea Rudolph was serving. He asked him about other things instead.

"Could you answer a few procedural questions? What is the system for ordering the reindeer feed? Who orders it, who signs off on it, and who comes into contact with it on an average day?"

Rudolph got glassy-eyed. "Um. I don't know. The RAT members feed us. They bring the barrels in using a forklift and roll them out once they're empty. As far as ordering the feed, we can check the paperwork. They hang it on the door. It's part of the compliance laws. If there is any bad feed circulating, they'll know which batch it came from and can pinpoint the problem."

Jax flipped through the paperwork attached to a clipboard hanging from a nail right inside the barn door. After he finished, he handed it to me, his expression solemn. I grasped why when I saw the name at the bottom of each order. Puck McHappy, the manager of the reindeer department. Was Puck involved?

"Oh, Jiminy Christmas," I said, a sinking feeling in the pit of my stomach. I thanked Rudolph for his help and pulled Jax aside.

"What is it?" he asked.

"Puck is an outlier. He's from outside the dome."

Jax ran a hand through his dark hair. "This doesn't look good, Tink."

"I know, but it can't be Puck. He's a good guy. Yes, he

can be..." I waved a hand around as I tried to come up with the right word. "...unconventional, but he's not a criminal."

I frowned, remembering Puck did indeed have a record. It was mostly for bar fights and minor assault. Not drugs. Not murder.

"We need to talk with him," said Jax. "Now."

When we went to Puck's office, however, the door was locked. "He took off five minutes ago," said Shimmy Pinesap, Puck's assistant. A short elf with beady eyes and a bad temper, guys like Shimmy were pretty much the norm for the reindeer department. Most were men. Most came from outlier communities. And most had a record of some kind. Some even had ankle bracelets to monitor their movements. Shimmy himself sported one on his right leg. Judging by how banged up it looked, he'd had it for a while.

"When will he be back?" I asked.

Shimmy scowled at us. "Hell if I know. I'm not his parole officer. It's not my job to keep track of him.

"I'm here at the request of the Elven High Council, Mr..." Jax leaned closer to read Shimmy's nametag. "Pinesap. What is your job exactly?"

Shimmy swallowed hard, aware he may have just poked a bear, and not in a good way. But Shimmy was not one to back down, so he stuck out his chin and squared his shoulders.

"Mainly I handle reindeer flight training, but when Puck is out of the office, I'm in charge."

"Let's ask this question again. Where is he?" Jax stood close enough to tower over Shimmy in an intimidating manner.

"He mentioned something about a meeting in Central City. He said he didn't know how long it would take. Should I give him a call?"

"No," said Jax, handing Shimmy a business card. "Let him know I'd like to speak with him as soon as possible."

We left the office and headed toward Jax's sled. "Where are we going?" I asked as we climbed inside.

"The police station," said Jax, a frown on his handsome face. "I want to talk to Officer Pudding about Puck."

I glanced out the window with a sigh. "I don't want it to be him. Puck is a friend."

"Everyone on the North Pole seems to be your friend. Or your ex. Or something." His tone was harsh, maybe harsher than he intended, because he placed his hand on mine, eyes still on the road. "Sorry. I agree with you. I like Puck. But I've learned the hard way it's sometimes the people we trust who disappoint us the most."

A sobering thought. I studied his profile, the firm jaw, and the straight, aristocratic nose. Who had disappointed Jax? It must have been someone important, and they must have done something significant.

My phone buzzed with a text from Win, and I read it, swearing under my breath. "It's from Win. The warehouse is empty. Not a barrel in sight, and no trace anyone has been there." I put my phone back into my purse. "Speaking of barrels, what was in the bottom of the one you opened back there? If it wasn't 'reindeer dust,' like the managers always told us."

"It was conactle. The residue left behind by candicocane."

I gaped at him. "You're kidding me, right?

He shot me a glance. "Why would I be kidding?"

"Uh, because I had it all over me on a daily basis. Wouldn't it make me high or something?"

"Not the residue. No." A muscle worked in his cheek. "I shouldn't have wiped the dust off my hands, but I wasn't thinking straight. Frank came at an inopportune time." He shook his head, as if irritated with himself. "If only we'd managed to get a sample. Even a small one. It would have helped."

"A sample?" I asked, my thoughts spinning. I sat up taller. "I can get you a sample if we're able to get into my apartment."

He made a sharp left-hand turn. "Let's go."

When we arrived at my building, the police tape was still up, but there was no one there. I unlocked the door and looked around the apartment with a sigh. It was a mess. I wish I could have blamed it on the police tearing the place apart, but the mess was all me. Still, I loved my place, and I missed it.

"Can I move back in soon?"

Jax glanced around. "Why would you want to?"

"Hey. Don't judge. I happen to like living here."

He shrugged, a nonchalant lift of one shoulder. "If you say so, but it's safer to stay at your grandmother's house for now. It's easier for me to protect you there."

"And she has food." I let out a sigh. "I cannot stress how nice it is to have a fully stocked fridge, but can I grab a few things?"

"Not unless they are essential. The police are still conducting an active investigation." As I considered whether my hair iron was essential or not, Jax interrupted my thoughts. "Tink. Focus. You said you could get me a sample of the dust?"

"Follow me."

I'd hoped to find a shirt or pants I'd worn to work, but Noelle, the neat freak, had washed everything in my hamper. Fortunately, Noelle did not look under my bed. I crawled beneath it and pulled out a bra with a satisfied smile on my face, holding it aloft with a pencil so I wouldn't knock any potential dust off it.

"Tada."

Jax raised one eyebrow at the lacey bit of lingerie. "And we're supposed to collect evidence from this?"

"Yes," I said, carefully sticking it into a plastic baggie. As soon as I did, it was evident the cloth was covered in the same fine dust we'd seen in the barrels. Jax grinned.

"Tink Holly," he said, giving me a firm kiss on the lips. "You are a genius."

I grinned back at him. "Yes, I am."

But my smile faded when we got back into Jax's sled. "We may have a sample of the dust, but what does that prove exactly?"

He squeezed my hand. "The closer we get, the more they'll try to cover up."

"Until when?"

"Until they run out of time."

Time. The one thing we had an unlimited supply of on the North Pole. Not that I wanted to mention it to Jax at the moment. I was happy to sit in silence, his warm hand covering mine.

When we arrived at the police station, we spoke with Officer Cherry, the rosy-cheeked young elf handling the front desk. His name fit, both because of the redness and because of his body shape.

"We'd like to speak with Officer Pudding, please."

"Sorry, miss. He's in a meeting." Jax gave him a business card, and Officer Cherry's eyes widened. "Elf Enforcement?"

"Yes. Could you let him know we need to see him? It's urgent. And is there somewhere private we might be able to wait for him?"

Officer Cherry led us to a small conference room. One wall of the room had nothing but a giant mirror on it, and I got excited.

"Is this one of those two-way mirrors?" I asked, making faces in it as soon as Officer Cherry left.

Jax barely glanced at it. "Most likely." He had his notebook out and was jotting things down, so I plopped onto a chair and waited. Officer Pudding showed up five minutes later.

"Sorry to keep you waiting," he said. "But it's good to see you. Did you hear the news about Nippy? He woke up this morning and spoke with one of the nurses."

I heaved a sigh of relief. "Great news."

"Yes, but unfortunately, he can't remember anything about what happened the night he got shot. I guess it's normal after a traumatic injury."

"It may come back to him eventually," said Jax.

"I hope it does. What can I help the two of you with today?"

"Well, there have been a few developments we wanted to make sure you were aware of." He pulled out his notebook, read from the pages, and told him about Joy's note and the powder inside the barrels.

Officer Pudding's eyes widened. "And the powder may be conactle?"

"Yes." Jax reached into his briefcase and pulled out the baggy with my bra inside. "Can you check this for traces of either conactle or candicocane? I suspect this may be covered in the stuff."

Officer Pudding took the bag from him. "Um, sure." He glanced at the bra, then at me, and back at the bra again. I had to guess poor Officer Pudding did not get a great deal of lingerie in his evidence room.

"And we have one more thing we need to tell you," said Jax, shooting me a sympathetic look. "We're concerned Puck McHappy might somehow be messed up in all of this."

Officer Pudding frowned. "Puck McHappy?"

"Yes," said Jax. "He's the manager of the reindeer department."

"Oh, I know who he is," said Officer Pudding. "But he's not involved. I can guarantee it."

Jax's brows furrowed in confusion. "Puck McHappy signed off on all the shipments of reindeer feed. He's right in the middle of everything. All factors seem to point to his involvement."

"I can see why you came to that conclusion," said Officer Pudding, getting to his feet. "But you're still wrong." He flicked on a switch near the wall, and the two-way mirror became like a window and left us staring into the adjoining conference room. Sitting on a chair, his feet on the table, was Puck McHappy. He couldn't see us, but we could see him. He didn't know that, however. It became obvious when he reached down to scratch his balls. Vigorously. He must have been super itchy.

Jax rose to his feet, dumbfounded. "You already have him in custody?"

Officer Pudding shook his head. "No, I was meeting with him when you stopped by." He turned back to us. "Puck isn't involved."

"What are you saying?" I asked, still confused.

"He isn't a criminal. Not anymore, at least. This is top secret information, and it had better stay that way," he said with a warning frown. "Puck McHappy works for me. And he's the best confidential informant we've ever had."

CHAPTER EIGHTEEN

Jax's frustration seemed to grow with each passing moment. The news that Puck was helping the police with illegal gambling on reindeer games, something that had nothing at all to do with candicocane came as a shock. For me, though, it was a good kind of shock. Unfortunately, it destroyed our entire theory regarding who might be behind putting the candicocane in the barrels of reindeer feed—if the white powder was indeed what Jax suspected.

"I may have been walking around with candicocane on my boobs," I said, hoping to elicit a smile from Jax. It worked.

"Judging by what you've told me, it wasn't limited to only that area."

"Oh, no. I had it in all my crevices." I giggled when he sent me a shocked look. Sometimes, for all his dark elf darkness, Jax Grayson could be oddly proper and easily shocked. I loved it about him. "Sorry. I shouldn't mess with you. When will the results be back?"

Jax glanced at his watch. "According to Officer Pudding, we should know by tomorrow."

"What do you want to do now?" I wiggled my eyebrows at him suggestively, and he laughed.

"How about we go through more files?"

"Mmmm. Filing. How sexy."

"You're ridiculous," he said, but I saw his lips twitch in another smile. "But at least your nose seems to have healed nicely from our last visit to Cookie's office."

I touched it gingerly. "Ah, the power of makeup."

Thanks to the ice, my bruising had been minimal, and my nose was barely even puffy at this point. Not that I wanted a repeat experience, but I was so relieved Puck was not a bad guy I didn't care about my swollen nose or sore face. I kept smiling. For once, my gut instinct had been correct. It was a banner day for me.

Although not the best time to say, "I told you so," to Jax, I couldn't stop myself. I said it anyway as we rode back to Grandma Gingersnap's house—several times. Jax reacted by shooting me a mildly hostile glare.

"Must you?"

I nodded happily, bouncing in my seat. "I can't help it. I'm so relieved Puck wasn't involved. He's always been nice to me."

"That's all it takes to inspire this kind of loyalty? For someone to be nice to you?"

"Yes. I've had enough betrayals and disappointments in my life. At least let me enjoy this one time my judgment was correct, okay? It doesn't happen often, so I want to revel in it."

He reached for my hand and brought it to his lips for a kiss. "You're right. I'm sorry. Revel away." Jax returned his hands to the steering wheel, and we drove a few moments in silence as I tried to process what was going on.

"It makes sense Puck would be involved in reindeer gaming," I finally said. "He's the perfect elf to do it. He's kind of got a reputation for betting on ridiculous things. Once, he bet me I couldn't drink three beers in five minutes. I sure showed him."

"Impressive," said Jax. "And yet not exactly useful."

"You're right. We need a new strategy. A new plan."

There was a long pause, and when Jax spoke, all traces of laughter had disappeared. "Or maybe a new detective."

"What do you mean?"

He stared straight ahead at the road, his expression even more somber than usual. "This is my first time on the North Pole. I'm stymied, to tell the truth."

"But what about what you said earlier? About how the closer we get, the more they'll try to cover it up."

"Yes, but this feels different. Officer Pudding is a good cop, but I had no idea Puck was an informant. I'm out of the loop, and it's hindering the investigation. Maybe I should turn this over to someone else."

I'd never heard this note in his voice before. It was the same defeated sound I'd heard in my own voice for years.

"Are you kidding? No way, Jaxy. We've got this. We'll figure it out."

He shook his head, his voice weary and resigned. "We have to face facts, Tink. You lack law enforcement experience, and I lack North Pole experience." He gave me a sidelong glance. "And stop calling me Jaxy."

"I can't stop calling you Jaxy. It's my super special name for you." When he opened his mouth to protest, I raised a hand to stop him. "But back to what you were saying, it's why we're a great team. The things you're weak on are my strengths. And vice versa."

He pulled up in front of my grandmother's house and turned to look at me. "What do you suggest we do next? Because I do not have a clue."

"I know exactly what we should do," I said as we got out of the sled and walked up the brick path to the front door. "Put on your dancing shoes, Jax Grayson. It's Friday night, and we're going out."

"Dancing shoes?" he asked as I unlocked the front door, and he followed me inside. "We don't have time for this, Tink. The elves behind all of this could easily strike again."

"Exactly. Which is why we're going to an outlier bar. Whoever shot Nippy was an outlier. I'm sure of it. And half the elves at the reindeer department are outliers. This is the easiest way to do some questioning, isn't it? They'll all be at the same place at once."

He rocked back on his heels. "Oh, my. You're right."

"See? I told you we make a great team. Now get dressed. We can grab dinner on the way. I'm starving."

"Of course you are. What does one wear to an outlier bar?"

I perused him from head to toe with a naughty grin before waving a finger at his ensemble. "Lose the suit, but dress in black, like you always do. Trust me. You'll fit right in."

A few hours later, after grabbing falafel wraps, tabouli, and some stuffed grape leaves from a food truck, we entered the largest and most famous outlier bar, appropriately named Wish You Were Beer. I'd only been at this place a few times, but it had a relaxed yet slightly dangerous vibe. And although they didn't serve The Grinch as one of their specialty cocktails, they did have something called Gettin' Blitzen, which I enjoyed, too.

I did a quick assessment of the room. Nearly everyone I knew from the reindeer department was here, including Puck, Shimmy, and Frank. When Puck saw us at the bar, he called us over to their table.

"Tink. Jax. Come join us."

Their table was in the corner, away from most of the action. Friday was live music night, and because these were outliers, that usually meant a metal band. I grabbed Jax's hand and led him over to the RAT table, getting some catcalls along the way. I wore a sparkly dress I found at Grandma Gingersnap's house. I hadn't worn it since my freshman year of college, and it was shorter and tighter than I remembered, but still a conservative choice for an outlier bar. One of the elves on the dance floor had on a mesh dress with nothing but a pair of panties beneath it. The poor girl would get frostbite if she wasn't careful.

Jax and I squeezed into the circular booth next to Puck. It was a tight fit, and I was nearly on Jax's lap. I wouldn't have minded under normal circumstances, but we were conducting an investigation. I needed to keep my wits about me.

"I heard the two of you had a busy day," said Puck, leaning close to me so no one else could hear. When I opened my mouth to respond, he gave his head a tiny shake. "Not here. We'll talk later. But I hope you know you can trust me."

"I do," I said. I wanted to explain I'd believed in his innocence all along, but had I? I couldn't say. I no longer knew who to trust. Things had grown murky, and I hated the doubt that had crept into my mind as soon as I'd seen Puck's name on the bills of lading.

"Can I get you guys a drink?" asked Frank as he stood up, on his way to get a refill of his own. "I know Tink likes Gettin' Blitzen. How about you, Jax?"

"A beer would be fine. Thank you."

There was a long moment of silence, a lull in what had been a loud and boisterous conversation. The guys at the table sat awkwardly, as if unsure what to say in front of Jax. He broke the ice, albeit inadvertently.

"What is getting blitzed, and why do you like it?" he asked with such honest confusion the entire table erupted in laughter.

"Tink loves getting blitzed. No shocker there, folks," said Puck, his big belly jiggling, as Frank returned to the table.

"It's a drink," I explained, thanking Frank and holding my glass up to Jax.

Jax lifted his beer. "Here's to getting blitzed. The next round is on me, guys."

And suddenly, Jax was everyone's best friend. As the conversation resumed around us, Jax glanced at my drink.

"Gettin' Blitzen, huh? What's in that thing anyway? It looks like mud."

"It's not mud. Here. Try some." I let him have a taste, and he grimaced in disgust.

"It's chocolate."

"Yes. The bartender makes it with chocolate ice cream combined with cream de cacao, Irish cream liquor, and vodka. He dips the rim of the glass in melted chocolate. And then adds chocolate sprinkles, of course."

"Of course," said Jax, taking a swig of his beer—likely to wash away the taste of my drink. The RAT elves were, as usual, telling dirty jokes about packages and snowballs. Jax leaned closer to whisper in my ear. "We should get started. Are you ready?"

Our goal was simple. First, we wanted to find out which outlier in the reindeer department had experience with guns. It turned out they all did. Guns were big in the outlier areas, primarily because of wolves and polar bears. But the gun discussion turned into a long conversation during which they all bragged about the many times they'd nearly gotten killed by a polar bear. I never grasped how much of an issue that was, especially due to the strict rules in place regarding hunting on the North Pole. Although the subject was fascinating, it got us no closer to figuring out who may have shot Nippy.

I decided it was time to play a rousing game of Never Have I Ever. Elves loved that game, especially outliers. They jumped in eagerly, but all I learned was everyone at the table, except for Jax and me, had done illicit drugs, gotten away with a serious crime, and made out with a cousin. The last one caught me by surprise. I didn't appreciate how interconnected the outlier communities were, or how isolated. It became even more apparent when Shimmy chose "Never have I ever...gotten intimate with a reindeer by accident" when it was his turn. That resulted in a whole bunch of stories involving drunken encounters I wish I'd never heard about.

I wasn't a total innocent on the subject. I'd worked around the reindeer, and the guys on the Reindeer Assistance Team, long enough to be aware this was a thing. I'd also heard rumors the outliers weren't the only ones. In Central City, for example, a place called the Ho, Ho Club was elite and very kinky. Reindeer encounters were supposedly one of the many things they offered, but it was only a rumor.

"They abuse animals?" asked Jax, looking like he might be ill. He held up one hand. "No. Please don't tell me anymore. I don't want to know."

Frank took one look at Jax and raised his eyebrows at me, pretending to throw up. Jax did look paler than usual, but he'd barely had anything to drink. It turned out Frank was right, though. Maybe it was the bestiality discussion, but Jax got so pale he could almost glow in the dark. Seconds later, he rose to his feet and staggered out of the booth.

"Pardon me. I need to find a restroom."

Frank sent me a triumphant grin, mouthing *I told you so*. Jax was heading in the wrong direction, so I stood up to help him. "Come on, big guy. I'll show you where to go. Are you okay?"

He shook his head, face pale. "It must have been something I ate. Maybe the falafel."

"Maybe." I didn't add I'd eaten the same thing and felt fine. I'd often heard dark elves couldn't handle spicy foods well, and the falafel had been on the spicy side.

By the time we reached the restroom, Jax was green. He flew inside, and I wondered if I should follow him. I opened the door of the men's room slightly, only enough to hear the sounds of Jax getting sick and closed it again.

"Jiminy Christmas," I said, certain Jax would rather die than ask for my help, but I had another problem as well. I needed to use the facilities, too, and the line for the ladies' room was twenty elves long.

Crossing my legs, I tried to hold it. I had only a few options. I could wait in line, but I knew I wouldn't last. Or I could join Jax in the men's room, but he would be mortified.

Or I could wet my pants, and that would not be cool at all. I decided on a different option. To pee al fresco. Yes, I might get arrested, but it was better than wetting my pants.

I was about to head toward the back exit of the club when Frank sidled up to me. "Are you okay?" he asked.

"Uh, no," I said, hopping back and forth from one leg to another. "I have to go to the bathroom, but the line is long. Also, Jax is getting sick. I don't want to leave him. Would it be weird if I went outside? You know, like a dude?"

Frank seemed flummoxed. "Uh, you're not a dude, and you're in an outlier bar in the middle of Central City, not in a forest somewhere."

"I've peed in weirder places."

He laughed. "True. Do you remember the time you got wasted and accidentally peed on Win's dog? Hilarious. I don't know who was angrier at you, Duke, or Win's evil mother."

"Stop. I'm going to pee my pants." I tried desperately to hold it, wiggling with the effort. "But to answer your question about who was angrier, it was a tie. I tried to apologize, but how do you say you're sorry for something like that?"

"Well, she was going to hate you no matter what. Whoever named her 'Angel' was either stupid or had an amazing gift for irony."

I snorted, in severe pain at this point. "Please don't make me laugh. You're a terrible person."

He grinned. "Nope. I'm a nice person who happens to live in an apartment right upstairs, where I have a bathroom with no line. Come on."

"What about Jax?"

Puck came up, seemingly unaware he wasn't in the restroom yet, because he'd already unbuckled his belt and was in the process of unzipping his pants. Frank grabbed his arm. "Hey, Puck, can you keep an eye on Jax for five minutes. Tinklebelle has to tinkle."

"Ha. Funny," I said.

"Sure, I will," said Puck, swaying on his feet and giving Frank some sort of salute. I did not feel like he was a responsible caretaker, but I didn't have a choice.

I stuck my head in the door. "Jax. I have to run upstairs and use the restroom. I will be back in five minutes. Puck is right here. He'll help you if you need anything, okay?"

Jax said something sounding vaguely like an affirmative, so I followed Frank up the staircase on the far side of the building and into a large and well-decorated apartment. It was much nicer than I'd expected, but I couldn't admire it when my bladder was about to explode.

"Where is the bathroom?"

He pointed me to a door, and I made it there just in time. Another five seconds would have been too late. When I went back into Frank's living room, I found he'd mixed a drink for me, and sexy music played from a speaker in the wall.

Frank was trying to seduce me. Oh, crap.

"I'd better get going—" I said, but he cut me off.

"Have one drink with me, Tink. For old time's sake."

My phone buzzed with a text. It was Jax, letting me know he was fine, but Puck had passed out in the restroom. Jax got him back to the table with the rest of the team, and they were trying to sober him up. He said he would wait for me in the bar.

I sent him a quick reply. *I'm upstairs in Frank Yummy's apartment. I'll be back in a few minutes. I'm going to ask him some questions since I have him here alone.*

I trusted Frank, and he knew all the outliers. He might be the connection I needed.

Also, to be honest, I didn't want to be rude to an old friend. I missed Frank. We barely spoke anymore. So I accepted the drink, something blue and sweet, and sipped it as I walked around the room, admiring his apartment.

"This is so much nicer than your old place. When did you move here?"

He leaned against the wall, arms crossed over his chest, as handsome and naughty as always, but in a familiar, non-threatening way. Like a sexy old sock, not that Frank would have appreciated that analogy, but there was something so comfortable about him.

"I moved in a few months ago. I inherited some money from a long-lost uncle, believe it or not. I used it to pay off some bills, buy a new sled, and rent this place."

"Good for you."

I smiled when I saw a bunch of old photos in frames on the wall. Frank had always been a sentimental guy.

"These are so nice. Look at us," I said, pointing to an adorable photo of Frank, Win, and me when we were small. Others were of people I didn't recognize. I knew Frank was an orphan, and Sugar had taken him in when his parents passed away. But I didn't know much more about his family.

"Are these your parents?" I asked, pointing to one of the pictures.

"Yes," he said.

"I thought so." I gave him a sad smile. "You look like your dad, you know, and your mom was breathtaking."

He studied the photo with a pained look on his face. "She was," he said, his voice tight with emotion. I understood the feeling.

"You never get over it, do you?"

He shook his head. "No, you don't." His phone rang,

and he glanced at the number. "Excuse me. I have to take this."

"Go ahead."

He went to another room to take the call, and I continued looking at his wall of photos. I stopped at the one from Frank's time on the professional North Pole ski team. He stood in the front of the group, smiling broadly. They must have taken the photo right after the team won something because they all had shiny medals around their necks. The man standing next to Frank looked vaguely familiar. I was going to ask him about it, but I forgot when I saw the worried expression on Frank's face.

"Is everything okay?"

"Yes, but I need to take off. Can I walk you back downstairs?"

"Sure. Thanks, Frank. And thanks for the use of your potty."

He smiled. "Once a friend, always a friend," he said.

I turned, oddly lightheaded. I must have had more to drink than I'd realized. I stumbled on the steps, and Frank caught me.

"Whoa," I said. "I feel strange. Maybe Jax was right. Maybe we did get some bad falafel."

Frank cupped my cheeks in his hands, his eyes sad. "I'm sorry, Tink." He kissed my forehead, and then he was gone, leaving me teetering on my heels at the entrance to the outlier bar. I turned, trying to find him to let him know I needed his help, but time seemed to move too slowly. Or maybe too quickly. I couldn't tell. But Frank was gone, and I was on my own. This was not cool. Not cool at all.

I pushed my way inside, the room spinning around me like a merry-go-round set on high speed. I squinted, trying to see into the dimly lit bar.

"Jax?"

I bumped into a burly outlier. He put out a hand to steady me, and I leaned against him, unable to stand up on my own anymore. I was either very ill or utterly wasted. If it was the first one, I blamed the falafel. If it was the second, I could only blame myself, but I had no idea how it had happened so quickly. I hadn't been this drunk in years.

"Please help me," I said. "I need to find Jax."

The bearded outlier seemed confused, like my words hadn't entirely made sense. I closed my eyes and felt myself falling, but strong arms gathered me up and held me close.

"Jax?"

I didn't know how I knew it was him, but I did. "It's okay, Tink. I've got you."

I leaned against his broad shoulder, sicker than I'd been in a long time. Something jabbed my leg, and I screamed. My mind was in a whirl of colors and confusion, and only Jax's voice kept me grounded. He told me I was fine, and he said he'd take care of me. I believed him, but I couldn't answer because my mouth wouldn't work.

After that, I saw nothing but flashes. Jax carrying me in his arms as he ran out of the bar. Jax putting me into some kind of vehicle and speeding away. Jax's hand in mine.

I turned toward him, wanting to speak, but I couldn't, even though it was necessary. I had to tell him I'd figured out something shocking, and it was where the puzzle began.

The man in the photo from Frank's apartment. The one on the ski team standing next to Frank. I knew exactly who he was, even though I hadn't recognized him immediately. He was Evergreen Berry. Joy's brother.

CHAPTER NINETEEN

I woke to a beeping noise and a pain in my head so intense I let out a moan. Reaching to the side of the bed, I searched for my alarm clock, but it wasn't there. And something pinched the back of my hand when I moved it.

"Jiminy Christmas," I said, my voice raspy and strange. My throat hurt, too. Badly.

"You can say that again."

I opened my eyes, which took incredible effort, and focused on the person sitting next to my bed. "Topper?"

"Hey, kiddo."

Why was my uncle's assistant in my bedroom? Opening my eyes a bit wider, I realized I was not in my bedroom. I was in a hospital room. And the beeping sound was a monitor measuring my heart rate.

"I'm in the hospital? What happened?"

Topper let out a sigh as only Topper could—a mix of regret tinged with disappointment, plus a healthy dash of disgust. I recognized that noise because I'd heard it many times before. "Things got out of hand last night. How much do you remember?"

I frowned. "I went to a bar with Jax. I used Frank Yummy's bathroom. And that's it. I can't remember anything else." Not entirely true, but I was too tired to get into it right now. I glanced around the room. "How did I end up here?"

He crossed one leg over the other, his expression resigned. "Let me fill in the blanks for you. You did drugs. Caused a scene. Accosted someone in an outlier bar. And..." He opened a small notebook and checked his notes. "Oh. Passed out on the sidewalk."

I put a hand to my head, confused. "None of that happened. I barely drank—"

He slammed his notebook shut. "Enough. This isn't the first time you blacked out, and I'm sorry to say it probably won't be the last. But drugs? That is too much."

"I didn't do any drugs, Topper. I swear."

"That's not what your blood test said." The disappointment in his eyes wounded me. "You had a dangerous level of candicocane in your system. If someone hadn't given you narzipan and rushed you over here, the consequences would have been dire. You're just lucky you didn't take the stuff laced with telezol. You're playing Russian roulette with your life. You need to pull yourself together, kid. And since you can't seem to do it on your own, we're stepping in to help."

"We?"

"Your uncle and I," he said, handing me an official-looking piece of paper. "It's tough love. Nothing else has worked. This is the last option we have left."

I stared at the paper, unable to believe my eyes. "Uncle Kris is sending me to the coal mines?" I asked, clearly recognizing the swirly, elegant signature at the bottom of the page.

"It's for your own good."

I willed myself not to cry, but I felt weak and sore and sick and confused. I'd screwed everything up once again. It was the story of my life. But none of it made sense.

"Look, you need to talk to Jax. He can explain what happened."

Topper wouldn't look at me directly. "Mr. Grayson has been sent back to Elf Central. His job is now in jeopardy. You will not be seeing him again."

"But—"

"Enough, Tink. I love you, kid. I wish I didn't have to be the one to do this, but your uncle thought it would be better coming from me."

"But—"

"Stop. Don't make things worse. This is hard enough as it is." The pity mixed with disappointment in his eyes bothered me more than my throbbing head. He let out a long sigh. "You'll be discharged from the hospital later today. My men will take you where you need to go."

I put a hand on his arm. "Topper. You have to listen to me. None of what you said actually happened."

"Bloodwork doesn't lie, Tink." Pulling away from me, he put his hands on his hips and stared out the window, almost as if he couldn't bear to look at me. "It's not forever. It's just until Christmas. Your uncle is in the middle of crucial negotiations with the Toymakers Union right now. Some of his adversaries are looking for any reason they can to demand his resignation. You've made him look bad, over and over again. If he can't control his niece, how can he be trusted to lead the entire North Pole?"

"But he's a great Santa. Everyone loves him."

"Not everyone. Not by a long shot." He glanced my way, his eyes as cold and hard as ice. "You are a liability right now, Tink. We can't trust you to behave, so this is our only option. I'm sorry. Your transport will be here shortly, and I've had a few things sent over from your apartment. I suggest you try to get some rest. You're going to need it."

He left, closing the door softly behind him, and I heard the faint click of a lock. I stared at the door, stunned. Was I a prisoner here?

I jumped to my feet, swaying as a wave of dizziness came over me, and fell back onto the bed. Even if I wanted to escape, and even if the door weren't locked, I doubted I could make it more than a few feet before collapsing.

I curled up on the bed, hoping this was all some kind of bad dream but knew it wasn't when members of Topper's private security force came to collect me later in the day. Two tall men with the same color hair, skin, and eyes, they dressed in matching dark blue uniforms. They didn't introduce themselves, and I didn't bother asking their names. In the grand scheme of things, it didn't matter.

They brought a small duffle bag containing a change of clothing, a comb, and a toothbrush. I got dressed in the bathroom, still shaky and lightheaded, but I'd managed to hold down a piece of dry toast and some orange juice, so I felt marginally better. Well, physically, at least. Mentally, I was a wreck.

I stared at myself in the bathroom mirror after getting dressed in a dark gray pair of sweats and a hoodie. My face was pale, and I had purple circles under my eyes. I had a big bruise on my thigh from the narzipan. I looked like I had some horrible disease. What the heck happened to me? And why couldn't I remember any of it?

A wave of nausea rolled over me, and it wasn't necessarily from whatever I'd done the night before. I was disgusted with myself. It seemed like the harder I tried, the worse I failed. I was done. I didn't want to try anymore.

A voice niggled in my brain. *But what about the file under Cookie's desk?*

I shook my head in annoyance. The file didn't matter. Nothing mattered. It was over. But I did want to call Jax to tell him I was sorry. I stepped outside of the bathroom and addressed one of Topper's guards.

"Excuse me. Could I have my cell phone, please?"

He stared right through me, his expression blank. "Sorry, miss. We don't have your cell phone."

I put a hand to my head. I'd had my cell phone in Frank's apartment. I was sure of it. Had I dropped it outside? I had no idea. It was all so fuzzy.

"Okay." I thought about asking him if I could use his phone, but who would I call? I didn't know Jax's number by heart, and no way I'd call my uncle, my grandmother, or even Noelle or Win. I was too ashamed. I was going down in a big way, and I refused to bring anyone else down with me. I was on my own.

The last time I'd been in an outlier area had been when I ran away to the reindeer ranch when I was a girl, and Topper dragged my sorry butt home. He'd been the first one on the scene when my parents died and my ally at a time when I'd needed one. He'd always have a special place in my heart. Even now, I couldn't be mad at him. This situation, like everything else in my life, was entirely of my own making. Tink Holly had screwed up yet again. What a shock.

"We're here, miss."

Our sled came to a halt in front of a concrete building with a weathered sign on the front that read North Pole Coal Mine Number Twenty-Five, Enter at Your Own Risk.

"Great," I muttered. "Home sweet home."

"Well, for the next few months at least," said the guard in the front seat, in what I had to assume was an attempt at reassuring me.

"Months?" I asked, my voice turning squeaky. "Topper said weeks. Just until Christmas."

The guards exchanged a long look but didn't respond. Instead, they got out of the sled, gathered my things, and opened the door to escort me out.

The wind nearly knocked me over when I stepped onto the road in front of Coal Mine Number Twenty-Five. The entire area was bleak and desolate. Not a single house or tree marked the landscape. Nothing but flat, empty waste-land surrounded me.

The guards had given me gloves, a wool stocking cap, and a parka. It covered me from my head to my knees, but the cold seemed to slice through all the layers of clothing and sink right into my bones. Within seconds, I was shivering so badly I could barely speak and was grateful for the warmth inside the building.

The facility's grand entrance consisted of a series of mismatched metal chairs placed against bare walls that were painted in a dingy shade of white. A reception desk, also made of metal, was in the center of the room, and a small elf with wire-rimmed glasses sat behind the desk, tapping away on a computer. He didn't look up when we entered or acknowledge our presence in any way. The guard standing next to me had to clear his throat three times before the receptionist deigned to glance at us.

"Yes?" he asked, his tone clipped and irritated.

"This is Tinklebelle Holly," said guard number one. "I believe you've been expecting her."

With a sigh of long-suffering, the elf shuffled through the piles of paperwork on his desk. A small plaque on his desk showed his name, Fiddle-dee Doo, in faded gold letters. "Ah. Here we are. Tinklebelle Holly. Miner number 5,263. Welcome to Coal Mine Number Twenty-Five. Do you have any dietary concerns, illnesses, allergies, or phobias we should be aware of?"

Did fear of ending up in the coal mines count as a phobia? That was likely not what Fiddle-dee Doo was asking about, so I decided not to mention it.

"Uh, no."

"Good. Because we don't care if you do, but, by law, I have to ask."

Fiddle-dee Doo rose to his feet. He was the same height he'd been while sitting, which meant he roughly came up to my waist.

"What? You've never seen a mining dwarf before, lady? Take a picture, it'll last longer."

I winced. "Sorry, I—"

He waved a hand. "Forget it," he said, and eyed me from head to toe. At first, I thought he was checking me out, but he was sizing me up. "I'd say you're about a medium. Not too big, and not too small."

"Just right?"

He lifted an eyebrow. "I wouldn't go that far."

He plunked a brown uniform on the desk, along with brown socks, brown shoes, and brown undies. I lifted them with one finger, horrified. They seemed to have already been used by someone else.

"Do I have to wear these?"

Fiddle-dee shrugged. "Your option. No one cares if you do or if you don't. But I will warn you, mine slugs are known to burrow into warm places—if you get my drift. Underpants are an added layer of protection."

I shoved the underpants into the pocket of my coat. "Got it. Anything else I should be aware of?"

He scowled at me. Well, I thought he scowled. It may have been his usual expression. I couldn't tell. "You will find what you need to know in your orientation packet. I suggest you read it. Since you have a background in collections, I'm assigning you to our collections office."

I closed my eyes, hoping this was a horrible dream, but it wasn't. "This is one of the seven circles of hell, isn't it?"

For the first time since I met him, Fiddle-dee smiled, but his words chilled me even more than the sub-zero winds outside. "This isn't one of the circles, Ms. Tinklebelle Holly. This is hell itself. Enjoy your stay."

I wish I could say Fiddle-dee had exaggerated. Sadly, Coal Mine Number Twenty-Five was indeed a dark, dank, cold version of hell. My living quarters were little more than a cell. My job, a nightmare. But things could have been worse. I could have been working in the mines themselves. I appreciated how horrible it was when a cave-in occurred, and I had to lend a hand in the medical wing. The wounds were awful, and two elves died, but the ones I handled only had minor scrapes and bruises. Even those were more than I could take. While holding one elf's hand as the doctor set a broken arm, I cried.

"Don't cry," said the elf. "I'll be off for Christmas thanks to this. I'm not complaining."

Christmas. It was only days away, and not a single person had reached out to me from home. It said a lot.

It also said a lot that these elves were excited about injuries received in a cave-in because it meant having time off. It didn't matter what they had done or not done. No one deserved to live like this. Outliers had it tough, their lives even more brutal than I'd realized.

I'd discovered most of the elves working in the mines had ended up here for petty reasons. A gal I met in collections had been sent to the coal mines because she had a vindictive ex-husband. "He decided if he wasn't happy, I couldn't be happy either. He had friends in high places. I did not. Also, I was an outlier, which was already a strike against me." She shook her head sadly. "But if you want to know the truth, I wouldn't change a thing. I'd rather be here than with him. Pretty sad, isn't it?"

It seemed many of the elves sent here had been transferred for similar reasons, and, sadly, those reasons often involved domers and members of the First Five. One elf told me he got sent to the coal mines for having a fender bender with a high-ranking member of the Tannenbaum family.

"The irony of it? I didn't even cause the accident. Tandy Tannenbaum ran into me if you can believe it. She was underage and under the influence, but *I'm* the one sent to the coal mines—because I refused to accept a payoff. Because I trusted our legal system."

It seemed most of the elves working in the mine were outliers or outsiders. I was the only one here from one of the First Five families. It made me an oddity among the oddities.

But I slowly adjusted to life in the colorless, depressing pit known as Coal Mine Number Twenty-Five. I made a few friends, people to share meals with at the cafeteria and chat with after work. There was nothing much to do in the evenings, so we told stories about our old lives and drank moonshine that one of the braver elves produced in a still he kept hidden in an underground tunnel. It tasted awful and could make us go blind, but we drank it anyway. The numbing effect it provided came as a welcome relief from the constant sadness we faced every day.

Living here sucked. Elves got lost in the tunnels or injured regularly. There was no hope, and there was no escape. I had to wonder if some of the elves who disappeared, never to be seen again, did it on purpose. It wouldn't be an easy way to go. You'd walk and walk and walk deeper and deeper into the darkness until you died. I shuddered at the thought. I preferred anything to that, even a cave-in. The only thing worse was freezing to death or getting eaten by polar bears. Or maybe getting eaten by polar bears as you froze to death. Now that would definitely suck.

I was sitting at my desk in the collections office, staring out the window at the endless sea of white tundra, recovering from both a hangover and the crying fit I'd had after the mine collapse when I heard a familiar voice behind me.

"The paperwork you sent me is wrong. Mr. Shenanigans specifically asked for the accounts due in September and October, not October and November. Please rectify this immediately. He does not want to be kept waiting."

I gasped as I turned around to face her. "Mince? Mince Mingle?"

She dropped the pile of papers she'd been holding and stared at me, disbelief mixed with dread on her sharp features. "Tinklebelle Holly. You finally ended up here. It's about time." I got up and helped her gather the papers she'd dropped. She took them from me grudgingly. "When did you arrive?"

I counted in my head. "Three weeks ago. At the end of November. How about you?"

"The same. Remember the day you and the dark elf showed up? The day Cookie disappeared?" I nodded, and she continued. "Well, the police were waiting for me when I left the building."

"Why were they waiting for you?"

She let out a huff, her eyes narrowing into slits. "As if you don't know. Stop playing with me."

I frowned. "I *don't* know, Mince. And why would I play with you? What's the point?"

It seemed to make sense to her. But she tried to hold onto her anger using the same tenacity with which she held the file close to her bony chest.

"They accused me of stealing something, which I did not. I assume you're the one who set me up?"

I stared at her blankly. "Mince, I have no idea what you're talking about."

She studied me, trying to assess if I was telling the truth or not. But I had no reason to lie, and we both knew it. Finally, she gave the tiniest shrug of her shoulders.

"It doesn't matter now. Cookie ran away and left me holding the bag, so to speak." She let out a sniff. "The scoundrel. I should have known better. That is the last time I ever fall in love with a married man. They promise you the world and leave you in the dirt. Anyway, maybe I should thank you. If it weren't for you, I would never have come here and met Mr. Tipsy Shenanigans."

"Tipsy Shenanigans?"

"My new boss. The CEO of Coal Mine Number Twenty-Five." She sighed. "And before you ask, yes, he is also married, but this is different. Tipsy is going to leave his wife for me. I'm certain of it."

251

We both paused a moment, absorbing the nonsense she'd just spouted. Fortunately, she seemed to grasp it was nonsense, too, which was a relief of sorts. "He's not going to leave his wife either, is he?" she asked.

I shook my head. "Nope."

"And I've made the same mistake all over again."

"Maybe, but a person who repeats their mistakes is an optimist. You do the same thing, but you hope it turns out differently. What could be more optimistic than that?"

"Optimistic or delusional?"

I considered her question. "Too close to call, but the important thing is you've learned from your mistake." I studied her face. "Want to drink?"

She looked at her watch with a sigh. "Definitely."

CHAPTER TWENTY

"I am such a fool," said Mince.

She'd already downed three or four glasses of a particularly potent batch of coal mine moonshine, mixed with cranberry juice, orange juice, and a swish of the peach schnapps someone had smuggled in from Central City. It was my version of Sex on the Beach. I called it Sex in the Shaft, which Mince found hilarious. She kept holding out her empty glass for a refill, saying, "I want to have Sex in the Shaft."

Mince and I shared the same sense of humor and the same love of alcohol. Who knew?

But poor Mince wasn't laughing now. We were out of ingredients to make more Sex in the Shaft, and her happy buzz had turned into a melancholy haze. I was still nursing my first drink, but even I felt it. It was depressing. And so was our conversation.

"Why did you think I'd set you up?" I asked.

"Money went missing a month or so ago from elven resources. A lot of money. It seemed like an awfully big coincidence you and the dark elf showed up, and minutes later, I was arrested. That's why I assumed it was you."

"It wasn't."

She winced. "I know that now. It was Cookie all along. He stole the money to finance his new life, and he made it look like I did it. Why are men so awful?"

At first, I assumed it was a rhetorical question, but she kept staring at me as if awaiting a response. Naturally, I responded.

"Not *all* of them are bad."

I couldn't help but think of Jax. I thought about him a lot. During many of the cold, snowy, miserable nights in Coal Mine Number Twenty-Five, thoughts about Jax Grayson were the only things that brought me any comfort at all.

Mince obviously needed comfort, too. She was currently splayed across the sofa of my tiny living quarters, an area consisting of a single bed, a shabbily appointed sitting area, and a small kitchen. The television in the corner was broken, but even if it had worked, the only channel they got here was the weather station, which was super exciting when you lived in the arctic circle. Reports typically ranged from "Today it's cold" to "Tomorrow it will also be cold."

It was one more way to torture us. As was the so-called library, which had an abundance of books on accounting, arctic wildlife, snowmobile safety for beginners, survival training, and, for some strange reason, magic. At this point, I knew how to balance a spreadsheet, recognize polar bear scat, drive a snowmobile, make it at least twenty-four hours outside with nothing but a switchblade and a lighter, and, if someone tied my hands with rope, I could get out of it faster than Harry Houdini. Not one of those skills had come in handy during my tenure here. Perhaps someday they would.

Mince let out a groan. "You only say that because *you* were dating *Winter Snow III*."

"We broke up years ago."

She pointed a finger at me. "*You* broke up with *him*. It bottles the mind."

I didn't bother correcting her. Bottles and boggles both worked for me. "Win and I have known each other forever. We're better as friends."

"Ha," she said with a snort. "Do you seriously believe that? He's still in love with you, stupid." She smacked me on the head, maybe harder than she intended, but it did drive the point home. Win was still in love with me, but I had serious trouble understanding why.

"He can do a lot better."

Mince squinted at me with concern, or maybe she was going blind from the moonshine. It would be the perfect ending to a perfect day.

"Love doesn't work like that, Tink. It's not done in half measures, not by people like Win. It's all or nothing. I recognize it in him since I'm the same way."

I started to reply, but she held up a hand.

"Hold on a minute, young lady. There is something else, too." She adjusted her glasses and managed to look prim even though she was lying sideways on my ratty-looking couch with her hair a mess and cranberry juice stains on her poo-colored uniform. "You deserve love. You know that, right?"

I sent her a sardonic half-smile. "Uh, yes. Of course, I do."

"I'm serious. Repeat after me. *I deserve love.*" She waved her hands like she was conducting an orchestra.

"I deserve love." The words seemed foreign on my tongue, clumsy and strange. I didn't like it but Mince the Merciless wasn't done yet.

"I deserve happiness," she said and glared at me until I repeated that phrase as well, and the next one, too. "I am a person of value."

By the time we said those things several times, I almost believed them. Or maybe it was the moonshine talking.

"You dumped Winter Snow III, the perfect man, and you hooked up with that hotter than hot dark elf, Jax Grayson. Cookie almost lost his mind when that happened."

"He did? Why?"

"Because the situation was getting beyond his control. Which is why I made a copy of all those documents. Did he seriously think I wouldn't read them all and keep copies for myself? Geesh. I'm not stupid. I put them in a safety deposit box for safety depositing."

"Good idea. What was in those documents, Mincie?"

"Oh, the usual. Stuff about you. Lots of stuff about you. Most of it lies, but some of it true." She snorted. "Hey, that rhymed."

"You have a gift."

"Also, Cookie *hated* you."

"Why? I don't understand what he had against me."

"Well," she said, leaning closer as if to impart something of great importance. "Cookie was convinced you might be the first female Santa someday. He had a big problem with that, since Cookie is kind of old school."

"And by 'old school' you mean a misogynistic asshole?"

She snorted. "Yes. Exactly."

I rolled my eyes. "He shouldn't have worried. No one in their right might would ever think I'd make a good Santa. I couldn't even handle the Mrs. Claus gig. Can you imagine me baking cookies and being a good little housewife? Not going to happen."

"No one ever said you'd make a good Mrs. Claus, Tink. But if something unexpected happened to our current Santa, well...who would be next in line?"

A chill went over my skin. "Mince. You need to tell me —what else did you see in those documents?"

"Lots of things. Secret things," she said in a loud whisper, putting a finger to her lips as if to silence me. "About a plan to get rid of Santa."

I sat up straighter in my chair. This conversation had taken an unexpected turn. "What do you mean? Is someone going to hurt Santa?"

"Hurt him?" she asked. "I don't know, but that's why Cookie took off. He didn't want to be a part of the whole 'Let's get Santa' thing. He's a—what'd you call him?"

"Misogynistic asshole?"

"Yeah. But he's not the kind of guy who goes after Santa. And when the Nipple man got shot, he finally realized he might be next."

"Nippy?"

"Yes. Nipple."

She seemed so confident, I let it slide. "But you said the police suspected foul play in Cookie's disappearance?"

"They did, but I later found out he's fine. He's living on a beach somewhere. Having Sex on the Beach with sexy bea-itches." She laughed at her joke, but her expression morphed into a confused frown. "He left both his wife and me. Both of us. What a jerk face."

"Repeat after me, Mince, you deserve love..."

She giggled, waving her hand as if to smack me again. She missed but grinned at me. "It's weird because I didn't like you before. You made Cookie's life so hard. He had to make up all those reasons to fire you and hope no one ever found out. Especially Santa. Santa would have fired Cookie if he'd known."

"You think?" I wasn't being sarcastic. My uncle relied heavily on Cookie.

She yawned, her eyelids drooping. "Santa loves you. He's an outstanding uncle. And a good person, too."

"If so, why would he send me here?" I asked softly.

Mince responded with a loud snore. So much for that conversation. I got up and removed her glasses so they wouldn't get bent and covered her with a blanket. I was about to climb into bed, but she surprised me by asking me, in a voice thick with sleep, "Is it true what they say about dark elves in the sack? I heard they can read your mind and know exactly what you want and how you want it."

I laughed. "No idea."

"Can you find out, please? Inquiring minds want to know." She slurred her words so badly I could barely under-stand them, and her eyes remained closed. This time she was down for the count. The rest of my questions would have to wait until morning.

I thought long and hard about what Mince had said as I climbed into bed, my mind a whirl. Did someone want to harm my uncle? It was hard to fathom. Uncle Kris was good. Like, genuinely perfect to his core. Which was why it had been relatively easy to accept he'd sent me here to rot. A person as saintly as my uncle would do things by the book, and, according to what he knew, I sort of deserved a one-way ticket to the coal mines. He didn't know Cookie had been falsifying documents and lying about me. Even I hadn't known. No one did.

I sat up with a start. Except someone did know because someone told Cookie to do it. Cookie was no more the brains than he was the brawn. But who was behind it?

I wracked my brain, trying to come up with an answer. It had been, as Jax stated, a long game, a plan put into place nearly five years ago and followed closely since. And I saw two possible scenarios. It was either someone above Cookie on the North Pole pay grade or someone who had dirt on him. If it was the first, I had only a few options. But the second? The list of suspects was almost limitless.

Sober now, and unable to sleep, I grabbed a pen and paper and sat at my kitchen table to take some notes. I had a plan, a vague and chancy idea, but to pull it off, I needed help. Who could I ask and how?

Jax was back in Elf Central doing who knows what. I wanted to believe he hadn't forgotten me, but it had been more than three weeks now, and if he hadn't, where was he? Win may still love me, but he was being all vice-presidenty and I refused to get him involved. Noelle was in Florida with her parents.

As much as I hated to admit it, Grandma Gingersnap was my best hope. Back in her big house all by herself, she had to wonder why I hadn't shown up for dinner. Or had Uncle Kris told her what happened? My misdeeds may very well have ended up in the papers. There are some secrets even Uncle Kris couldn't keep under wraps for long. Not to mention Topper, the bearer of bad news. The doer of the dirty work. He was so faithful to Uncle Kris, there was no way he'd listen to me. No, unless I wanted to appeal to my elderly grandmother, I was on my own.

With a sad sigh, I crumpled up the paper and threw it

into the garbage can. Even as my head told me to give up, though, I couldn't help considering alternatives, ways I could make it work on my own. That's when Plan B hit me. It was risky AF, and I'd most likely die, but I knew I had to do it anyway. But first, I needed to get some sleep. Tomorrow was going to be a big day, and my timing could not be better. No Christmas Elf needed a calendar to know the holiday was fast approaching, and tomorrow was winter solstice—the one day the sun didn't rise or set in the Arctic Circle. A day of complete and utter darkness.

Perfect.

I woke up at 5 a.m., which would have been dawn if there had been a sunrise. Mince still snored softly on my couch, one arm thrown over her head and a pinched frown on her lips. Poor Mince. She hadn't had it easy either. We weren't so different. She'd been set up, too. If my plan was successful, I vowed to help her get out of here. I owed her as much. She'd given me vital information last night, most notably that someone was after Uncle Kris.

As I thought of his sparkling blue eyes, kind smile, and merry laugh, I was more resolved. Even if I died today, at least I died trying. And that, in itself, was an accomplishment. To be on the safe side, I wrote out a letter detailing what I'd learned and addressed it to my uncle before tucking it into my pocket. If I didn't make it, perhaps the letter would—once they found my frozen, miserable body.

I dressed in as many layers as possible, put on my parka, gloves, and hat, grabbed a pair of snow boots, and left my apartment. The hallways were quiet because all the sensible elves were still sleeping. I grabbed all the gear I could carry from the supply room, shoving an emergency blanket and a small pop-up tent into a large expedition backpack. I also found a tiny kerosene cooking stove, a lighter, a radio, a compass, a map, and the all-important pen knife. The mine had no reason to keep these things locked away. Normal elves didn't steal this kind of stuff. Normal elves knew there was nowhere to go.

The snowmobiles were left unlocked and gassed up, with keys hanging on a board in the garage. Normal elves also didn't try to drive snowmobiles across the tundra in the dark. I was not a normal elf, but everyone knew that much already. I found goggles, too, and a balaclava, both handy.

After putting those on, I chose the snowmobile most like the model in the book I'd borrowed from the library and pushed it slowly out of the parking area. It was heavy but glided easily across the snow. Once I was far enough away from the building housing most of Coal Mine Number Twenty-Five, I checked my compass, made sure I was heading in the right direction, started the engine, and sped off into the darkness.

The waning moon hung like a silver sliver in the sky, and the stars sparkled brightly in a sea of black. Even without the compass to guide me, I had the North Star. It would lead me home. Or to my untimely death. Another distinct possibility.

The wind whipped over me. I'd never been so cold in my life, but I kept going. Hours passed, and yet still, there was nothing but the same expanse. The same darkness. The same cold. I was going to die out here, but I didn't care anymore. Dying wouldn't be so bad. Living was harder. Or, at least, as far as I could tell. But I kept going, worried that if I died, Uncle Kris would too.

That thought kept me moving through the bitterly cold day of pure darkness. It was the reason I couldn't stop.

I ran out of gas sometime around 10:00 am. I could no longer feel my fingers or toes. My face was frozen, too, despite the balaclava and goggles, my eyelashes covered in ice. But I kept going. I had to keep going. Step by step. Inch by painful inch. Carrying my survival gear strapped to my back.

When my legs finally refused to move any further, I dug into my backpack with my poor, frozen fingers and pulled out the pop-up tent. When I opened it, the pathetic little thing nearly blew away. I had to sit on it to make it stop. After several tries, I got it staked to the ground and climbed inside. There was enough room for me, my backpack, and the kerosene stove.

I pulled it out and carefully lit the wick with my lighter. Minutes later, I had heat. I was so happy I could have cried —if my tear ducts weren't currently frozen.

Sadly, warming up hurt more than being cold. It was agonizing. But I wrapped myself in the emergency blanket and whimpered through the pain. I knew better than to fall asleep, so, in a way, I was grateful my appendages throbbed so badly. The pain kept me awake and staying awake kept me alive.

Once I felt brave enough to look at my fingers and toes, I did. They were pale but not black, so it seemed they were not permanently destroyed despite how much they stung. It was a Christmas miracle.

Time passed slowly as I tried to figure out my next step. If my calculations were correct, there was an outlier settlement less than five miles away. I was so close. With a bit of luck, I could make it. But I'd never been lucky.

As I sat there, considering my options, I heard the growl

REBEL WITHOUT A CLAUS

of an animal outside. It sounded like a big animal, most likely a polar bear, and it also sounded like it was close.

Great. My worst nightmare had come true. I *was* going to both freeze to death and get eaten by a polar bear—a fitting end to the sad life of Tink Holly. I only wondered which would get me first—the cold, or the bear.

I readied my knife, but it looked so ridiculously small I had to laugh. I couldn't take on a bear with this thing. Its claws would be longer than my entire blade, and the knife wasn't even sharp enough to cut through its fur.

I was a goner.

For some strange reason, I pictured my parents. They wouldn't want me to die like this. Getting eaten by a polar bear was not a great way to go. But beggars can't be choosers, and I'd run out of ideas. It was game time.

I heard the animal's approach and smelled the dank scent of its wet fur and fishy breath. I may have imagined the last part, but the creature reeked. And it was so close to my tent I heard it moving, brushing against the side—toying with me.

"Didn't your mama bear teach you not to play with your food?" I asked, my voice soft. But the bear must have heard me because it came to a stop. I heard it huffing, and knew once again, my big mouth had gotten me into trouble. Probably for the last time.

A strange sound echoed through the night, a sharp, whistling noise. The bear grunted, and I heard the whistling sound again. This time the bear let out a yelp. Of pain? It sure sounded like pain, but I couldn't be certain. It also sounded like the bear tramped off, running away from my tent, but I couldn't be sure of that either. I was too scared to look outside. All I could do was sit in my tiny tent and wait.

A few minutes later, I heard a crunching sound in the

snow, signifying the approach of something new. I thought about turning off my kerosene heater, but what was the point? Whatever was out there had already spotted me. I may as well die warm.

I waited, barely breathing, until I heard the most beautiful sound in the world. The voice of someone I knew.

"Tink. You little idiot. Are you in there? Are you okay?"

It was Jax. He was here. He'd found me.

I let out a cry of pure joy and frantically unzipped the door of the tent. I crawled out, landing in a heap on the ground. I must have passed out because I woke up in a much larger, much warmer place—some kind of hunting cabin—wrapped in a sleeping bag. I wasn't alone in the sleeping bag, either. Jax was in there with me. And we both seemed to be naked, or at least partially naked. From what I could tell when I did a brief exploration, we had our underpants on, and I wore thick socks, but nothing else.

"Mr. Grayson. Would you mind explaining what happened to my clothing? It appears I misplaced it."

He laughed, his mouth resting against my hair. "I had to get you warmed up as quickly as possible. You were nearly frozen when I found you." He leaned back a tiny bit, his eyes scanning my face. "You've been asleep for hours. Are you injured?"

Shaking my head, I wrapped my arms around his neck and held him as closely as I possibly could. "There was a polar bear, and I ran out of gas but don't worry. We're five miles away from a large outlier community. We can make it. I know we can make it."

"I'm sure we can," he said, his voice oddly strained. "Since I have a state-of-the-art, all-terrain sled waiting outside. But I may not survive if you choke me to death."

"Sorry," I said, loosening my grip slightly so he could

breathe. I put my palm against his cheek. "Are you really here?"

He touched his forehead to mine. "I really am. Oh, Tink. You nearly scared the life out of me."

"I nearly scared the life out of me, too." I clung to him, loving the way his skin felt against mine. But there were questions I needed to ask. "How did you find me?" If Jax could find me, whoever was controlling Cookie could have found me, too.

He held me close, one hand stroking my bare back. "Well, it wasn't hard to track you once I found out where you'd been hiding out for the last month or so. Why didn't you contact me? Why didn't you tell me where you were?"

"Hiding out? I wasn't hiding out," I spluttered. "I was sent away, and had no way to contact you, or Win, or anyone."

"You considered contacting Win?" Jax's voice was as cold as the great outdoors.

"I didn't consider contacting anyone. I couldn't. I didn't have my cell phone or any of my things. But I also wasn't sure you wanted me to contact you. You left, after all. They told me you did, and I understood why you'd leave. I was sort of persona non grata. I didn't want to drag you down with me."

"I hardly left willingly," he said, making a tsking sound. "I was shipped back to Elf Central. Put on a plane and told to report to headquarters immediately. How much do you remember about what happened the night you were drugged?"

"I was drugged?" I asked, wanting to believe him so badly. "I didn't take whatever it was on my own?"

"Of course not," he said. "Why would you think such a thing? We both got sick. Someone put something in our drinks. Whatever they gave me made me ill, but what they gave you could have been fatal."

"Candicocane."

"Yes. I used the narzipan you had in your purse and brought you to the hospital. Thankfully, the narzipan worked pretty quickly. I stayed with you in the hospital that night and the next morning got my summons to return to Elf Central. The summons was delivered by members of what I thought were your uncle's secret service team. They didn't exactly give me an option. I had to leave, and since you were safely recovering in the hospital, I left you a note and took off. When I got there, however, I discovered it was a ruse. No one had summoned me back. My passport was revoked, and I couldn't get back to the North Pole until I resolved everything. It was all a big 'misunderstanding,' but it took weeks to correct. Weeks of not hearing from you. Weeks of not knowing what was going on. I tried calling everyone, including your uncle. I reached his assistant first and got nowhere with him."

"Topper?"

"Yes. Topper." He practically spit out the name. "He said any information regarding you, or a member of your family, was extremely confidential and could not be shared. But when he mentioned your family, I remembered the business card your uncle had given me—the one with his direct line. I called him, and do you know what he said?"

I shook my head. "What?"

"He was told you and I ran off together and were living in the Darklands. When he tried to track you down, he got a text he thought came from you asking that he leave you alone and let you lead your own life. I got one, too, saying you wanted nothing to do with me, and the whole investigation we conducted was nothing but a hoax perpetrated by me, a dark elf who hated Christmas. But I knew it didn't come from you."

"How? Because I know how much you like Christmas?"

He let out a soft laugh. "No. Because whoever sent it misspelled 'investigation.' You are far too clever for that. Your uncle agreed, and we launched our own inquiry, involving people on a need-to-know basis only. Your uncle was furious, and wanted to get to the bottom of this, which was why Noelle and Win are the only others involved." He said Win's name with a sneer, and I could easily imagine my ex was the last person Jax had wanted to go to for help, but it seemed like he'd had few options.

"Win isn't that bad."

"He is not," said Jax, still acting grumpy. It was so adorable, I fought the urge to smile.

"What happened next?"

"Noelle contacted the hospital from Florida and convinced them to send a copy of your discharge papers, but there was no record of who signed for your release. That seemed odd. One of her nursing friends remembered seeing you leave with two uniformed men in an unmarked vehicle. Win used his connections to find CCTV footage of you leaving the hospital, which was somewhat clever of him. Your uncle figured out who those men were and questioned them. That's how we found out you'd been sent to a coal mine, but they conveniently forgot which one."

"Oh, elf me."

"Exactly. Do you know there are fifty coal mines? When we asked for information, no one responded, so I had to visit each one personally." He grabbed my hand and brought it to his lips, kissing it softly. "I was halfway through the list when I spoke with Mr. Fiddle-dee Doo. And also the lovely and yet hungover Mince Mingle."

I snorted. "Mincie does not know how to hold her moonshine."

"Obviously not."

I sniffed, suddenly emotional. "Thank you, Jax. For coming after me. For taking care of the polar bear."

He frowned, feigning confusion. "What polar bear? I would never have harmed a threatened species. Not even with a dart gun. I swear. There are laws against that sort of thing, and I would not want to get into trouble."

"Well, thank you," I said, whispering the words against his lips as I kissed him. "Anyway."

That single kiss turned into another, and another, and soon Jax was on top of me, and I was in the process of ridding him of his skivvies when my poor, numb brain finally defrosted and came back to life.

"Jiminy Christmas." I wiggled out from beneath him and sat up so fast we bumped heads. "Ow. Sorry, Jax."

"It's okay," he said, rubbing his forehead. "But what's wrong?"

I crawled around the cabin, searching for my clothing. Thankfully, Jax had placed my things next to the fireplace to dry.

"It's my uncle Kris. He's in danger." I threw on my top before grabbing my pants. "Mince Mingle documented all of it. And there is something else, too." I pushed my hair out of the way so I could search for my boots. One was in the corner. It took me ten solid seconds to realize I was sitting on the other. As I tugged it on, I shot a look at Jax, still all sleepy and sexy and nearly naked. Unable to stop myself, I crawled over to him, kissing him firmly on the lips before I continued. "Guess who was on the ski team with Evergreen Berry?"

He frowned, his gaze snapping from my lips to my eyes as he tried to figure out what I was telling him. "Who?"

"Frank Yummy," I said, wishing I could curl back up in the sleeping bag with Jax but knowing I didn't have any time to waste. "Let's go. You and I have a job to do. We have to save Christmas—and my uncle—and we're running out of time."

CHAPTER TWENTY-ONE

On our way back to the dome, exactly forty-eight hours until Christmas Eve, Jax filled me in on more things I'd missed. During the time I spent at the coal mines, whoever was behind this managed to cover their tracks, and our investigation had slammed to a halt. After making a few calls to be sure my uncle was safe, Jax gave me the rundown.

"The barrels we saw with the residue inside are gone. The shed contains standard barrels full of nothing but reindeer feed now. The sample we gave the police." He shot me a sidelong glance. "The one on your...uh...underclothing has disappeared from the evidence room."

"Someone stole my bra?"

"I'm afraid so."

"I liked that bra," I said with more irritation than I intended.

"I'm sorry for your loss."

His apology, given with Jax's usual sincerity, made me giggle. Here I was bundled in blankets, safe and warm and not somewhere in the digestive tract of a polar bear right now, all thanks to him. And yet, I had the nerve to complain about a missing bra.

"You're right. I'm acting stupid."

He placed a hand over mine. "I wouldn't say that at all. You've been thrust into a horrible situation, all thanks to me, but you've handled it beautifully."

"I'm used to things going wrong," I said. "It's the story of my life."

"Through no fault of your own."

"Well, through some fault of my own."

Before we set out, I had a long phone conversation with my uncle. He'd reacted in his usual way—calm, methodical, and patient—but I sensed the tiniest bubble of anger beneath his Santa Claus demeanor. He promised he would find out the truth but wouldn't be able to do it himself until Christmas was over. He put Topper in charge. As usual.

"My uncle insists the thing with Topper was all a huge misunderstanding. He said Topper was concerned for my safety after the incident with Noelle. When Nippy got shot, Topper saw things escalating out of control, and he wanted me as far away as possible from the whole situation."

"And you believe him?" Jax's tone gave away nothing, but I knew him well enough at this point to see he didn't buy it.

"No, I don't. It was a move to protect my uncle's image from the scandal of Tink Holly."

"That sounds more likely." We were approaching the entrance to the dome. Jax grabbed our passports and readied them as he spoke. "What do you suggest we do now?"

I blew out a breath. "Well, first, I have an angry grand-mother to deal with. Want to come? For emotional support purposes?"

Jax handed the passports to the agent at the gate to stamp them. Seconds later, we were heading toward Morningstar Drive. "No, thank you. I've never met your grandmother, but I'd rather face a firing squad at dawn."

Jax wasn't too far off. He stayed long enough to meet Grandma Gingersnap, accept her profuse thanks for my rescue, and then took off. She was nice to *him*. He said he had paperwork to do regarding my recent tundra experience. I didn't believe him.

As soon as he left, my grandmother did the one thing she knew would bother me the most. She cried—a lot. In fact, she sobbed.

"I was so worried, Tink."

I could deal with her anger. I could take her disappointment. I could handle all the snark and guilt she chose to lay on me, but against her tears, I was utterly defenseless.

"I'm sorry." I patted her back awkwardly as she clung to me. "Really sorry. Not that I had the means to contact you anyway, but I thought Uncle Kris sent me to the coal mine, and I was so ashamed. I didn't want you to think less of me than you already do."

"Think less of you? What are you talking about?"

"Well, I know I'm not exactly the granddaughter you always wished for, but I will try to be better. I swear."

She leaned back, hands on my upper arms, an astonished look on her tearstained face. "Is that what you believe? Because it's not true at all. Do you know what I see when I look at you?" I shook my head, and she continued. "A world of possibilities, Tink. And a wealth of untapped potential."

I stared at her in confusion. "But I'm a screwup. I ruin everything I touch. I hurt everyone I care about."

"The only way you could hurt me would be if something happened to you. Don't you understand? I've already lost so much. Your parents. Your grandfather. I can't lose you, too, Tink. I couldn't bear it."

I held her as she cried, promised to be more careful, and let her make me a huge breakfast—purely for her benefit, of course. And when she insisted on blueberry pancakes, I allowed her to do it out of the kindness of my heart. Well, that and because my grandmother made the best pancakes in the whole world.

As we were finishing our meal, the doorbell sounded. To my chagrin, it was the Snow family. Angel, Winnie, Win, and even Duke, who snapped at me as soon as he saw me in the kitchen. I stood up, mostly to get away from the evil Yorkie.

"A dog always knows," said Mrs. Snow under her breath, but Win shushed her.

"Now is not the time, Mother." He turned to me, pulling me into a giant hug. Win gave the best hugs, and it made me remember all the times we'd been together and all the memories we shared. I sighed, leaning into it, enjoying the strength and familiarity of him. It would be so easy to go on holding him, to return to the way things were, but in my heart, I knew there was no going back.

I disentangled myself and stepped a few feet away. "Thanks for helping me," I said. "When I was sort of kidnapped or whatever."

He shoved his hands into the pockets of his pants. "I'll always be here for you, Tink."

"The same goes for you. Not that you'd ever be in this sort of situation."

"Of course he wouldn't," said Mrs. Snow with a huff. "My Win isn't that kind of boy."

"I'm warning you for the last time," said Win, sending her a death glare. "You need to stop it right now. We're here to apologize."

"For what?" I asked, genuinely confused.

"My parents," Win said, his voice filled with anger. "Have something to tell you, Tink. Something they should have mentioned weeks ago."

I looked at Win. He looked at me. My grandmother looked at both of us while Mr. and Mrs. Snow looked at the ground. Duke looked at Grandma Gingersnap's giant potted plant, and there was something in his beady eyes that told me he hoped to get his revenge for the time I accidentally tinkled on him.

"Perhaps we should all sit for this," said Grandma Gingersnap.

Win gave her a grateful nod. "Perhaps you're right."

It took nearly twenty minutes and several interruptions by Mrs. Snow, Mr. Snow, and Duke (when he had to go "tinkles," as Mrs. Snow called it—thankfully not on my grandmother's plant), but eventually, we heard the whole story. It turns out Win's stuffy, conservative parents were members of the Ho, Ho Club, the place where only the most elite members of North Pole society went for kinky sex. And reindeer encounters. When I thought of it, I nearly threw up my blueberry pancakes. But Mrs. Snow managed to look prim and proper even while discussing something as bizarre as their involvement in a sex club.

"We're *social* members, you see."

Mr. Snow agreed. "It's a great place for networking."

I tried to picture Mrs. Snow dressed as a dominatrix in black leather and Mr. Snow as the sub. It seemed like an insult to the BDSM community. I knew plenty of elves who practiced that lifestyle, and none of them were in any way as cruel as these two.

"To make a long story short, someone had photos of my parents taken at the club. In exchange for not going public with those photos, they asked for a favor."

Mr. Snow was sweating. "It seemed harmless..."

"It was not harmless," said Win, so mad he shook.

I looked from Win to his father and back to Win again. "What was it?"

"My dad was a mule. He dropped off those chocolates at your front door."

My grandmother gasped and put a hand to her chest. "The ones that nearly killed Noelle?"

"Yes." Win shot me an apologetic look, his heart in his eyes.

Grandma Gingersnap's expression went from shock to pure, unadulterated fury. She nearly vibrated with anger, and her normally cultured voice came out as a growl. "Winter Snow. I cannot believe you did that. If Tink had eaten those candies, she would have died. And Angel—you are just as bad. How could you let that happen? Over a few embarrassing photos? You've known her since she was a baby, and yet you were part of a plot to have her killed?"

"They were," said Win, swallowing hard as he stared at the floor. "And they nearly succeeded."

"Now hold on a second," said Mr. Snow. "I had no idea what was in those chocolates. I would never have done it if I had. I swear."

I stared at Win's parents, wanting to believe them, but

they had to have known the whole thing was fishy. And judging by the fact they couldn't meet my eyes, it seemed they had a lot to feel guilty about.

As they argued with my grandmother, who was rightfully upset, I stared at my hands. I'd known the Snows since I was a girl. I'd dated their son for almost a decade. They were like a second family to me, albeit a second family who despised me.

"Why?" I asked, my voice soft, but it caused the conversation to come to a halt. "Why do you hate me so much?"

"I have no idea what you're talking about," said Mrs. Snow, stroking Duke lovingly as she spoke. She could give affection to a mean Yorkie dog, but she'd never even said so much as a kind word to me.

"I overheard the two of you arguing the night Nippy got shot. I was by your back door."

Mrs. Snow bristled. "You were eavesdropping?"

"Not on purpose. I was cutting through your yard." I'd been sneaking through it but chose my words carefully. "And I heard you say 'the girl' deserved it after what she did to your son. Did you mean I deserved to die?"

She seemed momentarily stunned. I'd never seen Mrs. Snow at a loss for words before.

Remembering something else, I lifted a finger. "And why did you mention my mother? That was weird, too."

Mrs. Snow and my grandmother exchanged a long look. I had no idea what it was about, but Duke chose that moment to pee on the potted plant. Duke's tinkling distracted all of us. By the time we finished cleaning up Duke's mess (and let me say he had a large bladder for such a tiny dog), I lost track of what we'd been discussing. Frankly speaking, I was also too exhausted, both emotionally and physically, to care anymore.

"Never mind. It's irrelevant because you're irrelevant. But I'd like to go back to the part about how your husband nearly killed my roommate and what you plan to do about it."

Mrs. Snow opened her mouth as if she wanted to say something else, but Win sent her a look that stopped her in her tracks. "We're on our way to the police," he said, his expression wary and yet resigned. "They'll confess what they've done. But we wanted to apologize to you first since you were the one targeted. We'll have to call Noelle to apologize since she's still in Florida, but we plan to do that next."

"And?"

"And I expect you'll press charges, and my parents will go to jail—as they deserve."

As I watched them, I wondered when Win had become the adult in his family. Maybe he always had been. "I'm not sure what Noelle will want to do, but I'm not pressing charges, Win."

Mr. and Mrs. Snow let out a sigh of relief. "See? I told you she could be logical," Mr. Snow said. "No matter what others might say, she isn't stupid."

I ignored the last part. "But I can't promise anything on Noelle's behalf. Prepare yourselves."

"Oh, we are," said Mr. Snow, nodding so excitedly his chin wobbled. "Which is another reason we needed to speak with you. In order to hold it over our heads, it appears the person bribing us sent copies of the photos here as a precaution. They knew your grandmother was away on a cruise, but they didn't seem to know you were staying here. Once you went to the coal mines—"

Mrs. Snow muttered something along the lines of, "Where she belongs," but got a sharp nudge from her husband.

Mr. Snow continued. "Well, I used the key you'd left at our house, Gingersnap. I searched everywhere for the photos but never found them, so it must have been a bluff."

"Let me get this straight. You were part of a plot to assassinate my only granddaughter. You put her roommate, an innocent young woman, into the hospital. And now you're telling me you broke into my house, and searched through my belongings, and yet you want my help in order to get out of a situation entirely of your own making?" asked my grandmother, lifting one eyebrow in a way that told me she was about to crush Mr. Snow like a bug. "How dare you, Winter?"

He swallowed hard. "Wh...what are you going to do to us?"

"Following the lead of my generous and far too kind granddaughter, I'll do nothing legally—nothing at all except change my locks and never speak to either one of you again. Oh, and I will tell my son what you've done. Mark my words, he will not be as forgiving."

Mr. Snow paled. Mrs. Snow's eyes bulged. "You wouldn't."

"Oh, but I will." My grandmother turned to me. "Now, let's get to the bottom of this. Darling, did I get any packages while I was on my trip? I didn't see any on the bench in the mudroom."

"*On* the bench? I thought you wanted them *in* the bench."

The seat of the bench in my grandmother's mudroom lifted and had room for storage inside. When Mr. Snow's face fell, I recognized immediately he had not looked there.

Grandma Gingersnap put her hand on mine. "Would you grab those packages now, please?"

I got up and sped toward the mudroom. Lifting the seat

of the bench, I pulled out three small packages. Two were books, but the third was a large manilla envelope with no return address. My grandmother's name and address were scrawled on the outside in thick, black marker in a barely legible script.

When I gave it to my grandmother, she peeked inside, wrinkling her nose in disgust. "Well, it was not a bluff, Winnie."

Mr. Snow reached for the envelope, but Grandma Gingersnap kept it out of his grasp. "These will stay right here. And the next time you say or do anything to harm my granddaughter, the next time you or your horrible wife insult her in any way, shape, or form, I will make sure these are on the front page of the *North Pole Gazette*. And don't think I won't do it. Now, apologize to Tink and get out of my house. I never want to see either of you again."

"Gingersnap," said Mrs. Snow in her sweetest and most ingratiating voice. "Surely you aren't serious—"

"Oh, but I am. Apologize to my granddaughter. Now."

They did as she asked, albeit reluctantly, and left the house, with Duke growling at me the whole time. Win, however, stayed behind for a few minutes.

"Mrs. Holly," he said, his voice thick with emotion. "I'm so sorry."

She waved his apology away. "Not your fault, Win. None of it was ever your fault." She pulled him into a hug and kissed him on the cheek. "I'm tired, and I'm sure you have much to discuss. Goodnight. I love you both." Giving us a small smile, she turned and walked up the stairs, leaving us alone together.

He stared at me for a long moment. "You should press charges."

I shook my head. "No, I could never do that to you.

You're in line to be the next Santa, and you'll be a great one. I won't be the reason it doesn't happen for you, Win. I care about you way too much."

Without another word, he kissed me on the lips—softly, sadly—and left. I flopped onto the couch as the grandfather clock in the corner clanged. It was only ten o'clock in the morning. It had already been one of the longest days of my life, but it was far from over. As the wheels spun in my head, I thought about the chocolate and the Ho, Ho Club, and the drugs, and suddenly things clicked into place. Grabbing my grandmother's cell phone, I called Jax.

"Come and get me," I said. "Now. We need to talk to Frank."

Frank was at work inside the reindeer barn, exactly where I expected him to be. He had no idea I'd seen Evergreen Berry's photo in his apartment. It was the piece of the puzzle that made the rest all fall into place.

Joy had figured it out. Somehow, she'd found out where her brother had been getting his drugs—the drugs that killed him. That was why she quit her job, why she asked to be reassigned to the reindeer department. And there was only one connecting factor between Ever and this place.

Frank Yummy.

It had been staring me right in the face, but it wasn't until I recognized the handwriting on the envelope containing the pictures of Winnie and Angel Snow, Frank's messy, oddly tilted handwriting, that it finally clicked.

When Frank was a child, someone had forced him to write with his right hand, even though he was born left-handed. He did everything else with his left hand, including batting for baseball, dealing cards, and even pleasuring himself. I knew the last one because I walked in on him once when we were younger. The left-handedness was a little thing, a fluke, but it brought the whole picture into focus for me.

Well, most of it, at least.

Frank smiled when he saw me as if nothing at all was wrong. "Hey, Tink. What are you doing here? I heard you were out of town. Did you come to keep me company?"

I stared at him hard. Was that the way he planned to play it? Like nothing had happened?

Although all signs pointed to the fact that Frank most likely drugged me, a tiny part of me hoped it wasn't true. Or maybe it was an accident. Or maybe...sadly, I couldn't come up with any more ideas. The truth of the matter was, even if Frank hadn't drugged me, he'd left me when I'd barely been able to stand. If Jax hadn't been there, things could have ended up even worse.

I didn't respond to Frank's question immediately. Instead, I gazed around, taking stock of the situation. The whole area was strangely quiet. The reindeer were all resting for Christmas Eve, and the other members of the assistance team were having their annual luncheon celebration, a special treat from Santa. They looked forward to it all year. And when we'd drawn straws to see who would have to miss out this year and stay behind with the reindeer, Frank drew the short straw. He'd also drawn the short straw the year before. Frank was incredibly unlucky when it came to luncheons. And drawing straws. When I noticed Frank still awaited my answer, I let out a sigh.

"No, Frank," I said. "I'm here for a different reason."

Unbeknownst to Frank, Jax stood outside, close enough to get there quickly if I needed him, but far enough away that Frank couldn't see him. Jax had called members of his Elf Enforcement team for backup, not wanting to involve local law enforcement if he could help it. He trusted Officer Pudding, but not everyone else, which was understandable. His team was on their way, but we couldn't wait for them. If Frank sensed the noose tightening, he might split, and we'd be right back where we started.

I pulled the envelope out of my purse, the one with Frank's handwriting on the front. I saw him flinch, ever so slightly, but enough that I knew I was right. I'd played poker with Frank since I was a kid, so I knew all his tells. The problem was, he knew mine as well.

"You figured it out, huh?" he said with a laugh as he used a pitchfork to toss dry hay into a feeding trough for the reindeer. "But be honest now, Angel and Winnie deserved it."

He made a good point, but I was not going to let him charm me this time. "They deserved it, but I didn't."

Frank paused his hay tossing. "What do you mean? If I had photos of you, I wouldn't use them to blackmail you. First of all, you have no money. Secondly, I would keep the photos for myself. Now that would be something to see." He was trying to bluff again, trying to distract me, but I saw the guilt in his eyes as clear as day.

"You were my friend, Frank. I don't know why you did this." I shook my head sadly. "But it's not only about me. How could you do that to poor Joy? And Noelle? And Nippy? I was there when you shot Nippy, by the way. I saw it happen."

A noise outside made me turn my head. It was a loud whack, followed by a soft thump.

"Jax—are you okay?" I asked. When he didn't call out to

me or say anything, I knew something terrible had happened.

"Jiminy Christmas," I said and turned back to Frank in time to see him swinging the wooden part of the pitchfork toward my head like a bat. Left-handed.

CHAPTER TWENTY-TWO

I woke to the sound of arguing, the smell of reindeer sweat, and the sensation of warmth coming from a stinky kerosene heater located somewhere close by. I tried to open my eyes but couldn't. They felt like lead, and for a second, I panicked, largely due to confusion and the distinctive scent of kerosene. I thought maybe I was still stranded in the tiny tent in the snow, but as my brain slowly awakened, taking in the voices, and the reindeer stench, I realized that was not the case.

Gosh, I hated reindeer.

So far this week, I'd nearly frozen to death, almost got eaten by a polar bear, and learned my ex's parents tried to kill me. Now, it seemed likely I had a concussion. And the person who gave it to me, freaking Frank Yummy, was speaking right now

"Why do we have to kill her? I get that the dark elf needs to go. But—"

Someone cut Frank off in mid-sentence. They spoke in such a low voice I could barely make out the words. "It's your fault. I told you no selling on the North Pole. If you'd listened to me, none of this would ever have happened."

I frowned. The voice sounded familiar, but my poor addled mind couldn't place it. It hurt to even think at this point. I nearly moaned in pain but didn't want Frank and his friend to know I could hear them.

Frank spoke again. "Hey, the reindeer tranquilizer worked at first. Well, until we added too much, but it was an accident."

"Because of your 'accident,' things got out of control. You're going to have to answer for this. I protected you as much as I could."

The voices faded slightly, and even though I strained to hear them, I couldn't. Sensing a warm body on my right, I managed to open my eyes a crack and saw Jax's unconscious form on the ground next to me. His forehead and part of his face were covered in blood. I tried to reassure myself head wounds tended to bleed a lot, but Jax did not look good. I wanted to reach over and touch him, but my hands were tied. Literally. With rope. And on closer inspection, I saw poor Jax was tied up, too. Frank was definitely getting coal in his stocking for this one.

"She's awake," said Frank. "I saw her move."

Crap. Why couldn't I learn the art of subtle movement?

"You didn't hit her hard enough. You're such a fecking softie, Frank."

There it was again—the outlier word. But this time, spoken in a gentle and almost teasing way, and I recognized the voice immediately.

"Sugar?" I asked, turning my head toward her, too shocked to pretend I was still unconscious.

"Hey, Tink." Sugar must have come straight from work.

She still wore her Happypie's Hamburgers uniform. "I told you to go to Florida. I wish you'd listened."

I sat up and immediately regretted my actions since it caused the matter inside my skull to swish around like a boat on a stormy sea. "Ow." I winced, trying to work past the pain to fully open my eyes. I managed with one. The other refused to cooperate, but one was sufficient to allow me to make out my surroundings. The kerosene heater sat on the floor only a few feet away from me. The elves used them to warm up all the private reindeer stalls. At least I wasn't cold, a small consolation.

"What's going on?" I asked. "Why did you hit me?"

Frank had the decency to look ashamed. "You left me with no choice, Tink. I'm sorry."

Sugar rolled her eyes. "Don't apologize, Frankie. We love Tink, but she's a domer, like the others, which means she deserves it. They all deserve it. Don't forget who and what she is—not ever."

"I deserved to get whacked in the head? What did I do, Sugar? I've never harmed either of you, and neither has Jax." Before Sugar could answer, I heard a loud snort. Now I knew exactly which reindeer's stall I was in—Comet. Great.

"Hey, Tinklebelle Holly. I bet you wish you'd been nicer to me now, don't you?" He turned his big, brown eyes to Sugar. "We're going to have fun tonight, aren't we, Sugs?"

"We sure are." Sugar nuzzled Comet in a way that seemed vaguely...well, I couldn't exactly call it sexual, but it seemed romantic. Or at least abnormally affectionate.

Sugar caught me watching them. "Comet and I grew up together, on the same reindeer ranch." She pulled sugar cubes from her pocket and held them out to Comet. "He was my best friend. He still is."

"How nice for you."

I shifted slightly, trying to put myself between Jax and Sugar as I stalled for time, testing the ropes on my wrists. The knots were tight, but I had room to wiggle my hands and turn them slightly, and I knew it would be enough. I had, after all, practiced this back in the coal mines using the book on magic tricks. I didn't know how far away our backup was right now, but, with any luck, I might be able to Harry Houdini my way out of this. The problem was, I also had to get Jax out of here as well. To do so, I needed all the time I could get.

"It *was* nice, but our friendship was frowned upon. Can you believe it? A lonely girl and a lonely little reindeer. Where is the harm in that?"

"I don't get it. Why couldn't you and Comet be friends?"

"Are you seriously so clueless? Surely, you're aware interspecies relationships are taboo. Hey, even intertribal ones are frowned upon. How would you react if someone said you couldn't be with him?" She tilted her head to indicate Jax's prone form. "What if they told you, you were wrong for even considering such a thing?"

"I can't imagine," I said, playing with the rope as discreetly as possible. "But I'm not judging you. Live and let live. That's my motto."

Sugar laughed. The sound sent shivers down my spine. "A *Holly* who doesn't judge. How rich." She wiped a tear of mirth off her cheek.

I honestly had no idea what my old shake-making buddy meant but decided to let it go. Instead, I focused on her as I tried to buy some time.

"What happened?" I asked. "I'd really like to know."

Sugar continued petting Comet, a rapt expression on

her face. "It's a tale as old as time. No one cares about love. It's always about one person finding a way to feel like they are better than someone else. Reindeer are not good enough for elves. Outliers are not good enough for domers. And no one is good enough for a Holly, a Snow, or an Ivy, let alone a Tannenbaum or a Kringle. It's like a caste system, and we were always on the outside—in more ways than one."

"But my mom was your friend."

"When it suited her."

"And you were always so kind to me."

She laughed. "How could I not be kind to you? You were such a screwup, kiddo. Like a disaster waiting to happen. Mistake after mistake after mistake. Which was why you were the perfect scapegoat."

"What do you mean?"

Comet snickered. "You may as well tell her, Sugs. It's not like she's going to *RAT* on us, right?"

With a giggle, Sugar rubbed his nose with hers. As I wondered how she could handle the stench, she spoke again.

"When your friend started investigating our...business interests."

"Your drug ring?"

She gave me a slight smile. "Oh, it's so much more than drugs. It stretches far beyond a bit of candicocane. But we figured eventually someone would catch on, so we thought we'd better have a patsy lined up to take the fall. You know in case everything went South Pole."

"And you chose me as the patsy?"

"You're the perfect choice. Wealthy, troubled girl. Tragic past. Would anyone truly be surprised if you were caught doing something illegal, honey buns? You have a record a mile long."

"Not all of it was my fault." Jax stirred next to me, so I spoke in a louder voice. "But back to you, how did you do it? I saw the paperwork for how you got the shipments out, the bills of lading, and such, but the trail went cold. It was never delivered anywhere."

"And that is the most brilliant part. We used the reindeer. Show her, what you can do, sweetie." She smiled at Comet, who snorted before rising a few feet off the ground.

He was flying, but how? "He has his tag on. He can't fly with his tag on."

The tags kept the reindeer earthbound. Although members of the reindeer assistance team were authorized to remove them, it was a process. It required paperwork, two signatures, and a small machine that was fingerprint encoded. Every time a tag was removed, it was monitored and electronically recorded. And if someone removed it improperly, an alarm sounded, and it caused a great deal of pain to the animal involved. But Sugar stood in front of me, calm as could be, and slipped the tag off with one hand. There were no sounds. No alarms. No cries of pain from Comet. Just a smirk from Sugar at the look on my face.

"Oh, you mean this? It's fake, which was how we could send our product all over the elven world and the human world, too. Easy peasy."

"Lemon squeezy," chimed in Comet as he returned to the ground. "My girl is no dummy. She knew who to bribe and who to trick. And she also has dirt on everyone."

"Nothing is ever easy peasy." I frowned at Sugar. "I know that for a fact."

A bell sounded outside—reindeer roll call. The reindeer lined up three times a day to be counted, and the times varied. If any of the reindeer didn't show up, an alarm sounded, and a signal was sent both to the entire reindeer department and to Santa himself.

With a curse, Sugar put Comet's ear tag back in place. "Take him out," she said to Frank, handing him Comet's reins. "It'll only take five minutes. I'll grab what I need from my sled, and we can finish up here."

As Frank led the giant buck out of the stall, Sugar shot me a look. "Frank will be right outside the door. Don't try anything, Tink. You know it won't work. You know you'll mess up. Because that's what you do, isn't it?"

And with those parting words, she left Jax and me alone. I waited a long moment, counting in my head, making sure she was gone. Her words, and the way she assumed I'd fail, would have hit me like a physical blow not long ago. But I was a different person now. Sugar had no idea.

"Jax," I said his name softly as I struggled with the knot tying my hands together. "Jax. Are you okay?"

He let out a quiet grunt in response, wincing in pain. He was in bad shape.

"I need to get you out of here. Can you open your eyes? Come on, Jaxy."

"Don't. Call. Me. Jaxy." With effort, he opened his eyes, but he seemed dazed and confused. "Where are we? What happened?"

"We're in Comet's stall. I'll explain later, but we're in a lot of danger, and we have to move quickly." I gave the ropes on my wrists a final yank and let out a tiny squeal when I managed to get them off. I set to work on Jax's wrists, but those knots had been tied tighter. "We have to go now."

"I can't," he said, swallowing hard. "Save yourself, Tink. Get out of here while you can."

"I'm not leaving you, Jax."

"You must," he insisted. "It would take a miracle for both of us to make it, and miracles appear to be in short supply right now."

"You're wrong," I said, still pulling at the knots binding his hands. "Miracle is my middle name."

He frowned. "You're kidding. It's Miracle?"

"Tinklebelle Miracle Holly. I can't believe it took you so long to figure it out."

"Well, it suits you." He gave me a sad smile. "But look, Tink, there is something I need to tell you. Since we're about to die."

"No one is going to die." I listened to the roll call. *Blitzen. Comet. Cupid.* "Don't be a drama queen."

He let out a laugh and winced as if even that pained him. Whoever had hurt Jax—and my money was on Comet —had really done a number on him. I was angry now, angrier than I'd ever been. But I had to focus.

"You're so beautiful," Jax said dreamily. "And sparkly. Like a star. But you're funny, too. And smart. One might call you brilliant. You'd make a great Elf Enforcement officer someday. You're a natural. And did I mention how beautiful you are?"

Dancer, Dasher, Donner.

"You're super sweet, Jax, but you're hallucinating right now, and we don't have time for this." I freed him from the ropes with a final yank and pulled on his hands, struggling to get him to his feet. It was like lifting a bag of wet sand. I couldn't do it.

I leaned over him and tried to get him to move. I grabbed his shoulders and gave him a shake. "Come on. You have to try." I didn't know I was crying until one of my tears landed on his cheek.

Prancer.

"Fudgity fudge cakes." I was looking around the paddock, wondering what I could possibly use to haul Jax out of here, when the automated system called out Rudolph's name.

Rudolph.

We were almost at the end of the list. I needed to do something quickly, but I was running out of options. The only option I would not entertain was leaving Jax.

Rudolph...Rudolph...Rudolph.

I heard his name called again and again and again. A reindeer not showing up for roll call? In all my months of working here, it had never happened. I frowned, wondering what was going on, and that's when the alarm sounded.

"Feck."

Frank rushed back into the stall, Comet right behind him. Sugar came in through the opposite door, carrying a small cooler. I kept my hands in my lap, pretending to still be tied up, but the alarm gave me hope. Someone would be coming soon. I needed to keep both of us alive until they got here.

"What's going on?" asked Sugar, yelling to be heard over the noise.

"Rudolph is missing. It set off the alarm." He slammed a button on the wall, and the alarm went silent, but the sounds of reindeer fighting drifted in from outside. Maybe the alarm had upset them. Even Comet acted unsettled as he chuffed, eyes bugging out.

Sugar tried to soothe the frightened animal as she spoke to her nephew. "You turned it off. It's okay now. Good work, Frank."

"It doesn't matter. Whenever a reindeer does not show up for roll call, the alarm system sends an emergency notification to Santa and the team. It also continues to broadcast the warning internally, even though we can't hear it. We need to get out of here."

He made a move to leave, but his aunt stopped him. "We have to take care of these two first."

She reached into her cooler and pulled out a Happypie's milkshake cup, like the one I'd seen on the ground next to Joy's body. I stared at it in horror.

"This is how you killed Joy, isn't it? Murder by milkshake. I saw the cup on the sidewalk."

Frank looked at his aunt in disbelief. "You did it on purpose? You told me it was an accident."

Sugar pulled herself up to her full height. She was small, but mighty. "I had no choice. Because you were careless, Joy Berry figured out the drugs were coming from here. She followed her brother and realized this was where he'd purchased his drugs. But she never knew the reindeer were in on it, watching, and listening. Thanks to Comet we got to her before she blabbed to the dark elf. If we hadn't, it would have ruined all our hard work."

Frank put his face in his hands. "She was Ever's baby sister."

"We had no choice, Frankie. Like we had no choice with the chocolates. You're in this as deep as I am, and you need to grow up."

Frank didn't seem comfortable with the current situation. He crossed his arms over his chest, unable to look me in the eye, a muscle working in his jaw. He didn't want to kill me. I could tell.

I heard shuffling outside the door and a slight chuffing noise. I recognized the chuff. It was Rudolph, the only reindeer I trusted. At least there'd be a witness to my death and Jax's. I didn't hold out much hope for anything more. Rudy was half the size of Comet, and more a lover than a fighter. What could he do to help?

But Frank was more of a lover, too. I knew that from personal experience since he'd nearly been my lover on more than one occasion.

He ran a hand through his hair, his eyes darting back and forth in a panic. I thought he might cry, so I made one last attempt at reason. "There is nothing you can do to help Joy, and you can't take back shooting Nippy, but there is no reason to kill me. I'm your friend. I've always been your friend."

He frowned in confusion. "Nippy? Nippy Nibblewrap? What are you talking about—"

Sugarplum cut him off. "Stop talking and hold her down. It'll be easier that way. She won't suffer as much."

I shot a look at Frank, hoping he'd change his mind. "Frank. Please. It doesn't have to be like this."

Sadly, loyalty to his crazy aunt won out over allegiance to me. "I'm sorry, Tink. I really am. But there is nothing I can do. My aunt is right." He muttered a curse. "I wish things could be different. I never meant for it to be this way. I swear."

Comet snorted. "Kill her already. I'm bored."

Sugar approached with the shake. "Time's up, Tink," she said. "I made your favorite—chocolate raspberry with extra whipped cream and a cherry on top. I know how much you love having a cherry on top. Frank, stop dawdling and come here. We'll take care of her first, then the dark elf."

At that moment, Rudolph burst into the stall, placing himself between us. "Not on my watch," he said, breathing hard.

Comet and Sugar took one look at each other and

laughed. I guess I could see why. Rudolph was tiny, and he currently had a bright red bow around his neck. What he didn't have, however, was an anti-flying tag. I might not be able to save myself at this point, but I could save Jax, and I had seconds to do it.

I jumped to my feet, pulling Jax with me. I'm not sure how I managed it since I had zero upper body strength. I promised myself if I survived, I would work out more. Even Jax seemed amazed that I'd been able to do it—or maybe it was the concussion. He stared at me, still glassy-eyed, swaying, and barely able to stand.

"Help me, Rudy," I said.

"Sure thing, Tink." Rudolph lowered himself enough so I could shove Jax onto his back.

Jax slumped forward, and I patted the reindeer on his flank. "Get him out of here. Now."

As Rudolph ran out the door, already partially air born, Jax tried to grab me to pull me with him. But I knew I'd weigh them down, so I jumped backward...and slammed right into Sugarplum Happypie.

What happened next would probably haunt me for the rest of my life. Sugar fell onto her back, and the shake she'd been holding, the one laced with the deadly cocktail of candicocane and telazol, flew out of her hands and landed right on her face.

Unlike her usual shakes, this one wasn't particularly thick, which meant the pale pink liquid covered her quickly. Frank, Comet, and I stood, silently staring at her, and for a moment, she lay perfectly still before she opened her eyes and blinked.

I'd knocked the wind out of her. I also may have slammed her with the back of my head. All in all, it didn't work out well for Sugar. She had milkshake all over her eyes, her nose, and, most importantly, in her mouth. And when she tried to catch her breath, the liquid went into her lungs. It wasn't long before the drugs took effect.

I'd never killed anyone before, and I didn't intend to kill Sugarplum, but it wasn't my fault. She knew who she was dealing with. As she'd pointed out, I was a screwup. A *clumsy* screwup. But this time, maybe it had worked in my favor.

"Sugar," screamed Comet, leaping toward her. I moved out of the way just in time, but Frank did not. He took a reindeer hoof to his chin and was down for the count. I ran to the door of the stall, afraid Comet might come after me, but the giant buck wasn't paying attention. His focus was entirely on Sugarplum.

"Get up," he said, franticly licking the milkshake off her face. "You're going to be fine."

Sugarplum wasn't going to be fine, well, not if the blood coming from her orifices was any indication. "Comet..." she said, her voice a raspy gurgle. Her body spasmed, her back arching at an odd angle, before she went completely still.

"No. Don't die." Comet continued licking her, but he swayed on his feet as the reindeer tranquilizer took effect. He was a big deer, so there must have been a ridiculous amount of telazol in that shake. Sugar hadn't been taking any chances. She'd wanted me good and dead.

Comet fell onto his side, his nose still on Sugar's raspberry and chocolate-covered cheek. His back legs jerked in an involuntary movement, knocking over the kerosene heater. I watched as the flaming liquid poured out of it, quickly setting the hay on fire.

I didn't know what to do. The fire headed straight toward Sugar and Comet, and Frank was still unconscious near the stall's rear door.

"Frank. Wake up," I screamed as the fire crackled and burned, moving closer and closer to Comet and Sugar. But Frank didn't move. None of them moved.

As the flames climbed up the walls, I couldn't reach Frank, so I grabbed Sugar by the arm and tried to pull her out, but Comet's front leg was resting on her body, and I couldn't move her. Coughing from the smoke, I tried again. The flames had reached the roof now. It wouldn't be long before the whole place collapsed, but I refused to give up. No matter what Sugar and Comet had done, no one deserved to die like that. The smoke was so thick I couldn't see Frank at all. I got on my knees, trying to crawl toward him, but strong arms grabbed me around the waist and pulled me out. I kicked and screamed and tried with all my might to get away.

"Stop it, kiddo. It's too late. They're gone."

I looked up to see Topper, his face covered in ash, his eyebrows singed. He collapsed to his knees as Rudolph approached from the sky, Jax still on his back. They landed, and Jax stumbled toward me, his eyes slightly less glassy, grabbing my shoulders and asking if I was okay.

I was not okay. I wasn't sure if I'd ever be okay again, but I was alive, and Jax was alive, too. I'd gotten him to safety, and I hadn't screwed up.

I fell into his arms, my head resting on his chest as we half-sat, half-reclined on the hard, cold ground of the reindeer training area. Together, in silence, we watched the barn burn...with two people I'd known and loved my whole entire life inside.

CHAPTER TWENTY-THREE

Since the elves were all at their luncheon, the barn went up in flames quickly. The sprinkler system helped keep the fire contained but didn't put it out.

The Elf Enforcement agents Jax had called in earlier from Elf Central showed up when Topper did, but there wasn't much they could do other than help get the remaining reindeer away from the burning building. By the time the North Pole Fire Department arrived, with their candy cane striped ladders and sirens playing a warped version of "Jingle Bells," little of Comet's section of the barn remained.

"This is why kerosene stoves aren't permitted indoors," said the fire chief, his face dark with soot. "But no matter how many times we tell the reindeer, they refuse to listen. Kerosene is commonly used in the outlying areas, and they like it. The smell reminds them of home or something." He shook his head as he surveyed the damage. "What a waste."

Topper, Jax, and I went to the hospital to get checked out, but other than a few scrapes and burns, a mild concussion on my part, and a more serious one on Jax's, we were amazingly okay. I couldn't say the same for Sugar, Comet, and Frank, however. Later, I heard they'd managed to recover what seemed to be Sugarplum and Comet's bodies but still hadn't found Frank. Because the heat was so intense, and the barn a literal tinderbox, I feared they might never find him. The idea made me ill.

"How can you have any sympathy for him?" asked Jax, a bandage on his head. "He tried to kill you."

I bit my lip. "He didn't want to." I knew it for a fact, no matter what anyone else might believe.

"Are you sure?"

"Yes. He was being manipulated by his aunt. But he was still my friend." I closed my eyes, seeing Sugar's body, unmoving, as the flames rushed in. I had to open them again. "And although I don't fully understand Sugar's motives or her relationship with Comet—ew—she was right about the hierarchy here on the North Pole. We aren't a meritocracy, Jax. Not by a long shot. And it needs to change."

Topper, sitting next to me, with what remained of his eyebrows hovering on his face like two misshapen caterpillars, seemed oddly quiet. When Jax got up to make a phone call, he turned to look at me.

"Do you mean what you said?" he asked. "About things needing to change here?"

"I do. We've been living like two societies for so long. I never understood how unjust it was, or how bleak it made life for half our population." I folded my arms over my chest. "But, thanks to you, I got to experience the coal mines firsthand. It opened my eyes to things I never understood before. I saw how bad things are there and how unfair. It also made me appreciate what it's like to feel trapped and powerless."

He winced. "Sorry, Tink. I explained it to your uncle—"

I waved away his words. "Yeah, you did it for my own safety and blah, blah, blah. I'm not sure if I believe it or not since it was mostly to cover your bum regarding my uncle's public image, but I know your intentions were to protect him, and that's good. Misguided, but good. I learned a valuable lesson from the experience, and even if it ticked me off at the time, part of me understood. After all, I am a public relations nightmare just waiting to happen."

"You've got that right," he said.

I gave him the stink eye. "You were not supposed to agree with me on the last part, but I'll give you a pass since you saved my life today."

Topper pointed to his face. "And lost my eyebrows in the process. People have told me they were my best feature, and now they're gone, thanks to you."

Leaning back in my chair, I studied him. "They'll grow back, but I'm certain no one has ever told you that. You're making it up."

He lifted what was left of his eyebrows in a gesture so ridiculous, it made me giggle. "Would I lie to you, Tinklebelle?"

I let out a laugh. "You would."

He stood up and patted me on the shoulder. "I have to check on the reindeer. Since Vixen and Prancer were also involved in this whole mess, we're three reindeer short, and Christmas is hours away. Never a dull moment."

"How's Rudolph?"

Topper snorted. "Oh, he'll go down in history for this one. He's fine. He's kind of like you."

"What do you mean?"

He gave me a wink. "An outcast who is now a hero. Bye, kid. Try to stay out of trouble for a few minutes. Please."

After he left, a flurry of excitement erupted in the hall, and a few seconds later, my uncle appeared. Dressed for work in his red velvet suit with the long coat and white fur trim, he marched forward with a single-minded determination, his expression grave, but I sensed his relief as soon as he saw me. It was an almost tangible thing.

I rose to my feet, still unsteady. "Hi, Uncle Kris."

"Oh, Tink," he said, pulling me into his arms. He smelled like peppermint and cookies and happiness, and I inhaled deeply. Things like this used to bother me—his scent, his beard, his laugh, but now I felt comforted instead of saddened by it. He pulled back to look at my face, and I was shocked to see tears in his eyes.

"You scared me," he said, his voice thick with emotion.

"I'm sorry. I didn't mean to—"

He placed a white-gloved finger to my lips. "And you also made me proud."

Jax stood a few feet away, trying to give us space. My uncle called him over. "Good work. You managed to figure out who was distributing those horrible drugs and keep my niece alive in the process."

He shifted uncomfortably. "Sir, Tink saved me. And she's also the one who figured it out. She put all the pieces together."

I shook my head. "Not true, Jax. You also saved me. Several times. Are you forgetting about the night Frank drugged me? And how you found me after I escaped from the coal mines? And the polar bear?"

Uncle Kris frowned. "What polar bear?"

"Never mind," said Jax and I together.

My uncle raised an eyebrow. "Well, I'd like to hear more about that later, but it seems like the two of you make a good team. You may have saved hundreds of lives by figuring this out, and you saved me as well."

"What do you mean?" I asked.

"Thanks to the warning you gave me, I had Rudolph's tag removed as a precaution, just in case he had to get a message to me quickly. We also did an extra inspection on my sleigh. Someone had messed with the thruster. It would have exploded before I hit five thousand feet. I owe you my life." He smiled at me, his arm still around my shoulders. "Aunt Clarice is planning a giant party for you. Well, if your grandmother doesn't kill you first. And that is a real possibility. You made her extremely worried this time."

I cringed, mainly because we both knew my grandmother would likely make me pay for this for the next decade. I'd scared her badly with my disappearing act, even though none of it was my fault. Once she found out about the fire and Frank and Sugarplum, she'd lose her mind.

"I'll go see her as soon as we get discharged. I promise. By the way, you have Mince Mingle to thank for the warning."

"As requested, I made sure she was released from the coal mines as soon as you told me about her. She had documented everything and put it in a safety deposit box, but when she and Topper went to retrieve the information a few hours ago, it was gone."

"Gone?" I frowned. "How could it be gone?"

"Good question. We're looking into it." He kissed the top of my head. "Time for me to go, Tink. Those toys won't deliver themselves. Please try to stay out of trouble while I'm away."

I rolled my eyes. "Topper said the same thing."

He smiled. "Topper is a wise elf, and he knows you well."

"He told me once you hired him for his looks."

Uncle Kris let out a loud laugh, a cheerful, booming ho-ho-ho. "That too." As soon as the other elves in the ER heard him, a small crowd formed around us. Jax stared at the assembled elves in confusion.

"It's his laugh," I said softly in Jax's ear. "It's like catnip for elves. They can't resist it."

Jax didn't seem affected by it. "I see. Does he need help with crowd dispersal?"

"No, he can handle it."

My uncle nodded to the elves surrounding him, greeting each of them by name. He was always kind, always patient. But he was obviously in a hurry today because after he gently excused himself, he turned to Jax. "If you don't mind, Jax, I need a moment more with my niece."

"Certainly, sir," Jax said, giving my uncle a slight bow. To my astonishment, my uncle bowed back, but before I could question him on it, he linked his arm with mine.

"Would you mind walking me to the door, Tink? My sleigh is right outside."

"Uh, sure."

When we stepped out into the cold, the sky was growing dark, and light snow falling. He looked at me, his blue eyes filled with concern. "How are you holding up? I know this time of year isn't easy for you to begin with, but I'm sure things have been extra challenging this year. With what happened today, and to your friend, and your room-mate, and, of course, the coal mines."

"Oh, the coal mines weren't so bad. I might make it a yearly thing. You know how Grandma likes to go on a cruise? I'll head to Coal Mine Number 25. It's the new hot vacation spot."

"Can we be serious? For a moment?" He put his hands

on my shoulders and stared deeply into my eyes. "How are you, Tink?"

"I'm fine," I said, glancing at my watch. "You'd better go. It's getting late. You don't have much time."

"I have time for this. It's important." I heard an odd catch in his voice. "Every year, I've watched you slip further and further away. From me. From the rest of your family."

He stared at me, his expression as kind and earnest and familiar as always, and I sighed. "Don't take this the wrong way, Uncle Kris, but sometimes it's hard to look at you." When he lifted one eyebrow in confusion, I clarified. "Because you look like him. I see you, and sometimes I still see him, and it bothers me. A lot."

He blinked at me in shock. "I didn't understand..." He shook his head sadly. "Your parents were good elves. The accident wasn't your fault, you know."

I flinched, remembering the crash, the breaking glass, the blood. "I don't blame myself. Not anymore, at least."

His expression turned sad. "You blame Christmas."

"I did for a long time. But this year will be different. I feel oddly festive."

Uncle Kris gave me a slight smile. "As well you should. Speaking of which, that's what I wanted to discuss. The job overseeing the naughty list is yours if you want it, you know. After all you've done, after all you've been through, you deserve it."

"Thanks, but I might have other plans."

He cupped my face in his gloved hands and kissed my forehead. "Whatever you do, my favorite niece, I'm sure it will be amazing. Unpredictable, perhaps, and unconventional, but interesting."

"I'm your only niece, doofus."

He laughed, the merriest sound in all the worlds, human and elven alike. "Don't call me doofus, doofus."

"Wow. What a great comeback," I said as he turned and walked toward his waiting sleigh. "Hey, give Rudolph extra treats tonight. He deserves it. And be careful out there."

He must have heard the worry in my voice when I said the last part because he turned and smiled at me. "Merry Christmas, Tink. I love you, you know."

"Merry Christmas. I love you, too."

When I got back to Grandma Gingersnap's house, I was surprised and yet not surprised to see she'd been baking. She'd made what looked like a million cut-out cookies, a true indication of how stressed and worried she'd been about me.

Jax had to go to the police station to sort things out there. Against the advice of his doctors, who said he needed to rest, Jax insisted on going, but promised to come to Grandma Gingersnap's as soon as he was done. For now, however, it was just my grandmother and me. Alone. Well, except for the cookies.

I knew I'd scared her this time, which was why I let her hug me extra tight. And why I ate an entire plate full of Christmas cookies and drank a giant glass of milk at her request. When I finally finished, she laughed.

"You definitely have the Santa gene, Tink."

I dabbed at my mouth with a napkin. My head ached, but the combination of painkillers from the ER doctor and sugar from my grandmother's cookies helped.

"Funny you should say that..." I said, filling her in on Mince's theory regarding the reason behind Cookie's hatred of me. "He thought I might end up as the first female Santa someday, which is crazy."

She didn't bat an eye. "Why is it crazy?"

I let out a laugh. "Because I'm hardly Santa material. First of all, I'm a fu—" I froze at the look on her face. "—a bit of a mess, especially in the organizational department. Secondly, I'm the least jolly person I know. Thirdly, I hate reindeer."

"Understandable after what Comet tried to do to you."

"But yet another reason why I'd be awful at the job. Why would Cookie think such a thing?"

She picked up a Santa cookie and nibbled on it. Although it felt surreal to see Santa Claus's mother eating a Santa Claus cookie, it was nothing I hadn't seen before. Many times.

"Being Santa isn't about all of that stuff, Tink. It's about who you are...in your heart." She shot me a funny look. "Your mother used to say that, by the way. She had a unique ability to look past a person's exterior and see who they were on the inside. Where it mattered."

"Speaking of my mom," I said, frowning. "What was Mrs. Snow talking about? I saw the look the two of you exchanged. I know there is something you aren't telling me."

With a sigh, Grandma Gingersnap sat next to me. "I'd been meaning to talk with you about that very subject, but it never seemed like the right time. Now it does." She paused a moment as if to gather her thoughts. "With your mom and dad, it was love at first sight. They adored each other. And although your grandfather and I never had an issue with their union, others did."

"Why?"

She reached for my hand. "Your mother wasn't from

one of the First Five families. In fact, she wasn't a domer at all."

My eyes widened. "She was an outlier?"

My grandmother nodded. "And one of the best and kindest people I've ever met. But..." She paused. "It was a long time ago, and we decided as a family that no one else needed to know."

"You lied about it?"

She shrugged. "We never brought it up. We were vague. It was your mother's idea. She found she was treated differently if people knew she'd been born on a reindeer ranch, and she wanted to be judged by who she was, not where she came from. Does that make sense?" When I nodded, she continued. "It's where she met Sugarplum. They grew up together."

"Wow," I said, shaken by that information.

"Angel found out years ago, and always gave your mom a hard time. But none of it ever really mattered. Like your mother said, it's all about who you are as a person. So, who are you, Tink?"

"Who am I?" I ticked off my fingers. "I have no filter. I say and do things I shouldn't. I'm too impulsive. I'm horrible at following rules. And sometimes I do things because they amuse me, without any thought to the consequences. But today, I learned I'm tenacious AF."

She looked confused. "AF?"

"And Fierce," I said, keeping my expression neutral as I imagined all the ways my grandmother would misuse "AF." It reminded me of when I told her LOL meant "lots of love," and she used it on a sympathy card when her friend's sister passed away.

So sorry to hear about the loss of your dear sister. LOL. Gingersnap.

It took months for her to forgive me for that gem.

"You're a lot more than tenacious." We looked up to see Win standing in the doorway, leaning against the door jamb.

"I'm a lot more than what?" I asked as he came over to kiss me on the cheek. He kissed my grandmother, too. She tried to force him to sit and eat some cookies, but he begged off. No wonder he was so fit.

"More than tenacious," he said. "You're far braver than you realize, Tink Holly, and smarter than you give yourself credit for. You also do incredibly well under pressure. Not many elves can say the same."

I tried and failed not to blush. "Thank you." Coming from Win, it meant a lot. He'd seen me at my worst and still managed to like me anyway.

He gave me one of his trademark smiles. "You're welcome."

As Grandma Gingersnap washed up the mess she'd created with the cookie baking, I walked Win to the door. "How is it you never give up on me?"

Win tilted his head and looked up at the stars. "How could I? Whether we're together or not, you're a part of my heart, Tink, and you always will be."

His words made me sad, but not as much as they would have before. Win would be fine. We could love each other without being in love, and eventually, Win would see it, too.

"I have a question, though," I said. "Something has been bothering me. It's about Frank. What happened between the two of you? You were such good friends growing up."

His demeanor changed instantly. "Let me say I saw his true colors after he came back from his time on the ski team. And it wasn't just the drugs."

"The drugs?"

Win rubbed a hand over his chin. "I hate to speak ill of the dead, but Frank changed after his injury. It may have been the pain killers or the disappointment—I'm not sure. But he turned into someone I didn't recognize."

I hesitated with what I had to tell him, but he had to know. "Frank was the one who had the photos of your parents. That's how I knew he had to be involved. I recognized his handwriting on the envelope. I'm pretty sure that was how he blackmailed Cookie, too."

Win shrugged. "Makes sense. I heard he had something to do with the Ho, Ho Club. I don't blame him for the photos, Tink. After all, my parents chose to be there, and they chose to put themselves in that situation. But I do blame him for the chocolate." He swallowed hard. "He knew what you liked because I told him. He was with me years ago when I bought them for you. I guess I was showing off, both because they were expensive and because you were mine. I knew he liked you, even back then, and I was rubbing it in. Not my proudest moment."

I put a hand on his arm. "First of all, it's not your fault Frank tried to kill me. Secondly, I still like Snarkleberry Dingalings. You can buy them for me anytime."

He gave me a sad smile. "Promise?"

I wrapped my arms around his waist and held him close. "Promise."

Win left, and when Jax returned, I forced him to eat a cookie before we went outside to start a fire. We both needed to relax, so we sat, side by side, staring at the flames. I was bone tired, and my head ached, but I still had so much adrenaline flowing through my system that there was no way I could sleep yet.

"Did you mean what you said?" I asked.

He glanced at me. "Which part?"

I fluttered my eyelashes at him. "Don't you remember? You told me you were madly in love with me and asked me to marry you. You said you wanted me to have your babies."

Although I didn't think it was possible, Jax got even paler than usual. "Tink, I—"

I gave him a light punch on the arm. "I'm kidding. You never said any of that. But when you were concussed, and bleeding, and out of your mind, you said I'd make a great Elf Enforcement officer someday. Did you mean it?"

"Of course, I meant it. But it requires training as well as commitment. Are you truly interested?"

"Not at all. I only brought it up to mess with you."

He tilted his head and gave me one of those special Jax Grayson looks, the ones that told me he was trying hard to figure out if I was serious or being snarky. I lifted my hands in defeat because I was definitely being snarky.

"Fine. Yes, I am interested. Very interested. But I didn't think you were serious. I figured it was the head trauma talking."

"I was serious, Tink. You would be an asset. We could use a Christmas elf in our department, and I couldn't imagine anyone better suited for the job than you."

I ducked my head to hide how much his words affected me. "Speaking of head trauma—"

"Were we?"

"How are you, by the way?"

"Fine. Other than the throbbing pain in my frontal lobes."

I touched his forehead gently, wincing at the bruise there. "Does it feel as bad as it looks?"

"Worse." He reached out and laced his fingers with mine. "You saved my life today."

"Well, Rudolph helped."

"He did. And I got to ride on a flying reindeer thanks to you, so I owe you a debt of gratitude for that as well."

"Anytime you're stuck in a barn with a psycho milkshake maker, her druggie nephew, and a nasty, 400-pound rogue buck, I shall happily arrange reindeer transport for you."

"I appreciate the sentiment." His expression grew pensive. "But about the job in Elf Enforcement, the only difficulty may be that we'd have to work together."

I frowned. "Why would that be a difficulty? We get along great."

"Maybe too great." He tugged on a lock of my hair. "We've been straddling the line between personal and professional here."

"Like when we were naked in the sleeping bag?"

"Yes."

"And when I was naked in the kitchen?"

"Exactly."

"And when I kissed you—"

He pressed his lips against mine, but it was mostly to shut me up. "You know what I mean, Tink. It would have to stop." He gave me another kiss. "*This* would have to stop."

"I find it ironic you're kissing me as you say that."

He laughed, leaning back in his chair but didn't let go of my hand. "I found that ironic as well. I didn't say it would be easy. But as much as I've enjoyed..." He paused, apparently trying to come up with the right word, and failing miserably. "...everything, I take my job seriously. And out of respect for you, as well as the badge, we'd have to keep it professional. Do you understand?"

I knew he was right, but I still had a considerable problem following orders, which was why I put my hands on his cheeks and stared deeply into his eyes before kissing the poor man senseless. "I understand."

"Does that mean you're taking the job or not?" he asked, still bemused.

"What do you think? I've always wanted a badge, Jax. And a gun. Can I get a gun? I promise to try not to shoot anyone unless they deserve it."

He rolled his eyes. "Santa help us."

I laughed. "He already did."

EPILOGUE

Even with three substitute reindeer, Santa managed to deliver all the gifts without a hitch, and on December 25th, the party commenced. Although only a few hours had passed in the human world, precisely three months had passed in our world.

Time manipulation. The gift that keeps on giving.

I'd never been a particularly Christmas-y Christmas elf, but even I could get behind the idea of drunken revelry. And December 25th on the North Pole was the party to end all parties. It was also the day to acknowledge those who worked extra hard to make Christmas run smoothly. Surprisingly, I was one of the elves receiving an award this year.

Not that the day was all eggnog and Christmas stars. Before the ceremony, I'd stopped by to visit Holly and Jolly Berry. We sat together in their tidy living room, and they listened, hands clasped together, as I told them exactly what had happened to Joy and why. I'd had to wait until now, until all the paperwork had been filed and the dust settled, but I wanted to bring them some peace, and hopefully some closure.

"Frankincense Yummy," said Mrs. Berry with a shake of her head. "It's so hard to believe. He and Ever were such great friends, and he was always good to Joy, and to us."

"In his defense, he didn't know his aunt had killed Joy on purpose." I blew out a sigh. "I don't know why I feel the need to defend him, after all he's done, after all the people he's hurt, but I want to be fair, to his memory at least."

Frank hadn't been a good elf, but he hadn't been completely evil either. He'd been a charming fool, a great kisser, and a person way too influenced by those around him. Although I'd accepted Frank and I were alike in many ways (especially the good kisser part), we were also different. I'd never been very influenced by others, except maybe my grandmother, who gave me no choice. Anyone else though? No way. Which explained a lot.

"Thank you, Tink," said Mrs. Berry, pulling me into a hug. "It helps to have answers."

As I left their house and headed back to my grandmother's, I thought about what she said. Did it help? Joy was still gone. Frank was gone, too. And the rest of us, the ones remaining, would never be the same. But nothing I could do would bring anyone back. Perhaps that kind of closure was the only comfort many people got.

I rushed into Grandma Gingersnap's house and went straight to her closet to decide what to wear. She'd given me permission, and, frankly speaking, we both knew she had far better taste than I did. Deciding winter white would be the perfect color for the awards ceremony, I paired a white satin blouse with a matching wool skirt and coat. My heels weren't white, however. They were a bright and merry red —because nothing said "Christmas" like red stilettos.

Not wanting to be late, I hopped into an Ubersled. I hoped to get my license back soon, but until then I would enjoy being carted around. Plus, it gave me a chance to check the local news on my phone.

The candicocane scandal caused shock waves through the entire North Pole community. Happypie's was now closed, a tragedy, and the Ho, Ho Club was under new management. The reindeer encounters were a thing of the past. It was a regular kinky sex club at this point, which was a definite improvement.

We still had a long way to go, improving conditions for the reindeer and giving them more autonomy. We also had to stop using the coal mines as a penal facility. We still needed the coal—what else would we put in the stockings of naughty children? But we had to improve working conditions there and the quality of life for all outliers.

Win had taken the lead on it, stepping up as all good boy scouts do. He planned to run for office as a North Pole representative in the Tribal Senate and maybe even sit on Elven High Council someday. The career path suited him. He'd do a great job. It seemed, however, he'd be doing it without Candy by his side. They were taking a break until Win could sort himself out.

I saw the wisdom in it since I needed to sort myself out, too.

Noelle sent me a text. *Where are you? The ceremony is about to begin.*

I texted back quickly. *I'm here!*

I got out of the Ubersled with only minutes to spare, arriving in time to see Santa climb onto the podium, his eyes twinkling as he regarded the crowd. "This year, I'm proud to say we have a special commendation. This one is close to my heart because the recipient is close to my heart as well."

His eyes met mine, and I saw the love and pride in them. It made my heart swell with happiness. "I'd like to present this award to Tinklebelle Holly for outstanding bravery and remarkable intuition. Thank you for a job well done."

I climbed onto the podium to the sound of thunderous applause. Jax grinned at me from the front row. He'd come here from Elf Central especially for this celebration. Win sat next to him, looking every inch a future council elf. Grandma Gingersnap was there, too, beaming with pride, and so were Noelle and Nippy. They'd both recovered. Noelle had decided not to press charges against Win's parents, but she'd done something better. In exchange for not pressing charges, she'd asked that the Snows be assigned to six months of community service at an outlier settlement. They were currently up to their knees in reindeer droppings. Nothing could be better.

Nippy still had no memory of the night he got shot, but he concluded it was better that way. I wished I could block it out, too, but this moment, standing in the middle of the stage, and waving at my friends and family in the audience, was something I wanted to keep. The applause increased when Santa pulled me into a big hug.

"Nicely done, brat."

"Thanks, snitch."

Uncle Kris's wife, Auntie Clarice, and their three boys, Winken, Blinken, and Nod (don't ask—it's another idiotic Holly family tradition) stood behind him. I gave them hugs as well. We smiled for the cameras, dumped the confetti, and the party officially began. But not before Santa pulled me aside for one last word.

"Name it, Tink. What job do you want? The North Pole is yours."

I grinned at him. "Thanks, Santa, but I have other

plans." I pulled out the gold badge from inside my coat pocket. "Elf Enforcement Special Agent Holly, Christmas Crimes Division."

"Elf Enforcement?"

"I'm a civilian consultant right now, but I'll be a full-fledged agent soon. Sugarplum, Frank, and Comet were the tip of the iceberg. It's time to clean up the North Pole, and I'm the elf to do it."

ACKNOWLEDGMENTS

Thank you to my awesome critique partner, Kim Pierson, who is the most brilliant and helpful person I know. Thanks also to the entire Mindful Writing tribe, because this story began as a simple short story in the Mindful Writers Anthology Series. A big thanks to Demi Stevens for the initial anthology edits, Lara Parker for editing the book itself, and Maria Thomas and Gwen Jones for proofreading. Thanks also to my fabulous beta readers, Robin Webster, Erin Barker, Sue Boyd, Melissa Isenberg, Charlene Kowalski, and Shelby Crozier. You are all amazing. And a huge thank you to my cover artist, Najla Qamber. It takes a village, and I had the most wonderful village helping me with this book. Thank you all!

ABOUT THE AUTHOR

Abigail Drake is the award-winning author of seventeen novels, but she didn't start her career in writing. She majored in Japanese and economics in college, and spent years traveling the world, collecting stories wherever she visited. She collected a husband from Istanbul on her travels, too, and he happens to be her favorite souvenir.

Abigail is a coffee addict, a puppy wrangler, and the mother of three adult sons. To learn more about Abigail, please visit her website: https://www.abigaildrake.com

ALSO BY ABIGAIL DRAKE

Women's Fiction

The South Side Stories

The Dragonsong Law Offices

The Hocus Pocus Magic Shop

The Enchanted Garden Cafe

Passports and Promises

Delayed Departure

Sophie and Jake

Saying Goodbye

Other

Love, Chocolate, and a Dog Named Al Capone

Lola Flannigan

Traveller

Young Adult Fiction

The Bodyguard

Starr Valentine

Tiger Lily

Non-Fiction

The Reformed Pantser's Guide to Plotting

For more about Abigail, visit her website:

https://abigaildrake.com

Made in the USA
Monee, IL
05 November 2021

81170653R00194